GW01219275

Pamela Turton

SELLING SHORT

All characters in this publication are fictitious, and any resemblance to real persons, living or dead, is purely coincidental.

ISBN 10: 1456595830
ISBN 13: 9781456595838

To Ahmet Ç, for his pure heart
To Denise R. and the others who never had the
chance to tell their story

The story of the human race is the story of men and women selling themselves short.
Abraham Maslow

BARBA

Barba had a longing. It really had been the same since she was a little girl. One day she would meet her true husband, her eternal beau, her forever-knight. She would know when she met him because in his eyes she would see the stars of love, and no words would be needed. She would recognize those eyes because they would hold the same adoring light reflected in her father's eyes whenever he looked at her, from the day she was born. Daddy, nurturing, cherishing. In his eyes forever his princess.

The girlish vision was vivid and colourful, the teenage version somewhat tarnished by her forays into sexual experience and mediocre romance with a few local youths. Still it managed to persist, occasionally shining through the mud of disappointment and even abuse. Most times now, it was forgotten, then she might notice a couple, her age and older, holding hands. She would see through the husband's eyes, engaged with his partner's, and she would feel her throat bursting with lonely wanting. Oh, to have that, be that; always the young lovers beneath the greying hairs and sagging skin.

Steve used to call her 'Princess,' which is why she probably thought it was the real thing.

"Princess, Princess," he would murmur, over and over, the morning after.

"You know I don't mean to do anything to hurt

you."

He would follow her around as she picked up the fallout of broken furniture and crockery, reaching out to touch and guiltily pulling back, as her bruised limbs flinched reflexively.

"Princess, Princess," he repeated; dull, bleary eyes and matching voice when she told him she had lost the baby. Her prince. Literally, the life, her lights, punched out of her. She felt nothing then, just a kind of clarity which brought relief. The realization that with that death, the relationship was killed, having no reason to go on. It was as inexorable as the life of a grieving widow who throws herself on to the burning funeral pyre of her husband.

The striking image she had of her father the last time she saw him alive, his wasted body barely discernible under the hospital sheets, was not the signs of irrevocable disease, but that same light in his eyes. As soon as he saw her, he fluttered his bony hands, and became luminous, for her.

"My Barbara," he smiled with peace as she kissed him. "My princess."

No-one had called her by that name since her father left her. Sean had never addressed her that way, and now she really did not believe, anymore, that she was worthy of the title.

ATEK

Atek wondered if he could change; when he had changed. Was it in the military? Memories shuddered through his body. Huddled in a group on a cold mountainside on the border, chilled with fear, numbness and altitude. Waiting, waiting; waiting for what? Counting the days. Humour was a saviour. Nursing a glass of hot tea, laughing out loud. Too loud, as suddenly a brutal slap from behind jolts his head and the glass shoots out of his hand, spilling the amber liquid in the dust. Comrades with heads down, silently sipping as the officer strides away, mirthlessly. Then he was four again, sprawling in the dirt, watching the stick he was playing with jerk out of his grasp. Still, because he hopes his father will not kick him the way he has lifted the puppy he was playing with on his boot, and flung it off, as if it were excrement.

When his father was taken away, no-one explained. Atek had never asked, in case knowledge would make him materialize again in the seven year-old's life. He wanted just to come home from school with the other boys, without feeling his stomach drop in his gut like an iron ball if his father was smoking outside. To go quietly to the mosque, with his hand in the warm, dry grasp of his grandfather. Knowing that he would not be prodded and pushed around by the man stalking irritably every evening, while his mother scurried around, serving, placating. Was it his father who had forced his mother to tell him he could no longer drink from her breast, to show him the black hairs around the teats? "See, my son, it is dirty, now."

He used to desire sleep to enfold him like angels' wings. Soft, warm shelter he craved to stay within for eternity. Wrapped in grimy, rough blankets; boy and soldier clinging on to the feathers of sleep even when the shuffling shadow, the shallow breather, intrudes.

Remission: days of school routine, quietly performed chores, hypnotic hours at the mosque and undisturbed games swept over the wounds like dust in footprints.

Did he change when he came to Side? First, the tranquil thrill of each golden morning, as he brushed the sand and hoped for blonde girls to smile at him. When had that given way to the cynical agenda of guessing not only who would smile, but come back again, and better still, pay out? Flash their pounds and their euros as generously as their pearly teeth and their flesh.

In the few years before the hard school of compulsory army service, Atek had gained another form of education. He learnt from young men who had graduated, from heady, awkward, early days in tourist terrain. Boys who became maestros in the art of the attraction and manipulation of women on holiday. Facial expression, body language, words used; every response read and interpreted with marvellous acuity. Following his mentors, Atek practised the script of the accomplished Casanova; the posturing and the 'hand games', the faux-innocent brushes and strokes of skin and hair. A giggle was the green light.

4

Temperatures were high, even in the evenings. Atek put the chilled beer bottle against his forehead, then swigged. Maybe he would get some hashish from Berk later. He thumbed a quick text which he sent to Dusseldorf, Liverpool and Oslo.

'How are you darling? I miss you so. Kiss, kiss, kiss.'

Yawning, he mirrored Mehmet's head-to-toe appraisal of the females shimmying and wiggling in the lights, flashing like desperate sirens on the bar's little dance floor.

CHAPTER 1

She did not know why she had not noticed
before. The silhouetted figures against the interior lights
of each apartment. Women in different poses on every
balcony, figures in a dark and artful tableau. Marking out
the building with its reddening lights, the sky was
blushing with the last call of the sun for the day. Every
evening of their holiday so far, Barba had sat in the same
place, outside the Internet cafe, waiting for her partner to
finish checking his emails, he said, though she knew the
main purpose was to look at the horse-racing results.

She picked distractedly at the acrylic nails she
had done especially for the trip. Below the women, huge
Russian tour buses deposited groups. The majority were
female, most struggling with bulging, super-sized
suitcases, outside the hotel opposite. They were escorted
by glamorous reps with court shoes, clipboards,
inscrutable faces and crisp blue and yellow uniforms
which matched the buses.

It was a hotel, one though, which did not seem to
have a name. There was a front entrance, which was not
really a reception. No signs on the dusty, net-curtained
double doors, no-one ever seemed to come in and out of
them. The ground floor facade housed a mini-market and
a restaurant bar, popular with the English crowd for its
anglicised menu and nightly discos, hosted by gushing,
energetic, Turkish waiters. At some point in every

evening she had been there, the van of the Gendarme had been parked at the side-path to the left of the building, where the residents appeared to enter and exit. She presumed that the ochre-plastered walls surrounded a swimming pool, but the walls were high at each side, retaining the mystery.

Three Russian women passed into her frame of observation. Dressed differently from the waist down; a brief dress, shorts, hip-swathing skirt. Their uniform was the skimpy vests and body-clinging fabric. Exchanging a few barked words, they loped along with straight backs, glassy eyes and glossed mouths. Barba thought they had an odd air of purposelessness, except for their swinging hips, which moved as if to the beat of an unseen metronome. It slowed their progress, keeping the pace of their high-heeled sandals in unison.

"Hello, golden girl." Turkish accent.

Her head was bent as she rubbed a nuisance of a mosquito bite on the back of her heel. As she glanced up in response to the greeting, she felt the shape of the leg she held. She saw what he was seeing; a waxed-smooth, biscuit-coloured curve of skin. Pleasure blurted out in her smile, acknowledging the compliment in the caramel eyes of the man surveying her. The opposite of the look in Sean's eyes when she wore skirts as high as this. In defiant delight, she let her eyes follow her young admirer's rear through the doors of the Internet cafe. Holidays.

A little dizzily, she turned back to reappraise her legs and at once felt an abrupt nudge of her shoulder.

"Going for a paper," Sean mumbled without looking behind, as he strolled towards the mini-market next door. His hands were pushed into the low pockets of his baggy shorts causing him to stoop a little.

"Cigs," she called to his retreating back through cupped hands.

Still looking ahead, he held out a sidewards thumbs-up to show he had registered the request. Returning smugly a few minutes later with his imported copy of 'The Sun', he slapped her packet of Pall Mall Slims on the table. Seating himself opposite, he flicked open the tabloid.

"Thanks," she said to the Sports page. No answer.

The top of his head and forehead were visible over the top of the paper. The slight raise of his eyebrows indicated that he had begun with Page Three as usual, followed by a more studious frown as he hit the horse-racing page. Considering reminding him to use higher factor sun-block, she studied his crown through cigarette smoke. Wisps of ginger and white hairs straggled through shiny, reddened, thin skin. Instead she went to get herself a chilled vodka and fresh orange from the hotel bar, to ease the dragging loneliness of being tied to a person without togetherness.

"Going to the loo," she informed anyone who was listening.

The quickest access to the bar was through the Internet Cafe, which was mainly occupied on one side by Turkish men, from late teens to possibly forties. Barba found it hard to judge their age. There was a certain swarthy maturity about even the very young males, once out of puberty. Most of them peered over the top of their units as she passed, then back, closer to the screens before them, which she could not see. Which she did not want to see.

On the first night of their holiday, two days before, Sean had insisted they used an Internet Cafe near the bank on the main road. A gloomy little place, where the alcoves had been arranged in a square so the monitors were quite visible. There, the other customers were all Turkish men. She was left with an uncomfortable memory of frames of carnal imagery flicking off the screens as she glanced around the room.

Here, an English couple were talking through an internet phone on the other side, next to two tall teenage boys of Scandinavian appearance. None of the Europeans looked at her. Barba made a detour round the pool, pausing to admire the fairy grotto effect created by the lights amongst the foliage and flowers, and the soft night-lighting. The 'ladies' was paid a perfunctory visit first, to give herself a sense of integrity before going to the bar. Quiet, firm steps behind echoed hers. One of the customers was making his way to the toilets also. He held a mobile 'phone to his ear, a cigarette in the other hand. When she emerged from the washroom, he was stood outside the 'gents', smoking and smiling at her. Acknowledging him with a tentative 'Merhaba', she sidled round him. Relieved, she noted that the English couple had finished their online call and were perched on bar stools. Barba smoothed herself up on the empty stool at the end of the bar, next to the pair, so that no-one could join her.

"Hello, Lady," the barman grinned. "What can I do for you?"

"Hello, Sir," she replied, trying to keep her face

9

straight. "Vodka, with fresh orange juice, and a little ice, please."

"Sure, my lady."

Because of his generosity with the alcohol, she did not resent being asked for six lira when he presented the drink, with slices of orange and a gold cocktail stirrer. He asked her name. She gave it. He gave her his. Volkan.

"You have very nice blue eyes," the barman observed. "Amazing blue. Sky eyes."

"Thank you," she murmured, taking another sip and looking sideways at the English couple. They were turned away from her and the bar, to each other, forming an exclusive cocoon of romantic space.

"Where is your husband?" Volkan ventured.

"Oh, he's outside the Internet, reading his paper," she replied, in a bored tone.

"Oh?" The implied question, the expression of puzzlement and the shake of his head, made that simple exclamation seem profoundly flattering

Why was someone like her alone at the bar, indeed? She asked herself.

Glowing, she picked up her cooling glass, finishing the drink very quickly for her. Volkan came round to her side of the bar to clear some tables. His arm touched hers as he put out a hand for her glass, with a look that asked if she wanted more. She almost nodded. Yes, more, please. Instead, she demurred with a regretful smile and slipped off the stool reluctantly. The back of her little summer skirt stayed behind, caught on the cushion. Volkan stared at her legs openly as she descended.

"Thank you. Have to go, now." Hopping uneasily to release her skirt, she snatched her bag from the counter.

"Thank you, Barba. See you, Barba." Volkan shook her fingers with his, with a lavish smile.

Flustered and a little confused, she re-entered the Internet Cafe, passing sheepishly once more through the wave of raising and lowering heads. Sean was still occupied with his tabloid, this time scribbling with heavy pencil pressure on the lists before him. He would not tell her if she had been missed anyway. Without comment from either of them she rejoined him.

Any need for explanation was avoided by the arrival of their friends and holiday companions. Lucy settled herself self-consciously on the plastic chair beside Barba, wiggling her behind as if to establish stability, which always drew attention to her size. Voluptuous, clinically overweight and generously dimpled, from her peachy cheeks to her ankles, Lucy subdued her natural vivacity behind her layers of fat. Her husband, Alan, was tall, sinewy, with facial features and a body that looked gouged between muscle and bone. He scraped out the other chair and slid his lean frame next to Sean.

"How's it going?" He flicked Sean's paper mischievously.

Sean folded up his read, he and Barba nodded and smiled in response.

"You look nice," Barba said to Lucy.

Her friend laughed gratefully, as Alan looked away.

"Ready to eat?" he enquired, rubbing his

11

abdomen. "I know I am."

The other three all nodded and smiled again. Alan twisted round to indicate the open restaurant on the street about a hundred metres away. New, efficient, it was Turkish enough in food and ambience to satisfy the average tourist urge. It also offered familiar fast-food to console children, the simple-palated and the unadventurous.

"Shall we try Sultan's then?" Sean had already got up. No need to reply.

Lucy held out her hand. Alan gave her his, and without turning to her, helped her from her chair. She smoothed the ruffles of her bright-yellow, cotton sundress and flip-flopped after him, shaking her hair like a duck drying off.

"You coming?" Sean asked Barba with a snap of impatience. She gathered her sunglasses, 'phone and sequined straw bag even more leisurely.

"No hurry," she smiled, slowing down in passive resistance, when he began to walk off. Marching behind, she picked up speed to catch up with their friends as he did.

Lucy's teenagers were waiting at a table prepared for six. Sullen, mute blame exuded from their slumped bodies and apathetic expressions. Wayne looked up briefly from his DS.

"About time," he grunted and returned to the game.

Phee just gave a short, joyless laugh which translated as 'typical'.

"Well. You two having something different tonight? Try out some of the Turkish dishes? I'm drooling." Lucy attempted to persuade her children, after they had all studied the menu for a few minutes. They both frowned at her.

"I'll have Turkish pizza, cheese and sausage again, with fries and cola," Phee ordered rebelliously.

"Same," confirmed Wayne immediately.

"I'll have the 'chicken on the tile' with that gorgeous bread and dips. The lamb dish was to die for, last night. Same dips?" Lucy checked with the waiter, who stood nodding with his notepad and a patient smile.

"Can I have the special kebab?" Alan asked, pointing at the board.

"Dish from my home town," the waiter explained with a dash of pride.

"Ok, I'll have it too," Sean decided, "and four large Efes beers, please".

"Can't go wrong with a kebab, can you?" he announced to the group.

Barba was still deliberating when Lucy had already started on the flat bread, warm and irresistible, soft with a crisp edge. She wanted to try it all.

"What do you recommend?" she asked the waiter, holding the menu out for him. He leaned in.

"What do you like?" he enquired with a little side-ways look, through a fringe of black lashes.

"Almost everything, I think," she sighed.

"Take your time, Barba," Sean intervened sarcastically. Alan and Phee laughed.

"Stuffed aubergine, Chef's special to night, very, very nice."

"Thank you. Ok, yes, I'll have that," she agreed with a blink of appreciation, as the waiter took the menu from her with a bow of his handsome dark head.

No-one spoke for a while. Wayne was still playing with his DS under the table. Phee was looking out for her new Swedish friend. It engaged her in a round of coquetry with the youngest-looking waiter; looking, looking away when he caught her eye. Alan was, along with the waiters, whenever they had the opportunity, spectating women. Most were golden or bronzed, some provocatively dressed, strolling down the street. A beaming, bouncy, little greeter, dressed smartly in the restaurant colours, flattered and cajoled them to eat there as they approached. The light in Alan's eyes switched to full beam when two Russian women strolled in confidently, in shimmering, lycra, cropped tops and hip-gripping shorts. Munching and dipping contentedly, Lucy seemed oblivious to all. Sean was back in his tabloid. Barba watched couples; with empathy when the pair walked apart, with wandering eyes and apathetic expressions. Gazing after them wistfully, when their hands and hips were joined in an easy synchrony, as they walked and talked.

Sean stared at his plate like a sulky infant. "I ordered kebab," he muttered.

When Alan got the same dish placed before him a few seconds later, he shook his head and grabbed the waiter's arm.

"Kebab we ordered mate," he wagged his finger at the plates.

"Special kebab dish. Make this way in my home town."

"But it's not a kebab, mate." He stared pointedly at the minced meat and creamy sauce.

14

"Yes, this kebab, sir. Special one."

Alan shook his head. "You're lucky, mate, I'm starving so I'll try it. Funny kind of kebab, in my book." He picked up his fork condescendingly. Sean looked at his plate, then at Alan eating. Shaking his head disapprovingly to the waiter, whose face retained a mask of smooth civility, he shovelled up a mouthful too.

The waiter moved on, only returning to ask the women if their food was satisfactory, and to collect the cleaned plates from the men, who pushed them aside without comment.

"Mmm, thank you. That was delicious". Lucy delivered her feedback through lips glistening and rouged with oily tomato sauce.

Phee offered her plate with an approving pout. At that moment her friend, the fifteen year-old Anneka, breezed up to them; a Nordic nymph, with glacier-blue eyes, pale hair, rye-coloured skin and beige clothes.

"Hi guys," she greeted them airily, in a Scandinavian accent dipped in American inflexions. It was different from Lucy's, whose early years in Pennsylvania were layered by Northern English.

"Hey, Anneka." Phee hugged her friend effusively, transformed by the presence of a peer.

Even Wayne looked up briefly with a bashful smile of welcome. He accepted that, as two years junior, Phee and her friends usually considered themselves to be too mature and glamorous to consort with him. He continued his absorbed thumbing of the games console. Alan straightened himself up, twinkled a little and dragged a chair over for the sprite-like Anneka. She accepted it with a parting of thin lips over protruding, young stalactite teeth.

"Alan, you have many tattoos," the girl observed.

Phee groaned when her father began tracing the patterns and figures on his arms with manly satisfaction, ready to tell the stories which marked each one. Lucy ordered dessert and more beers as Alan pulled down his T-shirt to show Anneka his chest. Phee put her hand down on the table heavily.

"Dad," she protested.

"Anyway, I am too young for tattoo," announced Anneka abruptly, turning to Phee. Alan pulled up his t-shirt, looking rejected.

"Shall we walk now, Phee?" Anneka suggested.

Phee jumped up, eager and relieved. "Can I go, Mum?" she asked.

Her mother's mouth was occupied with a creamy chocolate rice dessert, so her brows did the questioning.

"Maybe to the beach, then along to Side centre." Anneka did the answering in a vanilla voice.

"Alright, honey. Got your phone 'cause you need to be back by ten-thirty. Ok?"

"Ok, Mum."

They disappeared like mist. The youngest waiter moved hurriedly as he realised they were planning to leave; too slow to catch their exit.

Barba felt sudden pangs of anxiety and envy simultaneously. She spooned her fruit as Sean and a deflated Alan took gulps of beer.

"I am totally full," Lucy declared with satisfaction, patting her tummy.

Barba felt hungry and empty, even though she

could not have eaten more.

"What do you fancy doing now?" she asked, without enthusiasm.

"What do you want to do?' replied Sean, without interest.

Lucy appeared to be stretched by the question. Alan shrugged, then brightened.

"We could check out the beach bar that Brummie couple told us about today," he suggested. "If we like it we could call the free bus to go there tomorrow, instead of the one the hotel uses."

None of them had a better alternative, and a walk in the August balm was appealing. There was a short cut from the boulevard where their hotel and Sultan's were located across a main road, down a dusty path, through scrubby grass and bushes growing amongst the Roman leftovers.

They had expected the beach bars to be bustling with holidaymakers reluctant to part from the sand and the waves. As they approached their target, the canopy with rows of flags like flamboyant rigging on a pirate ship, they noted that the bars were unlit and quiet. Noise came from the music escaping from the funfair of the huge German, all-inclusive hotel, a few hundred metres away. Four profiles could be made out, dipping amongst the stripped sunbeds. A torchlight arched towards them as they neared the decking of the bar area. A cheery voice hailed them, but they were motionless, dazzled like rabbits by the beam.

Barba averted her eyes for comfort; in her peripheral vision two shadows slipped from behind a bamboo and thatch hut advertising 'Masage'. She identified the outlines as girlish, and thought she heard muffled giggles, but they moved quickly and she was distracted by movement behind her, from the direction of the shore. As the torch-bearer lowered his tool and held a hand out to greet them, two young Turkish men, in bandanas, vests and cropped pants padded in their bare feet behind them. Everyone was grinning.

"Any chance of a beer, pal?" Sean requested.

The three dark heads all shook in harmony, sympathetically.

"Not permitted on beach at night. Gendarme," the torch-man said, as if that explained everything.

"Oh." Sean was looking bemused as well as disappointed.

"Sometimes we make beach party," the shortest one added quickly. "And you come tomorrow. We make good time here; music and we are dancing Turkish." He waved his arms and kick-stepped rhythmically a few times, to illustrate.

Barba and Lucy looked at each other and laughed. The other man, who had seemed more reserved than the torch-bearer and the dancer, stepped in between Alan and Sean, placing a chummy arm around their shoulders.

"Where do you stay? We send our bus for you tomorrow morning. Yeah? Free sunbeds. We have cold Turkish beer, Efes, ready for you, man," he winked at Sean and squeezed Alan's shoulders.

Obediently, they gave the name of the hotel and agreed the time for the pick-up.

Names were exchanged after some easy chit-chat. "Where you from?"

"Near Newcastle."

"Yes, the accents. Sometimes not easy to understand."

They joked about that.

"How long you here for?"

"Just the week, like. Four and a bit days left."

"You should stay longer."

"Aye, you're right. It's gone too quick already. I think we will next time."

The man with the torch introduced himself as Berk; the taller one was Mehmet, the shorter friend, the talkative dancer, was Musti.

"Bye Ladies. Bye Sean. Bye Alan. See you morning," they called after them. They waved back before continuing their separate progress along the beach path to the Antik centre, as it was called. They picked their way through crumbled pillars and monuments, stepping over ancient mosaic paving, in search of entertainment.

"Somewhere with a bit of life," Sean mumbled.

Phee and the Swedish girl flashed into Barba's thoughts. Her stomach muscles contracted momentarily, as the shadows on the beach flitted into her mind.

"Wonder where the girls got to?" she mused. Lucy did not seem to hear. She was mulling over the cocktail list.

They were paying the penalty for the cocktails, and several beers more for the men, the next morning. Assembling, dead-eyed, without conversation, in the foyer of the hotel, they waited silently for the beach bus, which was due at ten. Wayne lolled at the computer desk, surfing the internet. Phee tapped impatiently on the counter, the only one with any apparent energy. She stood, backs to them, eyes and fingers on the reception counter, watched by the young clerk behind, with his head of Roman curls and inquisitive brows. Barba knew she was avoiding any detailed explanation of where she and Anneka had been. She had arrived back on time, she had protested to her mother, after giving a vague account of a brief beach walk and a cruise around the town.

"Just around." Phee made it clear that, as far as she was concerned, the discussion was over.

A dull rattling and chunking of an engine turning over roughly, then the clerk's announcement that their beach bus had arrived, drove through their silence and inertia.

"It's here. Get your stuff. That all you're bringing, Wayne?"

Wayne, wearing beach shorts and a towel round his shoulders, carried his DS in one hand and his mobile in the other, from which the wires of the headset looped to his ears. Phee, also wired for sound, tripped along with a voluminous beach bag. The teenage driver nodded at them in greeting. A large dark birthmark stained the whole of his right cheek, accentuating his solemn eyes.

"Hallo, hallo. Good morning my friends. How are you?" Mehmet jumped down athletically, extending his arms and his smile to them. Patting Sean and Alan fraternally on the back, he slapped his hand affectionately on the back of Wayne's neck. The boy shrugged him off.

"Busy, eh?" Mehmet grinned nonchalantly, curving an arm solicitously behind the ladies as they stepped up. Phee smiled for the first time that day.

The interior of the bus was as dusty and worn as the exterior. A German family took up the back seats. The husband and frau sandwiched blonde, twin girls in sunhats, armbands and frilled swimsuits, clutching spades defensively. Mehmet smoothed the ten minutes of shaking and rattling with cheerful questions until they rolled up to the beach bar. They recognized the flags first, hung in rows like the masts of a pirate ship. The theme continued, as dark boys moved towards them from the beach, all wearing Jolly Roger bandanas and cut off pants.

Musti was quick to reach the door first, shadowed by Berk behind. Yanking open the door with the flourish of a cavalier, gallantly bowing them in turn down the steps, he addressed them individually with 'hellos' and 'good to see you's'. Except for Phee, who was last. With her he exchanged a brief little smile, observed by Barba, who had turned back to collect her bag, realising it was still on the bus.

Musti pointed in the direction of the sunbeds.

"Where do you want to lay?" he asked.

They settled for the front row, near the wooden aisle leading to the bar, closest to the sea.

"Good you come early," remarked Berk in his deep, hesitant tones. "Then you can choose."

As soon as they indicated a spot, another young Turk appeared, sprinting over to spring up the parasols and shake out the mattresses.

"Hello. Pleased to meet you. I am Atek," he introduced himself formally with a handshake, as they each thanked him for his attention.

"Merhaba. Sagol. Ben Barba," Barba returned, deciding on impulse that it was time for the debut of the smattering of Turkish she had learnt so far.

Sean raised an eyebrow before dumping himself on his lounger and screening his face with the newspaper. Atek looked at Barba, then Sean, then the others, who were busy arranging themselves and their accessories on and around the beds. Someone, not English, was calling for service further down the row, so he turned to attend to them. Barba followed him back to the bar when he was returning with his new order.

"Merhaba, Barba," he spoke softly. "What can I do for you?" Lifting his black crescent eyebrows over round, agate eyes, defined by lashes like kohl. He had a beak of a nose, noticeable ears, and a lithe but slightly squat body. Perversely, Barba was disconcerted to find, he was more than a little attractive to her.

"I'll have a large bottle of water for now," she said, pushing up her hair, with both hands. "It's very hot today." She blew through her lips to demonstrate the effect.

"For cold shower?" Atek joked.

Barba laughed and began rummaging in her bag for suncream. She could not believe she was blushing.

Minutes later, Atek approached their row with a notepad. Sean put his paper down and asked for a beer.

"Anyone else want anything?" he asked around their company, with uncharacteristic concern.

Atek began scribbling orders for food and drink from Lucy.

"I'll join Sean with a beer," Alan interrupted.

Phee hesitated, and looked over to the bar area.

"I'm going to get an ice-cream," she muttered, already on her way.

Barba watched her approach Musti, who was serving. He was stood beside Mehmet who was grinning like a stallion. A stocky, topless woman, in her late fifties, early sixties or badly sun-damaged and German, she guessed, was pulling his head over the counter. Closer to the breasts which rested as incongruously on the bar as the drying cow pats which came to Barba's mind. Apparently whispering in his ear, while he nodded, winked and beamed. Phee straightened her back and turned it on them. Musti, smiling and sprightly, led her to the ice-cream freezer. She seemed to be having trouble choosing. Looking into each tub ponderously, she was pointing and asking, smiling at Musti, fingers on lips.

Atek brought the beers and water.

"You like horse racing, Sean?' he remarked casually, after passing the Efes over the paper.

Sean was suddenly alert at the prospect of cold beer and an interest in his sport. Atek said he would bring a Turkish paper so they could choose some horses running in Istanbul that afternoon.

"Maybe you go shopping in Manavgat, Barba? You heard about that?" the waiter asked her.

"Yes, I've seen some tour information. Maybe later in the week, before we go home."

Atek tutted. "No need for tour. It's only a few kilometres from here. I could show you best shops and show Sean where we pick our horses."

Sean looked curious. Barba felt too interested, as she was not by nature a recreational shopper. Gulping water

23

she hid her embarrassment, again.

"We'll do that, mate." Sean took a slug of beer. Barba nodded.

Atek looked pleased as he went to collect Lucy's empty plate and Alan's empty Efes.

"Make that another two, mate." Sean was holding out his bottle too.

Phee asked her mother if she wanted an ice-cream too, once Atek was halfway back to the bar.

"Wouldn't mind a Calippo or something ," Lucy responded.

"I'll get it," Phee bounced up chirpily. "They said we can pay later," she informed them, already padding towards the bar, and Musti.

"Pay later?" Alan repeated, frowning. "Keep an eye on them, then."

"Who?" Lucy asked vaguely, closing her eyes.

Alan had closed his too.

Barba creamed her front, and leaned over to tickle Sean's chest. She ruffled the straggle of sandy hairs, threaded with a few grey ones.

"Do my shoulders, honey?"

Sean grunted and turned over without opening his eyes. Even though her request had been ignored, Barba smoothed the white fluid wordlessly on his back and legs. He did not speak or move, as she finished with the slightest of slaps on his thigh. She adjusted the shades to save their faces from burning, shook the sand off the greasy cover of her novel and looked around. Holidaymakers had settled on sunbeds, sprawled and supine like indulgent Roman nobility. The waiters flitted amongst the parasols, collecting and serving, sometimes engaged in conversation.

Some small children were excavating with colourful spades, laughing at the puppy that had left its box behind the bar to dig with them, flirting sand over their arms and legs.

Barba knew, without seeing, that she was being watched, too. Throughout lunch, when they all shuffled to the battered rattan furniture near the bar. As she tried not to notice the aggressively full and bare bosom of the German lady dining al fresco. When she shuddered under the capricious shower, waiting for it to release its chilling spray. When she lay, not quite hot beyond endurance yet, she knew she was observed. Whenever she rose, she recognized the sensation of moving down a gallery of pictures with the searing eyes of one portrait following her. She only once turned to meet the gaze. Atek's eyes were concealed behind dark glass; she would have said that he did not blink, nor was he smiling.

By four o'clock, four large beers and four food orders had sustained Sean, and finally finished him off.

"Going back to the hotel, Barb." He patted her with the sports page.

"You coming?" He tapped her again.

She shook her head, lifting from the lounger to reply.

"Having a swim first."

He just went. Alan followed, joined by Wayne, who pocketed his DS gratefully, to walk more steadily but just as lethargically, with the men.

Having declared her intent, Barba stretched and surveyed the scene. The guests were thinning out, more

25

had taken to the waves. The puppy scratched and frolicked more energetically with the children, now splashing and squealing in the surf. Closer to, and in view of the bar, Anneka and Phee were choreographing an affected game of frisbee. Lucy was sat, eating an ice-cream cornet, which she licked urgently, to catch the melting pearls before they dripped on to her exposed chest and stomach, which some had done.

"Going in the sea, Lucy. Fancy a swim?"

Her friend licked her fingers and lips, before issuing a tissue from her bag to finish the clean-up, then back to the bag for her camera. Breathing out heavily, she stood to swathe her form like a Buddha, with a capacious, turquoise sarong. Barbara wondered what she was doing, as Lucy combed her hair to her sturdy shoulders and pointed at a large rock with the comb.

"Just take a picture of me on that rock, Babe," she explained.

After changing from a position of straddling the rock, to a more poised, sideways pose, at Barba's suggestion, Lucy's image was taken.

Lucy reviewed the result on the screen of the digital camera.

"Hey, thanks honey." She was pleased. "I'll put that on my Talkbook profile. My cute Mermaid picture."

She threw off her wrap, and waddled to the sea. Barba, still aware of being watched, concentrated on the tattooed fairies, wobbling on the blubber struggling out of the under-sized bikini pants of her friend. Lucy glided into the sea as gracefully as a seal. Flipping and splashing Barba playfully, she nose-dived and surfaced with the ease of a dolphin. Paddling and splashing herself first to acclimatise, Barba threw herself into the comfortable waters, breast-stroking in rhythm with the waves, towards the sun.

As they swam, it was the wind that first gave a hint of what was to follow. As if in ill-mood, it took the huff, puffing and tugging provocatively at the bunting and flags, rattling the parasols, scattering light litter petulantly. Ten minutes later, the beach boys went into action; a damage limitation exercise, closing umbrellas with a snap, lifting and laying, as the wind worked itself into a frenzy. Most of the holidaymakers reacted quickly, snatching up their things and aiming for the shuttle bus back to their hotels. Barba and Lucy were about to follow, when the wind turned out to be a short-tempered freak and stormed off as abruptly as it had entered. The sky was now sulking. As she watched the blue topaz being washed out by greyness, Barba thought of Sean and wondered what he was doing.

The warnings could be heard several minutes before; the hints, the low grumbles, then the more ominous rumbles. The storm was coming. Barba could not resist the drama, and urged Lucy to stay at the edge of the tide with her. She glanced back once, to see Atek standing by a pillar at the front of the bar. Like a statue of a sentry, without movement or expression, his eyes were looking straight ahead, at her. Returning to the sea, she was enthralled. A bolt of fork lightning, like a glittering vein of precious metal exposed through muddy waters, flung out its thrilling trident and cut through the murk.

CHAPTER 2

The dirty yellow trucks were lined up by the side of the road, in convoy, as if preparing for a minor military invasion. Germans outnumbered the others, and were segregated into their own allocated trucks. The ten British, three Dutch and two Norwegians were directed to the one at the rear, which cemented their alliance from the outset.

The Truck Safari had been recommended by various people in the hotel they had chatted to. Once they were seated they were each issued with bottles of water. When their escort explained that it was not for drinking, but for attacking the other trucks, the Germans specifically, they began to anticipate fun.

The morning had started moodily, with an early rise to be ready for the pick-up car. Lucy was as cheerfully garrulous and irritatingly slow as usual, Wayne was neutralised by his DS, the men brusque and oily-eyed, from drinking too much and sleeping too little. It was Phee who radiated a force-field of resentment to which Barba, for once, felt uncomfortably empathic. Sensing that all Phee really wanted to do was get to the beach, to hover in Musti's radar. Even though she ignored what it might mean to her personally, she understood; she knew how it felt.

The trucks soon rumbled bullishly out of the town, onto the roads which led to the Taurus mountains.

The day- trippers were quiet, comfortable in the morning coolness but not on their seats. Past orange and lemon trees, rows of enticing melons in the dirt, they peered over the rails of the trucks to spot the little turtles basking on the concrete sides of the irrigation canals. Holding their breath and their talk as the three trucks, equidistant and hesitant, rolled their loads expertly over an ancient aqueduct. Barba marvelled at the beauty and durability of the Roman engineering and the skill of the Turkish drivers.

The first stop was at a reconstructed nomad dwelling. It consisted of a row of hovels and some low wooden and straw sheds. On one side some old people, with leather faces and peasant dress, sat surveying them silently, as if sleeping with their eyes open. Opposite were pens of jostling sheep with crumbly-looking wool. Lucy bent to peep inside one of the homes and nudged Barba, to show her the little television set winking in a dark corner.

"Hey, they're baking bread." Lucy pulled her over to a queue. A stomach-tickling smell of hot dough, cheese, spices and sugar intermingled with the heat. Two women were crouched over a flat stone oven.

The crisp-edged bread was thin and delicious; they chose between sweet and savoury toppings. Wayne and Lucy had both, the others shared theirs to sample. Sean and Alan bought chilled beers for themselves, bottled water for everyone else, and immediately became sociable and talkative. Barba, listening to Sean's jokes about the Germans and observing his sudden change of mood, felt a wave of unexpected and vehement pique rise against him. She recalled the scene the night before on the balcony.

Barba, Lucy and Phee had been dropped off at the hotel just before the storm advanced overhead. The rains descended as they reached cover, bouncing and hammering on roofs and outdoor furniture. The hotel pool looked as if someone was throwing pebbles in it. Barba found Sean asleep on the bed, surmising that he and Alan had had a few more beers, after leaving the beach. He was snuffling into the pillow, still wearing his shorts and flip-flops, feet suspended over the edge of the bed.

Leaving him to sleep, Barba showered, oiled her skin and put on make-up. She sat on the bed opposite the mirror. Looking more radiant with her darkening skin, she noticed. Eyes bluer and brighter, body glowing. Encouraged, she put on a new, oyster-grey, silk camisole and french knickers, slid her feet into pink leather, thong sandals. She clasped some simple silver hoops in her ears, dressing her middle toes with the toe-rings she was usually uncertain about, tending to remove them after a short period of wear.

It was still raining, though the tempo was softer, when she kneeled on the bed and shook Sean's shoulder. He mumbled a few words, his eyelids flickering.

"Want to eat, Sean?" she asked. "I'm starving, but it's really wet out there".

It took a few repeats before he sat up and rubbed his face and head to wake up. He stared and blinked his viscously-coated eyes. Putting out his tongue, he massaged his throat.

"Time is it?" he croaked.

"Sevenish. Thought we could order room service for tonight, seeing as the rain doesn't look like stopping. Plus we've got to get up at dawn, practically, for the Truck safari".

Sean yawned and nodded in agreement. Stretching and grunting, he raised himself and went over to the fridge. He took out a beer and a bottle of white wine, pouring out a glass for Barba, while she telephoned the order through to Reception. As she was talking she caught him looking at her appraisingly.

"That new?" He pointed at her with the bottle.

"What new?" she teased, stroking her hand down the silk, but he took his beer to the shower without answering.

The meal was better than they expected. They both appreciated a relaxed dinner in their rooms, rather than wandering about, hoping they would choose a good-enough restaurant. When the food arrived, the rain had died to a soft tap, and ceased completely by the time they had eaten. Barba cleared away the trays and brought more wine and another beer for Sean, who had moved out on to the balcony. Putting down her glass, she perched on his knee, brushing her lips from his temple, down his cheekbone. Her mouth reached his at the same time as the beer bottle. He took a swig and pushed her off as he rose.

"Need a pee," he had said, unapologetically.

"Wonder when the war begins?" Sean said to Alan, spilling his beer as he laughed.

"Well, things are warming up here. Could be soon." Alan looked over to the Germans, as if assessing their competence.

There was no sign of hostilities beginning, however, as they clambered back on to the hot seats of the vehicles. They trundled on past olives, giving way to pines, by the flashing river, below the layers of mountains. Gradually, random stones became piles, then discernible relics of structures. They parked, the guide explained, to visit the remains of the Roman town which had stood there two thousand years earlier.

"What's happening?" Wayne looked up from his DS.

The grandfather from Birmingham replied before anyone else.

"Stopping to look at a pile of old bricks, son," he said, with a strong Midlands accent and scornful emphasis on the words, 'pile' and 'bricks'.

Wayne's expression showed boredom verging on pain, Lucy appeared baffled. Barba was so annoyed she looked away, to avoid saying something regretful.

From the power of Barba's imagination, gorgeous white villas with terracotta roofs, walkways and forums, embellished with carvings and fountains, sprang up from broken pillars and grey rubble. Mosaics, blemished minutely so as not to offend the gods with their perfection, became complete beneath her sandaled feet. Divine statues rose from cracked, decapitated stone. Busy white ghosts in tunics and togas peopled the doorways and streets.

Wayne seemed fascinated too, as he beckoned Barba to join him and Phee, who had found the tiny square jail at the other end of the forum. Lucy was perched on the remains of a stone trough taking photographs, including a token one of Alan and Sean against the pillar at the entrance. They stood next to the seated grandfather who was smoking a cigarette with an air of weary tolerance. When the call came to move on, minutes later, Barba felt deprived, and lingered at the back of the groups returning.

The midday sun was spreading an inescapable blanket of heat, and many of the men, Sean included, had removed their shirts. Some relief was offered when they came to a halt by a lake and could rest in the shade of rocks and trees, or dabble and paddle in the coolness. Barba really felt the urge to swim, watching others, particularly the German women, push into the water. Instead, she hovered at the edge.

"You look as if you could do with some sunscreen, Sean." Barba reached to touch the reddening skin of his back.

Sean moved his shoulder away.

"Feels fine. Be fine," he answered. They were both distracted by the guide, calling and beckoning.

As with the history stop, the respite was brief, and efficiently they were summoned back to their vehicle. All seated and moving off, they began to grip the rails in front like thrill-seekers at a fair. Each of their trucks in turn mounted a rising bank, flinging them back and sending out dirty bouquets of mud from their tracks. The tourists squealed and groaned as they were bounced, rocked, shocked up and down rough terrain and ditches.

The cue to take up water bottles and attack came from the Turkish guide of the 'Allies' truck. When he launched the first arc of water, the joyous cry for battle to commence came from both sides. With whoops and yells, they bent down for their arms, shot and sprayed with intent glee. Gasping and shuddering when an enemy missile splashed home, they returned, drenched and determined, to the fray. Eventually, ammunition and energy were depleted. The tired, drying mob were happy to arrive at the hillside restaurant, for lunch overlooking the lake and the offer of a poolside swim.

Barba, to justify the party mood, swilled down her food with the local beer.

"Anyone taking the plunge with me?" she asked, picking up her glass and moving down the steps, followed by the others.

She managed a languorous few minutes in the pool, before, in keeping with the brisk space of the day so far, one of the guides called out.

"Donkeys ready for you to ride now, Ladies and Gentlemen." He repeated it in German with the same commanding tone.

"I'm up for that," Wayne responded with uncharacteristic enthusiasm. They were all apparently in the same mood, and got up to join him.

The donkeys clearly were less keen. Bearing a variety of colours, girth and fur-quality, some were doe-eyed, others with wilder expressions. All of them shared the same aura of apathy. Because there were too few of them for everyone to ride at once, the animals had to make three return journeys. Up and down the hillside they plodded with their jolly burdens, who had all just eaten and drunk heartily. Barba, Phee and Lucy watched the first cohort shamble up and trek back down the track, eager to be riders on the second journey. Alan and Sean quickly grew too bored and impatient.

"I'd rather have another beer," Sean declared lazily.

"Good idea," approved Alan, setting off with him back to the bar.

Wayne had planned to take the last ride. He had the ingenious idea of re-filling the water bottles from the drinking fountain, and was hastily gathering support from the grandson and the Norwegians. Some of the German children, returning from their ride, spied the action and began re-stocking too, furiously filling up each time the Allies carried their weapons to their trucks.

Lucy's donkey was so broad and burly, it seemed like a different breed to the one Barba was given. It was a meek creature, whose back was a mere step up for her to mount, while Lucy grunted and needed help to be hoisted up. Phee was ready, with an agile, gymnastic leg over her more average-sized ride. Straightening up, Barba did her best to look elegant for the photographers who were recording every event, though she was aware that her feet were dangling below her donkey's belly.

"Yee-ha!" Lucy called out lustily.

The animal bowed beneath her stopped to chew some leaves, started, and stopped again at the next branch. Barba found it hard to stop giggling after that. She contributed to the general hilarity by making a deadpan commentary on the progress of the donkeys, who all had numbered headbands. Hers was number seven. Lucky, she thought, laughing to herself.

The last stand of the water battle was conducted with renewed vigour and determination on their way back to their next destination, the waterfall. The supplies were soon exhausted, and they were too, with throwing, flak-catching, bawling and guffawing. Finally, they conceded peace with smiles and thumbs-up, with a few V-signs from each side. Retrieving the towels they had been advised to bring, which they had thought would be just for swimming, they became quietly absorbed in mopping, rubbing and patting away the consequences of war.

Before they could access the waterfall, they were forced to pass a stall selling their photographs. Surprised at the number of times they had been captured on film, they were also impressed to find their images already printed. The more one bought, the better the deal, so Barba grabbed one or two of the best for each of the highlights of the day. She then readily agreed to buy three bracelets of beads for one lira from a persistent local boy, guessing that there would only be a short time to enjoy the sight.

It was not spectacular as waterfalls go, still pleasing, with its pastel rocks, its verdant shade, the music and touch of its cool spray. Barba was entranced for a moment, before being brought back by the loud calls, in English with a Turkish voice, to move on.

Three times that day, first resonating authoritatively from the town centre, once closely, near a village, and thirdly, quite distantly, source unseen, they had heard the metallic call for prayer. Each time, Barba was reminded of the final activity on the day's agenda; a visit to a mosque. When she saw it, it was more palatial and breath-taking than she had anticipated. It had pure white walls, a golden–topped dome and minarets, a pristine expanse of finely-decorated tiles on the walls and floors.

"We see enough of these bloody things at home," mumbled the grandfather from Birmingham. Shortly after, he was the only one left behind, as he sat in silent protest in the truck. Barba looked back at the smoke curling over the back of his elderly head, and shook hers in disbelief.

"Not like this," she had retorted, scowling at him, then was disappointed with herself, for responding to such pitiful ignorance.

The others were intent on removing their footwear, washing off the dust at the four elaborate taps and stone bowls in the square fronting the building. Most of the women were required to stop by the box of fabrics at the entrance in order to select pieces to cover heads, shoulders and legs, before being allowed in to the holy, alien place. Barba chose blue because even if the effect could not be said to be attractive, the colour always flattered her. While Lucy had to spend more time rummaging for pieces big enough to cover herself adequately, Phee was mysterious and alluring within seconds.

It was her first experience of the interior of a mosque. This one had an exhilarating effect on Barba, because it was so magnificent, and yet so simple. She soaked up the quiet of the uncluttered, round prayer-hall. In the last few days, something powerful had stirred inside her, disturbing layers, shifting, like earth quaking. Heat, boiling and bubbling to the surface under pressure, like lava; choking, molten. In that space, she felt briefly expurgated, as if peace was pouring over her. Stood under a light-fall, washing over her, draining away. Feeling calm and clear.

Sean had been topless for most of the long day of the outing, replacing his shirt only when requested, before entering the mosque.

"Ouch. Caught the sun a bit," was all he had remarked as he pulled out the cotton fabric, away from his flesh.

Less than two hours later, Barba was gingerly peeling the shirt from his back with her fingertips, while he screwed his eyes and gnashed his teeth, as she revealed skin that was already blistering and weeping. That night, Sean was forced to take paracetamol, and attempt to sleep on his front on top of the bedcovers, while Barba shivered underneath because the air-conditioning was at maximum level.

"Where is your husband?" were the first words Atek said to her, when she arrived at the beach late the next morning.

"He is not my husband," were the first words she spoke to him, surprising herself.

"He got sunburnt yesterday, so today he is sore and feels unwell,"she explained, not sounding as sympathetic as she thought she should.

Mentally, she justified and acquitted herself of failing in her duty to her partner. She had delayed going to the beach. Gone to the shops to get aloe vera gel, put it on him, enduring his continuous moans and complaints. She had chilled plenty of water for him and made sure he was comfortable before she left.

"Where were you?" was the second thing he said.

She did not answer immediately. Dumbstruck by

the hint of reproach in his eyes, an almost censorious tone in his voice.

"I've brought some photos," she smiled, lifting out the envelope.

Each one was passed to Atek, who studied them for longer than most people do usually, she thought. They were placed carefully on the table, creating a collage of Truck Safari events.

"What are you laughing at?"

He was holding the picture of herself on the donkey to his chest, which was shaking with amusement. "The donkey. It is small." He began to laugh again.

She joined in as soon as she looked at the photograph again. Seeing through his eyes the timorous beast's body covered by her, her feet hanging comically close to the ground.

"You're right," she chuckled, "it should be a big white horse."

They were overcome with another bout of mirth, which continued even after Barba had collected the photographs up and put them way. It seemed very quiet when the laughter stopped.

"Where's Lucy and her family?" Barba asked, to fill in the awkward pause.

They had come earlier and she was ready to join them.

Atek pointed south-east; she squinted along the line of his direction and saw that Lucy had seen her, as if sensing her presence, and was waving. Barba took off her sandals to shake out the grit from the path, having walked instead of taking the beach bus. Stepping on to the sand, she immediately hopped, yelping, on to the nearest sunbed. Kicking her legs and shaking her feet like an infant at the climax of a tantrum. An amused German woman watched her, disturbed in her repose by Barba landing heavily on the lounger her husband had left to go to the bar.

"Hot, yes?" the German lady frowned in sympathy, clearly entertained.

"Oh yes. Ja. Sorry." Barba grimaced, suddenly seeing how funny she must have looked. She was laughing still when Atek came forward, holding her sandals, which she had promptly dropped when her soles hit the baking sand. He knelt down and placed them before her. For one moment she thought he was about to place them on her feet. She held her breath. Looking at her with lifted brows, his upper lip rippling, his eyes showing he wanted to laugh too. Instead, he lowered his eyes respectfully and stood.

"It's nearly fifty degrees, Barba," he told her in a stern teacher voice. With a backward glance as he walked away, he added very quietly, "so wear your shoes or you need someone to carry you."

She looked at her sandals, then at his back and his strong arms. Sighing, she put on her shoes.

As soon as she undressed and got on to the sunbed Lucy had reserved for her, Barba realised her energy level was low. She attributed the causes to the hectic trip the day before, the demands of Sean and the walk to the beach as the temperature rose. Checking she was fully shaded because she had no desire to join Sean, like a pair of chickens who have shared the same roasting tin. She spread her towels and massaged herself lazily with the tanning oil. Soothed into sloth by the sun, she sank readily. From time to time, she would surface reluctantly, when hooked with a question, an attempt at conversation, or a noise that broke through the hush of the surf and the background hum, of people doped with heat and hedonism.

With a jerk, similar to the involuntary spasms at the point of succumbing to sleep, Barba was hoisted abruptly, unexpectedly, into wakefulness. She blinked and looked around warily. Feeling the same sense of disorientation a sleepwalker feels when they find themselves conscious, in a different place to that which they believed they should safely be in. A shadow had fallen over her, blocking out the light and warmth of the sun. It lay over her upper body like the lead mats they use in X-ray units.

" Sorry, Barba. I disturb you?" It was Atek. She was alone with him. Lucy and the others were somewhere else.

"No, no. It's fine. Just dozing. You made me jump." Sitting up, smiling shakily.

"You leave soon, yes?" Sat on the next sunbed, facing her, under the shade, speaking softly, reminding her of a doctor at a bedside.

"Two more days, yes," she nodded, putting her head on one side to show her regret.

"Well, I was thinking tomorrow would be best day if you want me to show you good shops in Manavgat before you leave. They say rain again tomorrow, and Sean has burn," he reasoned, compassionately.

"Yes," Barba encouraged him.

"And I have a day off," he announced with a grin, as if that resolved it.

"I'll have to see what Sean says," Barba murmured indecisively.

Atek's tone switched to one of brisk formality as he glanced around. A piece of paper was slipped under her hand with the finesse of a magician.

"See what Sean says," he ordered, "text me."

Clutching the note in her fist, still reeling from the speed of the sleight of mouth and hand, she watched him walk up the decking path, past the bar and away from the beach.

After a day of solitary confinement and enforced sobriety, Sean did not feel like a better person. His face lightened when Barba came through the bedroom door, and he was more congenial to her suggestions.

"How are you feeling?" she asked, as she examined his back. "You managed a shower, then?" Sean had a thick white bath towel round his waist.

"Yep. A very cool one. And I'm feeling pissed off."

"Poor you," she commiserated, in role. "It's looking better, though. You don't look so hot now."

"Thanks," he answered dryly. "Feel more normal now, except for the pain when I stretch myself."

He sucked in his breath and squeezed his eyes as she tentatively patted blobs of green gel over his shoulders.

"Do you want to do anything this evening?" she enquired. What about eating?"

"Well, I've been crawling up the walls, having to stay in. Be nice to go out."

"Where do you fancy?"

"Maybe the harbour. We haven't tried the fish there yet, and only two more days left."

"Sounds good."

"And I could do with a walk."

"Even better. It'd be nice to go by the beach," Barba suggested, enjoying his enthusiasm and the prospect of a pleasant evening ahead.

It began auspiciously, as they reached the shore just before the sun sank. They were treated to its spectacular exeunt. Lifting up and spreading its majestic robes of gold, reds and purples, it let them fall as slowly, before bowing out for the day. Barba reached out for Sean's hand as they strolled by the breaking waves. He allowed her hold it limply, until they reached the end of the line of beach bars and restaurants, all closed and covered. His hand was reclaimed to find a cigarette. Barba watched the town lighting up, the reflections on the harbour, boats returning, from fishing and pleasure, others going out for the same. Reaching the ruins at the edge of the town, Sean stubbed out the smouldering remains of his smoke. Continuing, side by side, they walked apart to the main streets.

Pausing by the fish restaurants, gazing at the catch in the tanks at the doors, politely declining invitations from the men posted at every entrance, until they found the place they were looking for. Sean had done his research well.

"This looks nice," Barba commented.

The dining area was separated from the walkway by a charming screen of vines threaded through with twinkling leaf-like lights. When they were seated, they still had a view of the sea, the boats and the captivating mix of people moving, mingling and merging. Once they had decided and given their order, they settled back into their wicker tub chairs to savour the scene.

Anglo-Saxons, Huns and Vikings promenaded casually with their lovers, their wives, their children and their friends, by those Roman walls. Russians in groups pushed loudly and obliviously through the masses. A tall couple, striking because of their charisma, their good looks and their age-difference, walked close by them. They could hear the animated, easy conversation, see the rapport in the closeness of their mirrored bodies, their looks and smiles, as they talked and walked.

"You can see what he's after," commented Sean, sucking his teeth and putting his napkin down.

Barba did not answer. What she saw was a radiant, well-groomed woman with a relaxed face and shining eyes. A woman who looked comfortable and confident in herself. A woman, about her own age, clearly enjoying the attentions of her young and dashing Turkish lover. Whispering in her ear, holding her hand.

Later, passing through the temple of Apollo, they encountered them again. The woman, leaning against a pillar, being gently kissed by the man. Perhaps Mark Antony had embraced Cleopatra in the very same spot, Barba fantasised, having learnt something of the history of the place.

"Can we stop here for a bit, pet?" Barba asked.

The bar she liked the look of was quiet enough to hear the sea as well as see it, and a musician was strumming a Turkish guitar, singing in harmony with the tide.

"The fish was delicious, Sean. Good choice,

love," she complimented him. "I enjoyed the people-watching too. Just fancy a quiet drink here, before we walk back."

Sean hesitated before agreeing. Barba knew he really wanted to get back to Alan and the other Brits, gathered together at the Korner Bar near the hotel. There were chairs near the edge of the bank which slid to the beach, which they took. Barba looked down the list of cocktails offered.

"Sex On The Beach. Wonder what that's like?" Sean either did not hear, or chose to ignore the irony.

"I'll have a Roman Summer," she decided, knowing it would mean nothing to him.

Removing the tinsel and the unwanted lemon from the goblet, she drank her potion. It tasted of pomegranate and berries, reminding her of autumn fruits, rich and honeyed, with a bitter aftertaste that lingered on the tongue.

"Atek was asking where you were today," she told Sean; truthfully, she recalled.

"Oh?" Sean seemed pleased. "Missed me?" he smirked, "or my bar bill?"

Barba laughed to maintain the affable mood.

"Well, he suggested showing us round Manavgat tomorrow," she ventured. "He says the weather forecast doesn't look good, he's got the day off, and we're off home the day after."

"Good idea," Sean conceded, more readily than she had anticipated, or hoped for.

"What's the plan?" he asked.

"Oh, no plan, really. I said I'd have to ask you first, so he gave me his number so we could text him,"

45

she replied, mindful of the 'we'.

"Good," concluded Sean. "We'll text him first thing in the morning. We can ask Alan and co if they want to come, when we get to the Korner Bar."

That was a cue for Barba to finish her drink, which she was glad to, as she did not have to look at him, or say anymore, for the time being.

Back the way they had come, walking close to the waves without getting their feet wet. To take the track leading from the shore to the road where their hotel and the Korner Bar was situated, they had to pass the bar where Atek worked. The pirate flags were waving ahead of them, the white grinning skulls illuminated by the beam of the full moon behind. In front of her, large letters had been carved in the sand.

SENI SEVIYORUM

"What does that mean?" Sean said.

"It's Turkish for 'I love you'," she answered.

"Dirty bastards," he replied.

She did not ask who, or if he was joking. Walking round the words, her attention was drawn to a bamboo bower constructed ahead, around two of the sunbeds, at the end of the row nearest the sea. As they diverted towards the beach path, she looked again, to see the unmistakeable backs of Anneka and Mehmet. His arm, with its scrolled tattoos, crossed her hips, her long, pale braid swinging, as they disappeared behind the screen of leaves.

In Barba's mind, she saw pools of dried cow dung, pendulous udders, and a passive beast looking ahead, chewing the cud, seeing all, unseeing.

Surely the girl's mother knew about this? she

thought. She said nothing to Sean, or anyone else.

The beat of the 'Macarena' could be heard thumping out before they reached the end of the road, the volume beating the other bars. Barba and Sean eased into the crowd, through the overspill of the dance floor, nudged by floppy men, bumped by women with strapping thighs below strapless dresses. Shuffling past the cohort from Birmingham who were indulging in their last night revel.

One of the women shouted "Sex Bomb" so loudly in Barba's ear that she winced. She had seen enough drunken tourists and so many Turkish waiters performing for them, to understand that it was a request for one of them to jump on a table, remove his shirt and wiggle his hips to their tune. When the majority of the women present took up the call, chanting "Sex Bomb, Sex Bomb, Sex Bomb", a lithe figure strutted into the centre. Untucking his green uniform shirt from his trousers, revealing a 'Calvin Klein' band above his belt, as the music started up and the show began. The women gathered around him, clapping and cheering as he skipped up on to a counter, thrusting and swivelling his pelvis with the rhythm. Singing raucously along, out of tune, they pouted and pranced beneath him. A few of the more drunk or lascivious of the ladies unbuttoned his shirt, and caressed his chest, wet and heaving with exertion. For the finale, to bawdy applause, he ripped off the shirt, spun it and flung it dramatically in the air.

Barba found Lucy sat with Carol and her husband in the corner seats. They had retired early and were part of the British community who had bought homes and lived there most of the time.

"I see your girl's got friendly with the Swedish lass," Carol remarked to Lucy, indicating with her head towards Phee, who was jigging along with the crush.

"Anneka? Yes, they get on well. Godsend actually for Phee," Lucy answered.

"Have you met her mother?" Carol continued, with a hint of a smirk.

"Seen her from a distance. Haven't been introduced, talked or anything like that, have we, Barba?" Barba confirmed that they had not.

Carol seemed please to have an opportunity to prepare them for the event.

"Well, rum do, really, in my opinion," she confided. "Spend quite a bit of time here, the mother and daughter that is."

"They have their own apartment, don't they?" Lucy asked.

"Yes. Father is very well-off, apparently, and he bought it. Sometimes he shows up. But most of the time it's her and the girl," Carol explained. "Can't work out whether they're together or not. S'posed to be separated."

"Apparently, you name it, she's had it done." As Carol was warming to the subject, her voice, which had begun quite loudly, was growing stronger.

"Done?" Barba was interested now, but looked around uncomfortably.

"Plastic surgery. Botox, fillers, boobs, lipo, tummy tuck. Even down there, so I've heard." Carol illustrated the list by indicating her own body parts.

"Down there?" Lucy's eyes were widening.

"Labia. Trimmed," Carol mouthed the words,

nodding vigorously.

Barba began to chuckle, divining the meaning, even though she was ignorant of the scientific Latin terminology. Lucy guffawed, covering her face with her hands incredulously.

"Can't say how I know. Friend in the trade," Carol added, for credibility, tapping the side of her nose.

"Fond of the company of the young Turkish men, too," she revealed, her attention now on the Turkish Tom Jones.

"Oh, well," Barba equivocated. "Excuse me".

Sean was still thirsting at the bar. Barba managed to make Lucy and Alan understand the arrangements for the shopping trip, which they communicated that they were keen to join, and left them all to it.

In the hotel bedroom she found the ripped bill with Atek's name and number printed in red, folded tightly, in her purse. With trembling hands she tapped in his details on her mobile 'phone, as jittery as the first time a boy gave her his number.

CHAPTER 3

They were, unsurprisingly to Barba, all very sluggish at rising the next morning. She was doing her best to suppress her increasing anxiety that they would miss the opportunity, that Atek would do something without them, without her.

"Sean, we really shouldn't let Atek down. We haven't texted him yet, and he was good enough to offer us his time," she attempted to shame Sean into getting up. Each time she spoke to him she was consciously toning down the stridency she could hear rising in her voice.

"Text him now and say we're running a bit late," he mumbled under the sheet.

Relieved, she felt as if she had been given the permission she needed to activate.

Atek promptly returned her text.

'No problem. Could meet in Side instead. U shop there yet? 11 ok?'

Barba asked Sean, who consented easily to the change, then knocked on Lucy's apartment door. Thankfully, they were all out of bed and happy to go to Side too. Barba was pleased, because she loved the ambience of the Roman ruins, and had only been there once, the night before. The week had gone by so quickly. Next time, we will stay longer and do more, she promised herself.

' Ok, Atek. Good. See you at 11 at ampitheatre. Thank you. Barba x'

As soon as the text was sent, she realized she had added the x without thinking, out of habit, and wondered if she should have done. She deleted it guiltily. Ridiculous, she told herself.

Atek somehow looked younger away from the beach. She had thought he might be closer to thirty, but now considered him more likely to be in his mid-twenties at most. To her, generally, Turkish men were youthful-looking in their teens, then seemed to mature relatively soon, with men in their thirties she would have estimated to be over forty, at least. Was it the hard life, the military service, early-greying, the sun, or all combined? she pondered.

They waited for the buses and taxis, which could not go beyond the Roman gates, to turn round, so they could cross the road to him. With the ancient amphitheatre, ageing as gracefully as anything could be expected to, looming authoritatively behind him, he looked small. He also appeared unexpectedly belligerent, his black brows drawn together, scrutinising the passers-by, until he noticed them approaching. The frown changed to a smile as quickly as winking.

"Hello. Hello. Hello."

"How are you?"

"Good, thanks."

"Merhaba. Merhaba."

"Nasilsin?"

"Iyiyim. "

"You learning some Turkish good, Barba?" Atek praised.

"Trying. Thanks." Smiling modestly at him while Sean sniggered in the background.

51

"You know, when in Rome, do as the Romans do," she reasoned.

Atek looked unsure.

"Well, the weather's not too bad, is it Atek? This wind's quite nice, actually." Sean changed the subject.

"Nice here, but too much on the beach. Strong. Takes the umbrellas away, and people don't come."

"Oh, so it spoils your business," Lucy commented sympathetically.

"Yes, not so good for us", Atek shrugged.

"Anyway, so we shop and you can enjoy your last day. What do you want to buy?"

He listened intently to a few ideas from each of them, as they ambled towards the main shopping street.

Befuddling began in Barba's head as soon as they joined the crowd of bargain-hunters. Sensing the bargainers moving in, out of the dizzying show of goods stretching down each side of the main walk, with more shops branching off in each direction.

Some of it was sublime. Splendid rugs, hand-woven from silks and fine wools, draped over poles. Delicate, coloured glass lamps hung like dewdrops on leaves, above hookahs and ornaments. Skilfully carved, walnut boxes revealed their secret openings. Artefacts made from beads with the godly 'eyes' winked from shelves. Truly delightful confectionery assaulted their senses deliciously, joining forces with the spice stalls. Veils, tops and skirts in sequined and embroidered silk, for belly-dancing, swayed in groups.

There was also the ridiculous. Polyester harem pants, bras and headbands, in lurid synthetics, dripping with artificial coins, jangled from hangers. Tiny, leering, clay figures boasted massive phalluslie. Wooden couples copulated in implausible positions. Pharmacy windows were completely screened with stacks of cartons of Viagra. Pirated recordings of films and music could be bought alongside reproductions of all the latest gadgets, games and gimmicks. Faked, to near-perfection, in some cases.

The jaded tourists moved through like herded sheep, distracted here and there by something that took their fancy. The traders, as alert and purposeful as trained dogs, nipped at them constantly; yapping out compliments, jokes and offers, with practised familiarity.

Atek kept an attentive distance until Alan and Sean were showing an interest in jeans.

"You want jeans? I take you to my friend. He has quality, good price," he intervened, signalling for them to follow him.

A few doorways down, he led them into a shop dripping in denim.

The men were impressed when, having tried on a pair they liked, were told to come back in twenty minutes, as the length would be altered to fit.

"Hey, I call that service, mate," Sean praised. "In that case, I'm having another pair."

"You're right, pal," agreed Alan, joining in the pushing and pulling of hangers.

Lucy decided the opportunity, to have the jeans ready-fitted so economically, was too rare to waste.

"Wayne," she instructed, "find a couple of pairs you like too, while we're here. You know how hard it is to get the right fit for you."

Wayne began to look around apathetically.

"If you're buying him some, I'm having a pair, too," Phee demanded truculently.

Barba and Lucy got involved in her choosing, which led them to buy some also. The vendor encouraged and flattered throughout the process, whilst Atek monitored the process tactfully from the doorway.

Sean and Alan, finished with their purchases, had gone outside for a cigarette. Barba was checking the fit of hers in the mirror. First the frontal; smoothing her hips and buttocks she twisted to see her rear, to find herself facing Atek, who had moved forward. Returning to the mirror quickly, only to see his reflection behind her, smiling.

"These are perfect," she told the assistant, and escaped to the dressing-room.

Finally, all suited and measured, they were out into the street. Atek caught Sean's elbow.

"One moment, please. You continue, I'll be with you, one moment. Just I talk with my friend." He disappeared into the jeans shop they had just left.

Meandering on, in less than a minute he caught up with them, with an air of satisfaction. They continued past the troupes of dummies wearing many interpretations of all the present, past, and possibly future, fashions. The rainbow choruses of shoes, the flourishes of bags and belts gave way, on their left and right, to processions of glittering jewellers.

Alan, who had a penchant for heavy, ostentatious jewellery, was attracted to a designer watch. He hovered around the store window, until the others grew impatient, except Atek.

"If you like something, Alan, maybe I can get

you better price. My friend has jewellery shop. Best quality. I can show you if you like?" he intercepted.

"Do you think he has this one, Atek?" Alan asked hopefully.

"We can see," Atek replied, nodding.

Lucy rolled her eyes and turned away.

"C'mon Dad," complained Phee."I need to get some presents for my friends."

They were all visibly tiring of the intense retail experience. Consequently, the gift-shopping was brief and efficient, completed in one shop, which sold dried apple tea, boxes of Turkish Delight and bracelets of glass and leather.

"We need to eat", Lucy concluded firmly, when they were laden with bags and had collected the bespoke jeans.

"I'm going to the jewellery shop first with Atek," Alan asserted.

Trailing after them resentfully, they waited outside.

"Bet that's going to set him back a few hundred quid, good price or not," Lucy grumbled.

She discovered that her estimate had been modest, when Alan strutted out holding out his wrist effeminately to show off the chunk of gold. Atek followed him like a royal aide.

"Got nearly twenty-five percent off the other guy's price," Alan justified his indulgence.

"Let's go eat," sniffed Lucy.

Atek said he knew somewhere and led them to a small, shady pension near the harbour. It was just off the main street, with a board advertising 'Free Rooms' on

55

one of the walls. The owner was clearly another good friend, as he and Atek embraced warmly. They were all introduced, shaking hands in turn. Relieved, they dumped their bags on the floor and their seats on the rattan chairs. Gratefully they took the menus handed to them and began scanning the options.

"I will be back in few minutes," Atek announced, as soon as they had ordered their food and drinks. "My friends are waiting for me, but I am quick," he assured them with a smile and a wave, and was gone.

Barba realised she had intended to get some money from the cash machine.

"Sugar! Forgot to get more lira. Won't be long," she excused herself.

Back on the main street, she could see Atek ahead, walking briskly and talking into his mobile 'phone. When he disappeared from view, she realized he must have gone into one of the line of jewellers at the top of the street. The bank was just around the corner. Returning from withdrawing her money Barba saw Atek again. He had been joined by Musti and Berk, standing outside the shop where Alan had bought his watch. There were several bank notes in his hand, two of which he handed to each of his friends. Accepting, they slapped his back approvingly, before pocketing it, as Atek was doing with his wad. With arms around each others' shoulders, their backs to Barba, the three strode off in the direction of the pension. She knew she had not been seen. Somehow also knowing that it would be favourable not to be, she slowed her pace.

Everybody was eating, drinking and conversing contentedly when Barba entered the pension. Phee and

Lucy had brightened considerably with the arrival of Musti and Berk with Atek. Keen to ease her hunger and the puzzling discomfort she felt about the scene of the jewellers, she ordered a cold beer and bit into her sandwich appreciatively.

"How come you're not working, too?" Phee asked Musti, clearly thankful, whatever the reason.

"Wind too strong, today," explained Musti, with some concern. "But then we could meet in Side, for your last day," he told her.

Phee stretched her hand across the table towards him, and left it there, in reply.

Lucy was busy taking photographs of them all, in a combination of groupings and poses.

"We'll send them to you," Alan beamed generously." Give us your email addresses."

Three lines were written on the paper Barba quickly found in her handbag. She noted only one, 'Atek66@hitmail.com', before she watched it, with irrational jealousy, being relocated to Lucy's purse.

"Are you on Talkbook?" Lucy asked.

They nodded. Barba told herself it was time she put herself on this Talkbook thing, although she baulked in anticipation of doing it.

"Great," confirmed Lucy, "I'll put them on there too."

It was agreed they would all walk back together via the beach. When the bill came, Sean insisted on paying it all, declining the soft offers to contribute from their Turkish hosts.

"Please wait. I am going to get a sweatshirt from my room," Atek said, as they were about to leave.

57

"Your room?" Barba repeated.

"Didn't I tell you? We sleep here. Our rooms are there." He pointed towards three doors on the ground floor.

"Can you show me where the toilet is, please?" Barba asked, to none of the Turks in particular, specifically to Atek.

"I will show you," he offered.

He led her by the small garden, interesting because of its filched Roman statue, carved block of stone and two cut-off pillars, to a recess at the back of the building. Opening the door for her, he paused for what seemed an inappropriately long time, looking at her strangely; his eyes still, fixed on hers, his lips curving up and out.

"Sagol." Murmuring her thanks in Turkish she stepped in, momentarily having the feeling he intended to follow.

"Anytime," he said

Closing the door on him, listening to his footsteps fade, she breathed out, studied her cracking appearance in the old, tarnished mirror, hanging from one loose nail, and groaned.

Their route back took them past the largest and most popular discotheque in the town, 'The LightShip'.

"Have you been there, Alan?" Musti asked, glancing at Phee.

"No, we haven't," Phee replied objectionably, before her father had chance to, then abruptly changed her strategy with a plea. Knowing from experience that, with a few beers in his stomach and an expensive watch on his arm, her target was softened.

"Dad," she pleaded, sensing that she was silently urged on by Musti and the others, apart from Wayne, who acted horrified, and Sean, who seemed apathetic,

"Can we go here for our last night?" Phee begged.

"Well, I'm not sure, pet," Alan prevaricated, which was a good sign. He was feeling a slight sense of guilt about his indulgence.

"We haven't been anywhere I've chosen, exactly," she reproached.

"We have to see what the others want to do, too, don't we?" Alan looked round for support, hoping democracy would work in his favour.

Atek, Berk and Musti leaned on a wall, watching the process with interest.

"We will go anyway." Atek directed this information at Alan and Sean, cleverly, thus manipulating the whole group into a positive decision.

"Oh, alright, mate. Well, seeing it's the last night an' all," Alan reconsidered.

"I'm easy, pal," put in Sean. "As long as they've got Efes, cold like."

"Of course," Atek assured him, with a graceful bow of his head.

"I'd love a good dance," said Barba eagerly.

"It'll be fun, hun," was Lucy's verdict.

"I'm not going," Wayne sulked.

"You don't have to, Boring One," Phee replied nastily, her face close to his.

"Settled then," Alan confirmed, as if it had been his idea.

Through a short tunnel between walls of former

buildings, now habitats for creepers and bats, they came to the ruins where the old library and other buildings had existed. A square with a stone wall set with friezes and carved lettering, Barba learnt from a board, had been the location for crucifixions. She pointed this out to the others, prompting another photo-shoot from Lucy, who began capturing the others as they explored and re-grouped.

Barba's camera had been unpredictable throughout the holiday, but she spotted some resting camels and decided to see if she could get a decent shot. That scene recorded satisfactorily, she took one of Phee and her mother by the huge slab of the altar, another of Wayne wrestling hilariously with Musti, and a third of Berk, smoking with Sean and Alan, as they sat together on a stone block bearing three heads with chipped, eroded features.

Atek was standing alone, on a bank, apart from the others. He had put on his sweatshirt, the hood pulled over his head. With his hands in his pockets he struck a casual pose, flanked equidistantly by two twin, horn-shaped boulders, as high as his chest. Barba pressed the button. Nothing flashed.

"Can I see, Barba?" Atek stepped down and held out his hand.

"It's just a very shadowy figure, I'm afraid," she apologised.

'The Lightship' discotheque was not a boat, but a concrete prism extending from the ancient arched walls which formed part of the original temple. It looked out to sea, upon the real lighthouse, fulfilling its duty; warning of potential danger and averting wreckage.

The only connection between the two constructions was the intruding beams projecting from the disco into the night sky, like searchlights.

Shivering outside, Barba moved slowly with the others in the queue towards the entrance, though it was not really cold, just the same breeze tempering the heat, as it had all that day. She put her arm round Phee, who was scanning the clusters of Turkish males, some entering, some standing around the car park.

"Don't worry, he'll come," she whispered. "They'll probably meet us inside."

Just as the two Norwegian couples in front of their party reached the pay booth they arrived. After warm greetings, semi-air kisses and hearty handshakes were exchanged, Atek, Berk and Musti made a show of wriggling their hands deep in their pockets until Alan, who was already paying, held up eight tickets triumphantly.

"My treat," he announced . "Last night, eh? And Sean got us our lunch."

He was showered with thanks, profusely by the newcomers.

As they moved through the foyer, into the main body of the disco, a woman with a tight, shiny ponytail and a face and dress to match, swept round to Phee.

"Hi, Phee darling," she shrilled, releasing the arm of the young man she was holding, in order to hug the girl.

Phee lukewarmly accepted the embrace and made some brief, embarrassed introductions. "Mum, Dad, this is Ulva, Anneka's mother."

61

Guessing her identity before she was named, Barba assessed the success of her alleged enhancements, if Carol was to be believed. To her, she looked less youthful than slightly inhuman. The effect of her cosmetic procedures was paradoxically, natural, in the sense that she wore little make-up, and plastic, in that she had a strangely laminated appearance. When it was her turn to receive an insincere embrace, she was surprised at how hard and unyielding the woman's chest felt, poking into her own. Skipping away to the music, pulled along by her dark escort, Barba noted that neither Ulva nor Phee had mentioned where her daughter was.

Warming to their role as benefactors Sean and Alan went to the bar to get drinks for all of them, distracted by the girls in each corner, gyrating listlessly round bars in the centre of suspended cages. With hair extensions to their waist, sparse costumes of shimmery spandex, bare, oiled legs and hollowed-out eyes, cheeks, abdomens and buttocks.

In the centre was a large, oval dance-floor, already throbbing with movers, shakers and swingers, showered with flecks of coloured light, like confetti.

Atek and friends found a table and chairs between the dance area and the bar, seating themselves with their backs to the bar. Musti had an empty chair beside him, which Phee sat in as urgently as she used to play' Musical Chairs' at childhood parties. Barba and Lucy settled opposite, intending to join the action behind after a few drinks.

"We all scrubbed up well, didn't we?" commented Barba, after her first vodka and tonic, then had to lean over to explain the meaning to Atek, who relayed it to his friends, and everyone laughed.

Even Sean and Alan had made an extra effort with dressing for the evening. They were both wearing their new jeans and stylish, short-sleeved, cotton shirts they had found also in Side, advised by Atek. Barba had opted for her jeans too, deciding she would have a better time if she could dance confidently. Discarding the little dress she had chosen, putting on a rose-pink top with ribbons pulling in her waist, cut low so the sleeves draped rather than covered her shoulders, sandals with short chains of pearls tickling her toes. No item of make-up had been neglected by her that night; she was glossed, bronzed, lined, defined, shaded and highlighted. Lucy was in red cheesecloth; a long, crinkled skirt and smocked blouse, which amplified her ample bosom. It complemented her dark hair; with large gold hoops in her ears she resembled a buxom gypsy. Phee, in contrast, was eye-catching in a simple vest, miniskirt and metallic flip-flops, having
applied eye make-up lavishly and straightened her hair. The others, in pristine white T-shirts and leather-belted tight jeans, looked immaculately groomed in minimalist chic.

"Ok, honey, let's go strut our stuff," Barba summoned Lucy.

Her friend was ready too, compelled by the beat which had become less electronic, more African, and the effects of her second cocktail.

All except Alan and Sean, who preferred to drink, smoke and ogle, were swaying and stepping to the music, within seconds. Admiring how the Turkish men generally seemed to enjoy dance, Barba cheered as Atek,

Berk and Musti joined Lucy, Phee and her, forming a rhythmic circle of moving hips, arms and feet.

Concentrating on the vibrations, Barba averted her eyes from Atek's, which were on her, his back to Sean. Intermittently, intense strobes slashed the faces of the dancers like the weapons of anti-heroes in films, making their moves appear stilted, transforming them to crazed automatons. Only then would she look directly at him, as if protected by a spell, until the light-confetti broke it, setting all the robots free.

"Going for a drink," she mouthed and pointed. On cue, they all followed her to their table, where Sean and Alan, having returned to the bar twice since they left, had felt obliged to order more drinks each time for all.

"Come on, Barby," Lucy urged after more drinking and a visit to the ladies.

Lifting up her skirt with one hand she pulled Barba to the dance with the other. Barba shimmied obediently at her rear.

This time, Atek was watching from behind Sean, standing, drinking beer with Berk. Barba could feel herself undulating more noticeably, inserting some rotations into her sequence, to distract herself. Her hips were picking up the beat more fluidly, her arms extending more gracefully and openly, as Lucy's skirts were raised and swished increasingly higher, in keeping with her spirits.

Suddenly, Barba realised that not only had Musti left the others, but Phee was absent too. She could not see the pair anywhere near the four bars, nor in the dance area, though it was difficult to peer through the jostling bodies, and she was not tall. Still dancing, she turned her attention to the doorway, in time to see Phee and Musti, arms moving around each others' backs, slip through the exit. She was about to alert Lucy, who, trance-like, was wiggling further away from her, when she noticed Atek grinning broadly at her from his position. Glancing down, she saw that the right sleeve of her low, loose top had slipped right down. It was exposing not just her shoulder, but the complete black-and-pink-laced cup of her bra, the mound of breast above her nipple that was not covered by it. Yanking the top in place, checking around to see if anyone else had observed, then at Atek, who was still laughing behind an oblivious Sean's back. Laughing too, she danced towards Lucy to recover her composure.

"I need a drink, Luce," she said, when she had got her attention.

The friends, one looking disorientated, the other embarrassed, returned to their seats.

"Have a drink, love," offered Sean, slurring, handing her the fourth double vodka and orange of the night.

Starting on her fifth, she remembered with alarm that Phee had left with Musti. Guiltily, she wondered how much time had passed since that happened. Atek and Berk, who had sat down with them all again, had been entertaining them with jokes and witty anecdotes about the beach.

"Hi." Phee's voice interrupted them cheerfully, as she put an arm around her mother, addressing them all warmly.

Musti was talking to another man at the bar.

"Hi, honey," Lucy answered, hugging her daughter's waist. "You having a good time?"

Lucy noticed Barba staring at her neck, and covered it with her long hair before replying in a girlish voice.

"I am, Mum, but I was feeling a bit sick, so I went out to get some fresh air."

"You been drinking, chick?" Lucy attempted to sound stern.

"A bit. Not used to it, am I ?" Phee said, resting lightly on her mother's knee and looking in her eyes, like a child seeking assurance.

"Be careful, honey," Lucy reminded her, patting her arm indulgently.

Barba wanted to believe the excuse too, telling herself that it explained the smudged make-up and the dishevelled hair; perhaps even the flustered cheeks. But not the dark patch beneath the girl's ear, and the reddish ones on her arms, nor the wild new light in her eyes, she thought.

The decision was made to leave, taxis were called and last farewells made. In the cover of the taxi, Barba was horrified at how the words goodbye had stuck in her throat when leaving Atek, and her own ambivalence towards Phee. She watched her, wiping away tears and waving from the back window of the cab in front. Wanting to save her, like a mother. Wanting to slap her, like a mother. Wanting to applaud her, like a friend. Wanting to caution her, like a friend. Wanting to slap her, like a jealous rival.

Grappling with the feeling all the way home. Concealing it in the back seat of the car. Venting it in

furious packing. Gazing forlornly at the departing scenes
flashing by, on the coach, like someone drowning. High
in the sky, feigning sleep, riding out the turbulence.
Feeling caught between protectiveness and passion, until
the 'plane came down, and what she felt then was numb.

CHAPTER 4

When Sean went to fetch the car, Barba waited miserably at the edge of the road, smoking, not knowing whether it was the rain or her tears which made her feel so cold and wet. Thankful for the cover of the night and the excuse of fatigue when she joined Sean in the front seat.

It was as if they had never been away. Even though it was four in the morning when they finally opened the front door of their house, the cat greeted them with a plea for food.

"Oh, you're trying it on, aren't you? "she complained gently. "I know Elsie's been over-feeding you." She opened the cupboard to find a tin.

"Going straight up. I'm knackered," Sean declared.

She spooned the chunks sloppily into the dish and placed it on the floor. The duty-free bags were on the worktop. Despite having only had bouts of shallow sleep, Barba did not want to follow Sean upstairs. The vodka bottle was pulled from the carrier bag, a carton of orange juice out of the fridge.

James Morrison was fed into the CD player, she ignited the 'living flame' gas fire for warmth and settled with her glass on the sofa. She took up the refrain of the selected song tonelessly, as it tinkered with the strings of her heart; by proxy voicing her own willingness to take a risk, scary as it was, to follow it.

It was an hour before dawn when she found her way to bed in the dark.

She was grateful that the following day was Monday, and she only worked Tuesday to Thursday at the local travel agency. Sean slept in too, but had an afternoon shift beginning at four and ending at midnight, which Barba anticipated with relief also. It meant she only had a few hours in his presence. She filled them with relentless busyness; unpacking, washing and drying clothes while he kept company with the television and the cat in the living room. The only contact after breakfast was when she gave him a sandwich and tea mid-afternoon.

"What's on it?" was his response.

"Ham and cheese," was hers.

"Real ham at last," he approved.

He had made similar comments during their late breakfast, a 'full English' that Sean had requested.

"Great to have proper bacon again," he enthused. "I couldn't be a Muslim, me."

Her fists were clenched as she returned to the kitchen.

Fifteen minutes after Sean had left for work, Barba had filled a bath with hot fragrant water, and turned up the volume of the music she was enjoying. She was about to undress when Bethany called in with all five of Barba's grandchildren, on her way back from the school run.

"Hi, Nan," she heard her eldest granddaughter

shout from downstairs.

"Hi, darling. One second," she called back.

She put her hands on her hips, then waved them in the air with frustration, before twisting the tap fiercely to stop it running and jabbing the off switch on the CD player in her bedroom.

"Nana, Nana," the twins hugged her thighs.

"Hi, Mum. D'you have a good time?" Bethany pecked her on the head.

"Hello darlings." Barba put her arms around the twins' shoulders and air-kissed Bethany. "It's getting a bit cold for denim mini's, isn't it?" Bethany remarked, with more disapproval than concern.

Barba looked at her twenty-eight year old daughter in her long, unfitted, cotton skirt, t-shirt with cardigan and those German sandals, with two buckled bars and moulded soles, that lasted too long to be trendy.

"Beth, love. How are you?" she said pointedly. "We had a lovely time, thanks. I know summer's over, baby, but it's nice to show off a bit of colour."

"I think you look really nice, Nan," six-year-old Laura offered, with obvious sincerity.

"And so do you, pet. You and Ky, so smart in your new school uniform. How do you like your new teachers?"

"Mmm. Ok." Laura wrinkled her nose, contradicting herself.

"Mine's cool," affirmed Ky, who was a year older.

"Hey, and look at you two." Barba turned her attention to the twin girls, now proudly holding out their grey pleated skirts.

70

"Uniform for you too! Wow!" she exclaimed, tugging their braids. "My Grace and Joy at big school too, eh? How about that?"

"Just afternoons at first, Nan," Grace reminded her.

"We got to play in the sand and water, and did some fruit prints," added Joy, enthusiastically. "You can see them later."

"I'd like that," said Barba, reaching out for the baby in her daughter's arms.

"And how's your wee brother?" she asked, taking him from Bethany and stroking his hair with light touches. He bounced in her arm and threw out his dummy to chuckle at her.

"Nan, nan, nan, nan, nan," Lou chanted cheekily, showing his two-by-two teeth, still bouncing.

They moved merrily into the kitchen, where Barba put Lou in a big, empty laundry basket which he rocked in until it moved forward, jerk by jerk, on the laminated wood floor, to his great satisfaction.

"Now then, these busy schoolchildren must be hungry." Barba was opening cupboards, finding fruit squash and biscuits.

"Sorry, Beth, not much to offer really, until I go shopping tomorrow."

"Oh, don't worry, Mum. We'll be having dinner with Richard soon," Beth assured her.

When they had cups of tea, and were sat down with the children, snacking at the kitchen table, she showed them the photographs.

"I'd love to go abroad," Bethany said dreamily.

"D'you know, I've never thought about that,"

Barba answered, wondering why she sounded apologetic. "You've never flown, have you, baby?"

"No, practically always with child for the past ten years," continued Beth, with only a hint of ruefulness. "Bless them, they're worth it," she added, smiling at them brightly in turn.

"Aye," agreed Barba, vaguely.

Her daughter nudged her hand.

"I have thought it'd be nice if we could all go away abroad, sometime."

"All?" enquired her mother, knowing the answer.

"Us and the kids, you, Dad, maybe even Gran," Beth clarified.

'Us' referred to her husband of ten years, whom she had married at the same age as Barba, and in similar circumstances, being pregnant. However, in contrast to her own, her daughter's marriage looked set to continue to be as content and enduring as it was fruitful.

"Talk to Dad about it," Barba side-lined the suggestion, only able to visualise sticky days of washing, wiping, life-guard duty and baby-sitting.

Bethany began to call Sean 'Dad' the day after he had moved in, thirteen years previously. Barba assumed it helped to snuff out lingering reminders of the absence of her real father, the man who Barba divorced six years after Beth was born, after he had effectively murdered her brother in the womb. Barba could not bear children after that.

"Nan's got something from Turkey for you all, before you go," she declared, getting up from the table to fetch and distribute their gifts.

An hour after their arrival, she waved them off,

the girls swaying exotically to the car, shaking the coins on their headbands and their bracelets, Ky using the path as a runway for his Turkish Air-Force aeroplane. Lou flapped his furry helicopter around, making it hard for his mother to keep her grip on him, her large can of apple tea and a box of Turkish Delight for Richard. Barba blew six kisses and closed the door.

Her bath, when she finally got into it, was not the lingering affair she had hoped for. Lukewarm, the scent diluted, it was disappointing and therefore short. Immersing herself briefly, she felt the unfamiliar, inexplicable restlessness creep through her again. The unnerving niggle, a just-perceptible but undeniable ache, had come over her in the earliest hours of that day. For the following hours before she decided to put herself to bed, she attempted to chew it away with a bowlful of microwaved tinned tuna and baked beans, iron it away with the creases in their laundered holiday clothes, and beat it out with the voice of her mother.

"Hello, Mum," she greeted her in the upbeat tone she mentally rehearsed before each call.

"Oh, Barba, love," her mother exclaimed, as if she was the last person she expected to call. "When did you get back?"

"Early hours this morning."

"Oh, you must be shattered? Did you get much sleep?"

"Not too bad. We managed to sleep for several hours." Barba realised her mother would find it hard to anticipate that anyone might readily stay in bed after seven in the morning, unless they were ill or disabled.

"No work then, today?" her mother continued.

"No. Usual, Mum. Mondays and Fridays off."

"That worked out well, then. What about Sean?"

"He went in at four this afternoon. Working Thursday, then four days off and days next week."

"Poor Sean".

"Anyway, Mother, how are you?"

"Oh, alright really. Had a bit of a tummy bug mid-week."

"That's not good, Mum. Do you know what caused it?"

"Think it was a virus, love. Not something I ate. Anyway, I just had to ask Phyllis next door to get me a few bits of pieces from the shops," she explained.

"Good of Phyllis," Barba commented.

"Well, I had no one else to ask, with you being away." She sounded accusing. "And I couldn't put on poor Bethany, with all she has to do."

"Ok," Barba complied, hoping to shift the direction of the conversation.

"To tell the truth," her mother persisted, "she could do with someone helping her."

"Have you seen her?" asked Barba, still hopeful, knowing the 'someone' was herself.

"Nooo," was the reply, as if she had suggested the impossible. "Have you?"

This gave Barba a chance to inject a positive note.

"Actually, yes, she called round with the children after school today, for an hour or so. It was lovely to see them."

"Yes, it would be," came the doleful response.

"Well, Mother, I'm calling because it would be

lovely to see you on my day off, Friday", Barba put in quickly. "Are you doing anything?"

"Oh no," she retorted, her tone implying that was a ridiculous question.

"Good, good," Barba concluded. "Alright if I pick you up around midday, drop you off after tea?"

"Yes, love."

"See you then, Mum. I'll call tomorrow."

"Yes, love. 'Bye."

"'Bye, Mum."

She went into the kitchen to find the duty-free vodka. By ten o'clock she was relaxed and weary enough to be fast asleep before Sean arrived, according to plan.

Sean was slumbering as deeply as she had, when she woke before the alarm sounded. She knew he would not stir before she left for work. Even though it was not unusual for them to have little interaction when his shifts fell on evenings or nights, she was grateful for that. Enjoying the peace and the extra time she had, she lingered in the shower. Her hair was dried and styled more attentively. Eye-liner was added as well as the lipstick and mascara she normally flicked on. Dressed, in front of the mirror, she perceived her uniform coral shirt and teal suit to be more flattering than usual. Completing the process with her tan leather court shoes, she decided to wear the gold chains and earrings she normally reserved for special occasions.

"Wooh, you look like you've been on a spa break," Nicole appraised her from behind her work station as she pushed open the door of the local branch of the Douglas Scott travel agency.

"Thank you, and hello, chick," she returned the greeting.

"You're welcome, hun. Did you have a good time?"

"Fab, thanks."

"Would you go again?" Nicole asked.

"I would, yes," Barba enthused. "I wasn't sure about Turkey, y'know. Never really fancied it, but I've changed my mind now."

"Oh, only I once went with my mate, about five years ago," Nicole recalled, "and I was right put off, to be honest."

"Oh?" prompted Barba.

"It was the blokes. They gave us the creeps."

"Why was that?" asked Barba, feeling disturbingly irritated. She switched on her computer so she could divert her face from her colleague.

"Well, they were everywhere, all over us, and some were so hard to shake off", Nicole reminisced with a shudder of her petite shoulders. "But then again," she noted ingenuously, picking up the papers she had begun working on, "we were only eighteen, so I expect it was very different for you."

"I expect so," Barba responded calmly, wanting to throw the mouse at Nicole's pretty, highlighted head.

Instead, she walked to the office door of their manageress and tapped lightly before opening it. The glamorous woman behind the desk, with pearl-white hair swirled round in a chignon and heather-grey eyes, removed her designer glasses and looked up with a hospitable smile.

"Good morning, Mo," Barba greeted her boss.

"Barba! Good to see you back. Your holiday looks as if it's done you good. How was it?"

"Thanks, I'd be lying if I said I wouldn't jump at the chance to be back there."

"Take it that it went well, then?" Mo nodded her head approvingly. "You must tell me more later. We missed you, anyway."

Barba accepted that as a discreet cue to go back to her work.

"Nice to be missed. I'll open up now, Mo?"

"Please." Mo had replaced her glasses and was typing distractedly.

Barba was just about to turn the sign over, when she was startled by a brown face being pressed against the glass. The nose was grotesquely squashed, the eyes opened into a cross-eyed stare. She twisted the handle quickly and pulled it. A young Asian man tripped in comically.

"Good morning, my professional young colleague," Barba addressed him without betraying her irony, as he straightened up.

She strained to keep her expression stern. Hilarity bubbled up inside her and then she, Kash and Nicole were laughing so much they had to use the work counters for support.

"So you didn't run off with a Turkish love rat, then Barba?" Kash winked.

His words acted like a bung on her frivolity. She fluttered her eyelashes theatrically to mask the effect.

"Apparently not, sir," she said, contriving a demure voice and manner. "It seems you've been overdoing the womens' weeklies again. You really must get a life, Kash."

Emitting another gust of jocularity, he vanished into the bureau de change cubicle.

Shaking her head, she sat at the computer and opened her inbox.

"Four hundred and bloody two emails," she complained aloud, because they had no clients.

Just a few seconds later, two young men walked in hesitantly.

She asked if she could help and indicated the chairs at her desk. They sat.

"Er, we're hoping to find a decent package deal for the end of September," one of them spoke loudly from under his baseball cap.

"Where did you have in mind?" Barba began.

"Thinking of Spain, really," the spokesman informed her.

"We'll consider other places, like, though, won't we?" his friend added, tentatively.

"Oh aye, we're not too fussed, so long as it's warm enough and the booze is cheap," the other deferred. "Oh, and a bit of nightlife." The friends exchanged conspiratorial grins.

Barba entered the main details into the computer, and began discussing the possibilities. Showing them the photographs as they came up, she selected the important criteria from their responses.

They were considering Benidorm and had enquired about Lanzarote.

"The Turkish lira has a good exchange rate. Turkey is generally good value. I know, I've just come back from there," she proposed, almost with pride.

Before they had time to react, she had re-routed the search and was cheerily pointing out resorts, hotels, pools, beaches and activities, citing so many nights for so many pounds. Half an hour later, the dazed pair handed over a credit card, to buy a fortnight in an apartment in Marmaris for a few hundred pounds each.

Once they had gone, Barba returned to the backlog of emails, deciding to begin with the elimination of the obviously pointless and trivial content without reading it. She was occupied with that task for forty-five minutes when the door jangled again and an older couple entered.

She assumed they were retired. They dropped the other's hand they were holding to sit before her, exuding mild excitement.

"Good morning. How can I help you?"

They looked at each other. The woman nodded at the man to speak.

"We've decided to have a little adventure," he told her, in a confidentially quiet way.

"Sounds good. What do you have in mind?"

"Well, a last minute deal somewhere quiet and sunny, by the sea," we thought.

The anticipation in the air increased palpably.

"Ok". Barba manoeuvred the mouse around the screen, clicking and selecting.

"Have you thought about Turkey?, she heard herself suggesting. "It's very pleasant at this time of the year. I was there myself just two days ago,", she added, for verification. "Ideal spots for relaxing and sightseeing."

To her satisfaction, they sat up with interest, leaning in and murmuring approvingly as she guided them virtually around coasts and historical sites. In fifteen minutes they were destined for a boutique hotel in Bodrum at the end of the week.

Fifty more messages had been decisively deleted when Barba was presented with more clients. A thirty-something, affluent-looking Asian couple waved at Kash through his little window, before joining her.

"Look after my friends, Barba," he called.

She put her thumb up, smiling at them.

They were thinking of Egypt or Morocco, the following May, they explained.

"Just those two locations?" she determined.

"It's the food issue really," the wife expanded. "We don't want to be worrying about whether the food is halal or not, so Muslim countries make the choice easy."

"I really enjoyed the cuisine in Turkey when I was there last week." Barba was warming to her subject and quite familiar with the options by this time.

She immediately conjured up feasts before their eyes and recited restaurant reviews for a few of the more salubrious areas. It was a converted traditional Turkish cottage, with pool and modern facilities, near Cesme, that won them over.

When the door closed behind them she leant back in her office chair and swivelled in it like a happy child.

"You're obsessed with Turkey," Nicole observed.

This jolted Barba into the realisation that she had been acting as if she had been hypnotised. Better be careful, she thought.

"Going for lunch now," she digressed. "You need anything?"

"Get me a sandwich, will you, pet?"

Barba made a note of her preferences, then did the same for Kash. Mo was already daintily eating a tossed salad she had prepared herself when Barba peeped round the door.

Before she went to the snack display in the supermarket across the road, she stopped at the Fotoshop counter. She inserted the memory card from her camera into the processing machine. As the five photographs printed out, she peeked at each one as it dropped, with infantile impatience and curiousity. They were stacked carefully into the envelope and placed into her handbag. She patted it, as furtively and with as much satisfaction, as if they were fifty new banknotes.

They took their paper bags into the tiny kitchen-diner to eat.

"Who's for a brew?" Kash said, filling the kettle.

Nicole and Barba, mouths full, put their hands up.

Companionably silent, they finished their lunch and sipped tea. When there were three scrunched paper balls on the table, Barba brushed off the crumbs and laid her photos on it.

"Is this all you've got?" Nicole commented.

"'Fraid so. My camera was playing up. We've got some of the Truck Safari and Lucy's taken loads, so I'll bring them in if you're interested."

"Yeah," Nicole said, apathetically.

"Who are these guys?" Kash pointed at Atek, Berk and Musti in turn.

81

"Oh, they're the ones from the beach bar we got friendly with."

This prompted Nicole to repeat her experience in Turkey to Kash, who made knowing nods as she retold it.

"Oh, there was another guy called Mehmet, who seemed a bit that way," Barba added, as if that exonerated the three depicted.

This entertained Kash immensely. "Oh, Mehmet. Mehmet," he mused. "Did I ever tell you about the time I went to Turkey with my mates?" he asked them.

They shook their heads.

"For a laugh, and to see if we could pull some girls," he went on, "we decided to call ourselves Mehmet."

Barba found that so amusing she had to gulp hard to stop herself spraying her tea over her photographs.

"What? All of you?" Nicole was looking at him as if he was a very naughty, but adorable, child.

"Yes, yes. All of us." This elicited another bout of chortling.

"Did it work?" Barba prodded him.

Kash responded as if he were being tickled, but was not giving anything away.

"Ah, our code is what goes on, on holiday, stays on holiday," he smirked secretively.

Nicole thumped him, half-playfully, half with exasperation.

"Back to what you were saying, though, Nic," Kash spoke in a more serious tone, as if to placate her. "A lot of those Turkish guys do play about."

Nicole was interested. Barba wanted to cover her

ears.

"How do you know, Kash?" She wanted him to justify his words.

"Because it was easy for us to get friendly with them. 'Cause we're Asian, and Muslim, you know, they told us more. Brothers, man," he grinned, making a gesture of bonding with his fingers.

"Such as?" Nicole demanded, in the tone of a child's nanny.

"Well, they showed us photos of different girl-friends they had in different places. Different cities, different countries."

"Huh!" Nicole exclaimed with disgust.

"We asked how they kept it all going," Kash elaborated. "Apparently, they just keep saying, I love you, I love you." He was clearly suppressing a tinge of admiration.

"Very cheesy," Nicole sniffed, and got up from the table to signal the end of the narrative.

Barba collected up the teacups, washing them more thoroughly and noisily than usual.
For the next two days, she determinedly avoided leading clients, or the in-between chats with her colleagues, in the direction of Turkey. Privately however, when the inbox was cleared and the paperwork shuffled, she would allow herself the safe indulgence of being transported to Arabian Nights. Over domes and minarets, gliding into warm currents; full of eastern promise. A magic carpet to fly you there whenever you want; a magic lamp to give you whatever you might wish for.

She had been cleaning for two hours when Sean came

down on Friday morning around ten o'clock. She was taking a second load out of the washing machine.

"Mornin'," he mumbled as he passed her.

"Mornin'," she answered, picking up the basket of clothes to take outside. "Bet you're glad you've finished for a few days?" The thought that she was not occurred to her, guiltily.

"Aye. Have we got any eggs?" That was a cue for her to cook some.

"I promised my mother I'd pick her up at eleven and bring her over for the afternoon, seeing as I've not seen her for two weeks," she said as she put the fried eggs and toast in front of him. "Have you got any plans for today," she asked, knowing he soon would have, if not already.

"Right", he answered thoughtfully. "Well, it's a nice day, like. I was thinking to get a bit of fresh air and exercise at the golf club this after."

"Aye, why not?" You forgot to say 'and beverages', she thought to herself.

He glanced at her, surprised at her encouragement. Barba was mentally predicting that the afternoon would blend into the evening, once refreshments started.

"Well, I'd better get going. Mum'll be waiting." She picked up her bag and car keys.

"You'll still be here when I get back?"

"Probably, for a short while anyways."

The drive to her mother's home took less than fifteen minutes, and even though she was only five minutes late, her mother was stood on the pavement outside her terraced house, dressed as if she was going to church, with matching cream cardigan, gloves, handbag and shoes.

Barba pushed open the passenger door for her then got out to help her fold herself in the car.

Barba leaned in.

"Hi Mum. How are you doing?"

"Oh, can't grumble." Her mother lifted her chin to accept the kiss and the seat belt offered her.

"What on earth are you wearing, Barbara?" she asked, as her daughter slipped back into the driver's seat. She was clearly referring to her skirt, as she was glaring at Barba's legs.

"Oh, it's not as short as it looks, Mum," she answered, pulling down the hem around her thighs like a rebellious schoolgirl.

Driving back to her house, she listened to the shortcomings of most people, events and things in her mother's environment. She threw in a question occasionally to demonstrate her attentiveness. Meanwhile, she was planning how she and Lucy would spend their usual Friday night together. Anticipating that this one would be a little different, causing a frisson to ripple up her body, making her shiver at the wheel.

When they arrived, Sean was prepared to leave, dressed in his golfing clothes with his clubs waiting by the front door, he was making his intentions clear, in order to limit questions.

"Hello Dot." He gave her a loose hug which was reciprocated with vigour. "Good to see you."

Hovering around her mother dutifully for the next twenty minutes, he made them all a cup of tea and brought it in with biscuits. Barba deduced that this was to avoid too much conversation. Not successfully, however. Barba smiled as her mother followed him into the kitchen.

"And how was your holiday, Sean?" she heard her enquire, as if he had been somewhere different.

"Don't make us any dinner, like," he said to Barba when he found the right moment to take his leave. "I don't know what time I'll be back exactly. You know what it's like, with rounds and all," he justified himself lamely.

For the second time that day, Barba felt him scrutinising her face when she approved his stated course of action.

"Ok, pet." She pulled a cat hair from his shirt. "Text us when you know what you're doing."

He kissed the air very close to her lips, then over her mother's cheekbone, gathering up his clubs quickly.

"Poor Sean," Dot remarked, as soon as he had closed the door.

"Why?" Barba could feel her neck muscles tense.

"He got badly burnt, by the sound of it. Did you not warn him?" she rebuked her.

"Yes, I told him. More than once."

"Well, you should have made him protect himself."

"He's a grown man!"

Barba turned the television on remotely, judging the action less rude than anything she might say to her mother at that point.

"You know what they're like," her mother went on, undeterred.

"You want to watch 'Loose Women', Mum?"

"Men are like children," Barba was reminded.

She steered through the rest of the afternoon more skilfully, with a cold meal accompanied by lunchtime television, which gave her mother more diversity in subjects she had an opinion on. That was followed by some shopping. Barba was careful to choose an area with a number of bargain stores. Half-irritated to be dodging allusions to her flaws and past mistakes, like a console game where you are unsure from which direction the missiles will come, Barba also felt some relief. It gave her something else to think about.

By tea-time, fatigue and several hours of free speech had mellowed Dot. They prepared and ate cottage pie together in relative conviviality, with Dot's favourite quiz show on the television.

On her return from driving her mother home, she heard the gong on her mobile 'phone signalling a text message, as she threw her car keys on the table. It was Sean.

"Going to eat here. See you later."
The 'phone sounded again as she plugged in the laptop, this time startling her. An edginess had crept over her.

"Am I still good for coming over? ☺ I'll bring the vino. U got nibbles? XXX"

She replied at once.

"Def. good, Luce. Got both ☺ Bring Turkey pics. See you bout 7.30?"

Forgivably unpunctual, Lucy pattered in, chattering and bountiful. Her arms clutched two bottles of wine to her chest, the largest-sized bag of tortilla chips available grasped in her hands. Barba relieved her of the goods in the kitchen, and joined her in a heartfelt hug.

"Hi babe. How's your week been?" Lucy started to open the tortilla chips.

"Ok, so-so. Rather be back in Turkey, I can tell you."

"Me too, babe," crunched Lucy.

"I got two, too", she smiled naughtily, as she put a bottle of white in the fridge next to another.

"Oh, well. See how we go. Better get started."

Barba poured a generous glass of white wine for Lucy, a red for herself. Barba slipped a Latin-American music disc into the player. With mock-intense expressions they exaggerated their movements. Re-living farcical moments from their classes, they salsa-ed in and out of the kitchen, holding out the drinks and bowls to keep them stable.

"Hey, Barb, we'll have to take it up again." Lucy caroused around the room.

"Yeah." Barba swung round nostalgically, then stopped abruptly, excited at her next idea.

"Let's do belly-dancing instead," she urged, slowing to flick her hips from side to side.

"Community Centre. Friday nights too!"

When they tired, they settled in armchairs and reviewed the days since their return from holiday.

"Presume Sean is at the Golf Club?"

"Where else? Alan not with him?"

"He's gone on a golfing weekend with three others. Surprised Sean didn't go."

"Mmm, strange. He's usually up for anything like that. Maybe he hadn't sorted his shifts out before it was arranged," agreed Barba. "How are the kids?"

"Wayne seemed glad to be back with all his

home comforts. Phee has been pining, horribly in both senses of the word, for Musti. She caused a stink about going to their grandparents tonight because she can't go on msn to talk to him."

Barba reflected on this information for a moment, before getting up to fill their glasses.

"Did you bring your photos?"

Lucy reached for her bag and brought out a bundle. Barba perused them all, returning to the group shots from the last day, particularly to the ones with Atek posing.

"That Berk was dying to flirt with you, Lucy."

"Noo!" Lucy cackled, flapping a hand dismissively.

"What about Atek? Couldn't take his eyes off you." She nudged Barba suggestively.

"Really?" Barba's eyes were wide. "You really think that?"

"I really do, hun."Lucy pursed her mouth knowingly.

"Have you sent the photos to them yet?" Barba had a purposeful air now.

"No, haven't had time. Want to put them on Talkbook too."

"Been thinking about that, Lucy. Will you help me set up on it?"

"Sure, pass me your glass and I'll do the honours while you switch on. I'll get my camera. Can put my mermaid piccie on my profile too, while we're at it."

Lucy joined Barba at the dining table and pulled up a chair next to hers. She plugged in her camera, downloaded the photographs and created a folder for them.

"Great, I'm impressed, chick. Shall we send them to the guys now?"

"Sure." Lucy laughed at her childish impatience. "Open your inbox then."

Barba opened the box for a new message. In the address book, she entered 'Atek66@hitmail.com' without reference to any piece of paper.

Lucy was intrigued. "You remembered?" She looked very directly into her friend's eyes.

"Easy to," Barba dismissed the unspoken implication, attaching the new folder of photographs.

'Hi Atek

Hope you like these. How are you?

Barba x'

A text box asked if she would like to add him as a contact. She clicked to confirm.

"You can send them to Berk," she told Lucy slyly.

"Maybe I will, maybe I won't," teased Lucy.

"Get your Talkbook thingy on now, Luce. More wine needed." Barba sounded giddy.

Lucy had replaced the coy portrait on her profile picture with the mermaid when Barba came back. She guided her through the setting up of her account, completing her profile and inserting the photograph Barba chose, asking her preferences throughout.

"Want your age showing, hun?"

"God, no!"

"Religion? Political Views?"

"Pass, pass."

"Ok, I'll write that." Lucy typed in 'Pass' for

both, chuckling.

"Family?"

"No, too much information. Tee hee."

"Education?"

"What education? University of Life, babe."

"Relationship?"

"Now, that is funny." Barba held her belly, mock-hysterically. "Options?"

"Single, married, engaged, in a relationship, it's complicated."

"Can we leave that out?"

"We can hide it."

"Right, do that then, please."

"Do you want to add some friends, now?" asked Lucy, once the profile was finished and the holiday photos were displayed in Barba's 'albums'.
Barba, who had grown increasingly vague throughout the process, was taken aback.

"I only know you on Talkbook, babe."

"Well, add me and you can search for other people later. What about Atek? She gave her a sideways look.

"Oh yeah," Barba spoke dreamily. "Oh, but I don't know his surname." She looked crestfallen.

"That's fine," Lucy soothed, "put in his email address."
Barba squealed adolescently when Atek's profile showed up on the screen.

"Add him. Add him as my friend," she urged breathlessly.

"Calm down, babe." He was added.
An amber light began flashing at the bottom of the

screen. Barba put her hands to her face histrionically, bouncing on the spot.

"It's him, it's him." She squeezed Lucy's shoulder with both hands, her face a shade of pale fuchsia.

She almost ran to the kitchen, peeking round the doorframe and beckoning urgently for her friend to follow, as if they could be seen.

"Barba, get a grip, girl." Lucy managed to convey the feeling that this was at the same time extremely foolish and extraordinarily funny. "Do you want to chat with him or not?"

Barba slapped her cheeks and took exaggerated, deep breaths, followed by an explosion of abandoned laughter, which set Lucy off.

"Yes, yes, I want to talk," Barba finally said, wiping tears away with a tissue and gulping a few mouthfuls of wine.

Smoothing her hair, suddenly remarkably composed, she opened the chat window.

Atek: Hi Barba, are u there?

Barba: Hi, I'm here now

Atek: How are u?

Barba: Good, miss being there. How are you?

Atek: Ok thank u. We miss u too. Beach more quiet this week.

Barba: Lucy is with me

Atek: Your husbands?

Barba: I told you. I don't have one. :D Just Lucy here with me tonight

Atek: Do you have cam?

Barba: I will have to find it

Atek: Next time, maybe?

They were disturbed by the sound of metal tapping on metal, at the front door.

Barba: Sorry, got to go.

Atek: Ok, bye. See u

Barba: Goodnight. See u

She closed the programme just as Sean lurched into the porch and pushed through the living room door.

Delivering a few sloppy words of greeting, blindly making eye contact, he pointed to the stairs, which he ascended clumsily and noisily.

Barba turned the computer and the music off while Lucy ordered a taxi to go home. They waited quietly, sipping the remains of the wine, listening to Sean thudding around before hitting the bed.

"That was fun, hun." Barba hugged Lucy before she clambered into the cab.

"Thanks, babe. See you next Friday. Talk soon."

In the interim, Barba marvelled at the serendipity of the universe. Two unexpected events, which would have otherwise annoyed and disturbed her in turn, unfolded, paving the way for escape and adventure.

By the time Sean rose at midday, Barba was shopping for groceries. When she returned he was just leaving the house.

"Just going to put a few bob on a horse," he explained, leaving her to carry several plastic bags of food inside.

"Bye," she replied impassively, to his retreating figure.

He reappeared briefly after thirty minutes, made

them a cup of tea, added his cup to the dishes he had used earlier and picked up his jacket again.

"Think I'll catch a round at the club," he announced.

"Bye," she repeated.

She knew he would be back for his evening meal as it was Saturday, then would probably stretch out on the sofa with a beer by his side to watch the sport. What was unpredictable were his elevated spirits when he appeared.

"Have you won on the horses?" she quizzed him.

"Hey no, but I've had a stroke of luck all the same."

"Oh, what's that then?" She consciously adjusted her expression to show interest.

"Do you remember that golf trip to Portugal I missed out on? There weren't many places and it got booked up quick, like."

"Go on," she frowned, thinking it best to show a modicum of resistance.

"Well, Chad's had to drop out and I've been offered his place. It fits in perfectly with my shifts 'cause I've just got the four nights before and my eight days off after that."

"Good for you," she remarked coolly, hoping he would not sense the voice cheering inside her.

"I'm made up, I am," he called as he ran up the stairs with untypical boisterousness. "Seven nights. Middle of October," he yelled from the landing.

Barba looked at the calendar and shouted to him to confirm the dates, then concerned herself with planning activities to colour in between the lines of the next day and Monday, when he would be at home with her if the weather was too poor to justify spending it at the golf club. Checking the weather forecast she decided to invite Bethany, Richard and the children over for Sunday dinner, as it was predicted to be changeable, with a fine, dry day following.

Their interactions turned out to be more congenial than usual, between the hectic family meal and Sean's comings and goings. His proposed vacation, which would normally have been a source of contention, had uplifted them both. Carefully maintaining the harmony, even though it puzzled him.

Barba was soon presented with another reason to be grateful for his trip, when an opportunity arose out of inauspicious circumstances. She often spoke to Lucy on the 'phone during the week and decided to call on Tuesday night, when Sean had begun his night shift.

"Hi babe. How are things?"

"Hi, hun. Fine thanks. How about you?" Lucy sounded as if she was in a bubble.

Barba told her about Sean and Portugal, hesitantly, aware that in effect she was talking to herself.

"Everything alright, Luce?"

"Not really. Can't say just now. Do you mind if I call you back tomorrow? Alan's just come in and there's something we need to talk about." Her words were clipped, her voice strained.

"Not at all. Ring me when you're ready." Barba put the 'phone down, biting her upper lip as she speculated.

The last holiday had been sold near the end of her

working day when she heard the gong. Lucy's name flashed on the screen of her 'phone.

'Really need 2 talk 2 u. X'

She sensed a crisis and acknowledged it at once.

'Sean nite shift – cum mine anytime after 7.30pm? X'

There barely seemed enough time for her message to travel through cyberspace when the response came.

'Thx babe. U wont blv it. C u soon xxx'

If it was about Alan, she thought, she would believe. No extraordinary foresight needed.

What did shock her, however was the appearance and demeanour of Lucy when she arrived that evening, clutching a bottle of vodka. An uncontained, volatile energy was seeping out of her like electricity seeking earth; her hair looked as it was channelling it, her eyes sparking dementedly.

"My God, Lucy. What's wrong?" She pulled her inside firmly and sat her down.

Lucy sprang up immediately and re-seated herself in front of the laptop on the table.

"I swear I could kill him. And her. Get that vodka poured. I want to show you something very, very cheap, and very, very nasty," she demanded with such uncharacteristic venom that Barba, with wide eyes and tight lips, obliged.

Handing Lucy the drink, she joined her at the computer. As soon as she typed in her password, Lucy pounced on the keyboard, tearing into the Talkbook log-in procedure. Breathing shallowly with unvented fury, she found her profile, then Alan's, summoning the list of his friends. Banging her finger on the key, she opened a window of a photo of a woman. Around the age of thirty, Barba estimated. Photographed in a baby-doll nightdress, one hand teased up the hem to give a glimpse of matching briefs. The other hand was on her hip, allowing her to thrust out her bosom as forcefully as her lips. Difficult to judge her attractiveness; she had the ubiquitous long, straightened, streaked hair, coloured-in eyes and orange skin. Kerrie from Eastley had something to say to her visitors, clearly not intended to be female.

"Is there anything your wife or girlfriend won't do for you?"

"Ooooh, boob job too." Barba sucked in breath and shook her head, noting the cereal bowl effect under thin skin. "What's it all about, babe?"

"Well, see if you can complete the jigsaw too. I'll give you a couple of pieces to get you started," she laughed scornfully. "A hotel bill and restaurant matches from a place not far from Eastley". She was looking at the obliging Kerrie's wall, pointing to entries from the week before.

Monday: Glad my baby's back from Turkey!
Wednesday: Lucky girly got hot weekend planned!
Thursday: Good girl taking my vitamins! LOL!!!
Friday: Soooo excited!

"Are you sure it's her?" Barba wondered why she was whispering.

"Trust me, there's more," Lucy spoke through clenched teeth.

Barba fetched more drinks. Lucy's agitation was so unfamiliar it was unnerving her.

"Here, calm down a bit, hun. Tell me."

"Did you get the bit about the hotel bill and the matches? The bill had Sunday's date, for two nights, double room. So, no golf! Bastard," she sputtered. "They were in his jacket pocket. Idiot! Could hear the box rattling when I moved his clothes in the wardrobe."

"What did he say?"

"Well, I waited. He was shattered, of course," she sneered. "Fell asleep on the settee, and got a text. Miss you already. Every way, it said. She was listed as A Kerry." Lucy snorted derisively.

"What did you do?"

"So I wrote down her number."

"And?"

"Called her on Monday. Five times before she answered."

Barba swallowed. "Go on."

"Said hi, I'm Alan's wife and you are the dead slag who has been shagging my husband this weekend."

"Restrained, then?" Lucy managed a laugh at that.

"Oh, I got a few really psychotic things in."

"Luce, I'm sorry." Barba reached to hug her. "I've never seen or heard you like this. What did she do?"

"Hung up. Guilty as charged. Then the phone was switched off."

"And Alan?"

"Got all angry. Denying. Saying ask so and so. Complete shit." She began to sob. "Then I showed him the bill and the matches. Told him about Talkbook, the text, the call," she babbled, wiping her nose roughly, like an infant, with the tissues Barba pressed in her hand.

"Where were the kids?"

"I sent them to his mother's. Just told her something serious had happened."

"What now?"

"Called in sick at work. Put his clothes in bin bags today. All waiting for him when he got home."

"Where is he?

"At his parents."

"The kids?"

"Told them Dad had to have space to work out something important about his life."

"What did they all say? Do?"

"Kids don't seem phased at all. Doesn't interfere with their usual stuff. Actually think they're more relaxed when he's away."

"His Mum and Dad?"

"Think his mum's secretly delighted. His dad looked completely pissed off with him. Mortified, really."

"What are you going to do now?"

"Oh. I don't know, honey," Lucy wailed. She gripped the sides of her head and flopped on the sofa, where she lay, eyes closed; storm-wrecked and stranded.

Barba stayed still and watched her for several minutes, praying to be shown the means to keep her friend afloat. She was about to go to her when Lucy flipped up, suddenly buoyant.

"I know what I'm damn well going to do," she declared loudly, with a determined hardness.

Barba raised her eyebrows.

"I spoke to my mother for ages last night. She never really trusted Alan anyway."

"So?" prompted Barba.

"Well apart from assuming I'll take the kids to the States for Christmas this year, she told me to book a spa retreat or something and she would pay for it."

"Nice idea," Barba approved.

"But I've got a better one," Lucy asserted." Let's go to Turkey."

The flash of ecstatic hope which overwhelmed Barba at that moment, was as quickly extinguished by doubt.

"Us?" she queried tentatively.

"Yes. Us. We've got the funds". She strode over to the laptop, in full flow. "What's stopping you?"

Barba's mouth opened and shut a few times, without uttering words of reason.

"You're right," she conceded finally, clapping her hands. "Nothing to stop me. Especially if we can go the same week Sean goes to Portugal." She rubbed her hands and held her fists to her mouth in excitement.

"Babe, let's do it," Lucy thumped the table and laughed, a little manically.

The dates of Sean's trip were entered into the flight search engine Lucy had found.

"Oh, that is so affordable. Let's sort out the rooms now."

Barba felt as if she was being carried away with the current of Lucy's resolve.

"You got Atek's mobile number still?"

"Yes, think so. Why?"

"Great. Get your phone and text him to come online," Lucy commanded. "We'll ask him how much those rooms are at his friend's place. Must be pretty cheap."

The text message was sent. Within ten minutes Barba was looking into Atek's keen face through a webcam.

Atek was in turn fascinated, pleased, discreet and efficient, when they explained the plan. Half an hour was all it took to arrange two double rooms at the pension for a week at twenty pounds each per night, including Turkish breakfast. With Lucy's credit card, return flights costing three hundred pounds for both of them were booked online. Berk would borrow a car and collect them from the airport for less than the usual transfer fees, Atek assured them.

Barba sat on the rug on the living room floor, steadying herself, as if a powerful wave had swept over her and knocked her off her feet. Lucy was a tornado, gyrating around her, and they were laughing.

Barba decided it would be more propitious to share the scheme with Sean at teatime on Friday. It was the last night of his shift, which meant he would be too tired to resist too much. He would be looking forward to his eight days off, unaware that it had been expedited so early and thoroughly.

"Have you spoken to Alan this week?" She introduced the topic indirectly as they began to eat.

"Texted me at work," Sean nodded, without emotion.

"Do you know what's happened with him and Lucy?" she prodded.

"'Course," he answered with a look that ordered her not to ask him to discuss the situation.

"Lucy wants to get away for a bit. I said I'd go to Turkey with her for a break."

Sean stared at her incredulously and put his fork down.

"So I said I'd go with her the week you go to Portugal." She smiled as if she had just delivered good news. "Lucy's Mum's sent her money for a holiday so she's treating me," she concluded.

Sean gripped his cutlery and chewed fiercely, looking around the room as if he could pluck a reason to challenge or deny her from the ether. Defeated, he assented with a nod, masticating slowly, deliberately and mutely, until his plate was empty and he got up to leave.

CHAPTER 5

It had taken almost half of Barba's life to drain the pot that was her inner life, of colourful desires, meaty passions and the flavours of intense feelings. In just the transition from summer to autumn, the pot had begun to be refilled, the lid replaced and slow-cooking.

The double doors of Antalya airport parted like glass curtains as Barba rolled her baggage through. She could feel the pressure build inside the pot, the contents rising, the lid cracking open and falling away. Feeling surreal, as if the boundaries of her body had become unclear, merging with the scene of travellers in the night, seeking and finding, being found.

"I think that's Atek." Lucy pointed to a figure walking briskly through the space between tour agency meeting points.

Immediately conscious of the coldness of the air, Barba became grounded again. She squinted to see him.

"Hi." Atek kissed them on both cheeks. "How was your flight?" Taking the handles of their cases from them, one in each hand. "Here," he indicated their direction with his head.

"Good. Good," they both murmured through bashful smiles, following him.

Wearing a broad grin of welcome on his dusky face, Berk was waiting, leaning on the car. He repeated the cheek-kissing ritual and opened the rear doors for them. They wriggled in, thanking them profusely for coming at so inconvenient an hour and for arranging everything so smoothly.

"So, ladies," Atek turned to them, leaning his chin on his lower arm which rested on the top of his seat. "What brings you back so soon to Turkey?" he enquired lightly.

Barba judged it best that Lucy should choose the level of response and kept silent. Lucy looked at her hesitantly before replying.

"Oh, we'll save that story for later," she postponed revelation.

Atek was clearly curious to glean some information.

"Why you come alone, not with your husbands?"

"We don't have husbands!" Lucy threw her hands apart and shrugged her shoulders with an insouciant smile on her face.

Berk repeated first, keeping his vision on the road ahead.

"You don't have husbands?" He and Atek exchanged brief glances.

They all shook their heads and chuckled, the women with frivolity and freedom, the men with intrigue and anticipation.

Berk pressed a button to play some plaintive Turkish music, which lasted for a few tracks, then gave way to more coaxing and sensuous melodies. The atmosphere relaxed as they settled into the journey, chatting about the beach, the weather, their work, watching the dark shapes of mosques and palms flit by.

"It's Ramadan, isn't it?" Barba remembered. "Are you fasting?"

Atek laughed. Berk echoed him. "Do you think I am fasting?"

"No," answered Barba, without having to think about it.

It was permitted to drive through the Roman gates after midnight, so Berk was able to park right outside the pension. He and Atek, with notable courtesy, opened the car doors for them and insisted on bringing their luggage for them. The courtyard was shadowy, but in the bar area four figures were huddled around a table in the dimly lit square. The women were shown up a wrought metal staircase to rooms with balconies overlooking the bar and garden. They were marble-tiled; sparse, though bright and clean, with everything they would need. Each had a double bed, as Atek had explained, which filled most of the floor area, with just enough room for a single wardrobe with mirror and shelf. Berk took Lucy's suitcase in the next room, while Atek went in the first room with Barba. She inspected the shower room.

"Everything is okay?" he asked earnestly.

"Yes, yes, it's just fine, thank you?"

She sniffed around. There was a slight odour, possibly the drains, she thought, which Atek had noticed too, for he dashed out of the room holding his index finger up, and back, holding a spray bottle. The chemically-scented contents were squirted liberally around the bathroom. Barba squeezed her nose and held her hand up.

"That's enough, please," she said nasally.

105

"Is there anything I can do for you?" Atek asked politely, but his eyes were playing with hers.

Pretending to search in her handbag she considered her response, then delved into a carrier bag on the bed.

"Any chance of us having a drink? I know it's late, but I'm not really sleepy yet." She held up a bottle of vodka she had purchased while waiting for the flight.

"Sure."

She could hear Lucy and Berk sharing a joke outside, the tap of her heels echoing on the tiles.

"Good, we'll be down in a few minutes." She instructed Atek to find orange juice, tonic water and lemons so they could share their airport vodka.

Lucy came into her room as the men went downstairs.

"Quick glam job if possible," she whispered to her friend, pulling out her cosmetic bag, perfume and comb.

"Me too," tittered Lucy, copying her actions.

Downstairs, two of the people they had seen were Musti and Mehmet, with two young women in their late teens, whom Atek introduced as the daughter of one of their guests from Sheffield, and her friend.

"Staying here also," he explained." Maggie, our friend, comes three times a year. More, sometimes. She is here also with a friend and her cousin. They have gone to disco."

Barba was finding all the information mildly confusing and largely unnecessary.
"Merhaba, Musti. Merhaba, Mehmet." She hugged the two men who had stood to welcome them, Musti

noticeably sheepish, Mehmet as usual, with an air of vague amusement.

Barba thought of Phee.

"Hello, I'm Barba," she smiled with her mouth at the other guests. Lucy, more warmly, did the same.

The girls introduced themselves.

"Hi, I'm Jade, Maggie's daughter." The unshapely, plump one with straight brown hair spoke confidently, appraising them with small, greenish eyes.

Her friend, who was leaner, taller, with rounded shoulders and acne-blotched features, blinked at them from under her blonde and brown striped fringe.

"I'm Leanne," she said, her eyes roving around them.

"How long are you staying for?" enquired Lucy.

"Oh, we came last week. We're going home the day after tomorrow," Jade replied, in a bored, flat tone.

"How's the weather been?" Barba small-talked.

"Good up to today, but saying it's gonna rain for a couple of days," grimaced Jade.

Barba and Lucy groaned.

"If it does, you can be sure sun will follow." Atek cheered them with his forecast and the mixers. Berk put down glasses and a dish of sliced limes as well as lemons. The others faded away like frames from a slideshow. Suppressed squeals and sounds of lively activity gave away their presence from the living quarters.

The alcohol was poured free-handedly by Berk. Lemonade was added for the men, who wanted it sweet, juice for Barba, tonic for Lucy.

"So," began Atek suavely, "you are back so

soon."

"Yes." Lucy lifted up her drink. "Cheers! Here's to a holiday for the girls."

"Cheers!" They chinked and toasted together merrily.

"What happened to your husband, Lucy?" Berk pulled up his chair to her attentively.

Lucy delivered a matter-of-fact synopsis of her marital mess.

"And you do not love him anymore?" Berk seemed to be making sure.

"I can tell you." Lucy was firing up. "At first I was ready to murder him and that woman. You know, kill?"

The men flinched a little. They knew.

"But as soon as the rat had run out of the house, I just felt relief. Pure, blessed relief." Lucy slammed down her glass in a gesture of finality, and picked the vodka bottle. They all held their glasses out meekly, while she filled them with an air of resolute intemperance.

"Relief?" repeated Atek.

"You know, when something bad has ended, and you get a good feeling. Like pain, like toothache," she searched for illustrations.

"Yes, I understood."

"She is welcome to him," continued Lucy, keen now to elaborate on the details of her release. "I mean, she must think he has money." She looked at Barba for substantiation. "And as for her." Contempt distorted her placid face. "She must get passed round the internet like a spliff in a shebeen."

Berk and Atek were showing signs of confusion.

"Spliff?" sought Berk.

"Joint. Hashish," Barba translated helpfully, entertained by Lucy's cathartic outrage.

"Thinks she's some kind of celebrity, the more creeps use her photo on Talkbook."

The men clearly got the gist. They began fumbling with their lighters uncomfortably.

"But cheap's not built to last, is it?" Lucy concluded with disdain.

Atek looked down at his mobile 'phone. He stood and walked over to the bar, face over the screen. Berk followed and bent to see what Atek was sharing with him.

Barba became aware of the cold and the gloom in the pre-dawn air. She had an ambiguous sensation of being very weary, yet worryingly alert. Like a child who enthusiastically embarks on a swim in the ocean, then begins to tire. Realising it is out of its depth, unable to go on at that point, wondering if it can reach the safety of the shore.

"I'm ready for my bed." Grabbing her things, she called over to the men. "Thanks again. See you tomorrow. Goodnight." Waving graciously, she stepped on to the stairs.

Hastily finishing her drink, Lucy picked up her bag to follow her. Looking up from the screen, the men returned their sudden bedtime wishes with uncomprehending stares.

Barba waited for her friend to clatter up to her and hugged her closely.

"You alright, babe?"

"Oh yes! Oh yes. Especially now I've got that off

my chest."

"Sleep well, hun. See you tomorrow."

"Can't wait. Goodnight hun."

Barba sent two texts, before sliding, in her underwear and make-up, into the double bed.

'Arrived safe B x' to Sean. Same words to Bethany, except for 'Mum x' at the end. She hoped it would not disturb their sleep.

For some time, whether minutes or hours passed she could not measure, there were noises. Footsteps, running, resounding, unruly cackles and doors banging, heaved her out of the tunnel of unconsciousness, flinging her back, finally still and silent.

It was midday before she was fully awake, aware of a cool, malodorous draught from the open window in the bathroom. The sound of dripping beat a rhythm on the floor, beneath the steady hammering on the roofs and balconies. Barba checked the time, recognising the sound of monstrous rain. Her thoughts turned to the unexpected problem of keeping dry and warm. Layers, she decided, and the shoes and jacket she had worn to begin her journey.

Lucy opened the door, rubbing her shoulders under a black pashmina, frowning.

"Good morning. Not quite the beach scene we had in mind, eh Barbs?"

Barba closed the door and sat on the bed.

"Morning, Luce. We'll have to work out what we're going to do, won't we? Did you sleep alright?"

"Not really. Not until some drunken woman stopped her antics. How about you?"

"Same, only I was half-awake and didn't know

where the noise was coming from."

"I was pretty annoyed, so I got up after a while." Lucy pinched the skin between her eyebrows.

"They were drinking downstairs and she was in and out of their rooms, ran up here, knocked on your door, I think. Laughing and shouting out."

"Why my door?" Barba was puzzled. "Whose rooms?"

"Not sure. Definitely Atek's and Berk's, because I heard their voices. And Atek was drinking with her. You can see from the balcony."

Barba's sense of provocation was at a level still high enough to be dangerous, she judged, when they went down. They were instantly offered a Turkish breakfast and an introduction to Maggie, bleary-eyed and subdued, from Sheffield. She could have been her daughter's aged clone, with the same thin hair and the large-breasted, androgynously portly body. Barba allowed Lucy to provide the polite returns. She found the furthest table from the bar, where Maggie was facing Atek on the other side, preparing their coffee. He carried it over to them.

"Good morning, ladies. How did you sleep?"

"Good morning. Good question." Barba sweetened a little. "Slept when someone stopped banging about." She looked over to the bar, where Maggie was smoking, her face turned away.

Atek made sympathetic noises, though his eyes showed his amusement at her pique.

"Maggie came back very late. She was little crazy, I think." Sitting down by Barba, he asked with concern. "What do you think you will do, today? We are told it will rain all day, all night."

"What do you think, Lucy? We could do a bit of shopping, the shops are so close. Find an umbrella, just so we don't get homesick." She rolled her eyes.

Lucy finished off a black olive and a piece of the soft white cheese. "Good idea. What do you think about visiting the Roman baths?"

Barba began to feel more optimistic. Atek had also been planning.

"We were thinking maybe we could all go to the cinema in Manavgat later, too," he suggested.

The invitation pleased them, although Barba suspected that Lucy, like herself, wished it had been more exclusive. Assuming, rightly, that 'we' meant all the 'friends' staying at the pension.

An hour later, they were about to turn into the main street of shops when they heard their names being called. From the round seating area of the cafe in the middle of the square, Maggie was hailing them in a sandpaper voice. Hesitating, another shower ruined any excuse and it would have seemed churlish not to join her.

Smiling around the group, they heard that Maggie's best friend was Paula, her cousin was Steve. Maggie and Steve were drinking beer, Paula tea, Jade and Leanne had Diet Coke. They ordered Nescafe, as they found the Turkish coffee too small, too strong and too sweet, the tea insipid. Barba took the cigarette Maggie offered her, even though she had been promising herself to be free of the habit for a year, regularly relapsing from periods of abstinence.

"How do you know Atek, then?" Maggie began

the conversation in her rough-textured tones.

"We were here on holiday in August," Barba replied."We kept in touch and fancied a cheap break."

"Emphasis being on cheap," interrupted Paula, with an accusing glare at Maggie."Stay with the locals, she said," indicating her friend again. Steve's wry smile showed assent.

Maggie, apparently nonplussed, ignored her.

"I've been friends with them for years," she claimed. "I used to go out with Atek's uncle, for about six years."

"It didn't work out?" Barba asked, in tones of condolence, interested to hear more.

"He's married to a Swedish woman now."

Interpreting the story between the words, Barba saw the nostalgic glaze in Maggie's eyes, the downturn of the corners of her mouth.

"Hey, Jade. Remember when we surprised them by turning up in their home town? The guys are from the same place, you know," she crackled." It's nearly four hundred miles east," she informed them. "We called Atek on his mobile in the High Street, didn't we, Jade? Jade's been seeing Musti since she was sixteen, haven't you love?"

Jade appeared too bored to respond, though even Lucy registered the history. She sat up straight, holding her coffee cup to her lips. Barba made a show of finishing hers, signalling to the waiter to pay while Maggie carried on with her anecdotal demonstrations of her familiarity with Atek and friends. Fortuitously, the rain had trickled away, making it seem opportunistic that they were leaving.

"Better find us a brolly." Barba took leave of them brightly. "Nice to chat. See you later."

Maggie waved goodbye with her cigarette.

"Did she say she comes here four or five times a year?" Lucy asked, as they turned the corner.

"She did," recalled Barba grimly.

The shopping was brief, since they gave up when they had found and purchased two folding umbrellas at an inflated price. The relief at seeing the previously teeming streets quiet and unhurried gave way to another stress. Diminished tourists meant greater attention and pressure to buy.

With a renewed assault of rain, against which their new umbrellas seemed flimsy, they escaped to the shelter of the Roman baths. Unlike the spas at Bath and Cheltenham, the main pool area was missing but the ante-rooms were well-preserved. Barba was especially inspired by the parade of statues; the gods, goddesses, the eagles and lions, in their immortalised states of graceful beauty.

"What time did they say for the cinema?" Lucy's time-keeping moved her out of her awe.

"Oh God," Barba glanced at her mobile. "We'd better go".

Everyone was waiting for them in the bar area when they arrived back, so with hurried apologies they made for their rooms to refresh their appearances as quickly as they could. Barba was ready and at Lucy's door when Atek came up.

"Hi. I come to tell you, you need to pay for rooms now," he reminded her in a firm but slightly regretful tone.

114

Embarrassed, Barba relayed the message to her friend inside. Lucy called him in and genially counted out thirty of her twenty lira notes, under Atek's brightening eyes.

"Thank you. We wait down for you." He sprung to the stairs, clutching the money, while they stayed to check they had what they needed and locked their doors.

When they joined the assembly by the bar, Atek and his friends emerged from the room he shared with Berk and led them out into the street. By the spot-lit amphitheatre, through the ancient gates, onto the patchy mosaics, stepping by columns and foundations to the area where buses and taxis collected.

Atek started to approach a taxi, when Maggie surprised them all by shouting at him.

"What are you doing, Atek?" she barked with exasperation. "Who's paying?" The scorn in the question implied no answer was required.

She boarded a small bus determinedly, her company behind her, including Musti and Mehmet. Barba, Lucy and Berk all watched them get on. Atek, with a furious scowl, held his hands out and accompanied them on the bus. Berk slid on to the seat next to Lucy, who shuffled with pleasure. Atek gestured Barba to take a window seat and moved in beside her, which felt inevitable, significant and disturbing to her.

The ticket man came, fumbling and clanking, with his machine. The four Turkish friends each handed him a twenty lira note, while the English found or shared coins for the exact fare. Twice during the twenty-minute journey, Barba felt simultaneously rejected and relieved, when Atek moved to the back of the bus in response to

115

texts on his mobile. Between the stop where they alighted in Manavgat and the cinema, he fell back once more as they walked.

The cinema was unexpectedly modern, with enough films offered to require a choice. After a short discussion the majority opted for an American comedy. Paula and Steve made an independent decision and went off to watch something else. Atek went to the booth first, buying two tickets. He handed one to Barba, which astonished her, and apparently Maggie, who was behind her in the queue. She regarded the transaction with thin lips pressed together so hard they were hidden, as she stepped up, her turn to pay. No visible offence registered on her face when Lucy blithely accepted a ticket from Berk as they all moved towards the theatre.

Inside, in the aisle at the end of an empty row of seats halfway up the auditorium, Atek was positioned. He seemed to have given some consideration to the logistics of the seating. Jade edged in first, Musti close behind, then Leanne, Mehmet and Berk, who made sure Lucy followed. Barba was then gently pushed through by Atek, who neatly took the next seat in between her and Maggie, who slumped in last.

From the moment the space was darkened and the Turkish sub-titles showed up, Barba failed to be fully entertained. The heavy reliance on flatulence and slapstick could not be used as an excuse. It was Atek's thigh, lightly touching, but in effect melded to hers throughout, which blurred her faculties.

There were sequences of consciousness. Hearing herself laughing with the crowd, checking there was a gap between Maggie's combat trousers and Atek's jeans, noticing that Lucy was leaning closely towards Berk, away from her.

Dazzled, she stood and blinked around at the end. Musti was peeling his arm from Jade's shoulders, Mehmet removing Leanne's hand from his lap.

It was twilight when they had entered the building at twilight. Emerging, it was darker, colder, the pavements still glistening, the sky showing signs of clearing, as stars flickered between straggling clouds.

Hungry, they bought kebabs of spiced chicken and meltingly fresh flatbread, from a shop with an open counter on the street.

"So, what do you want to do on your last night, Maggie? Atek consulted her.

"I know what I'm doing," Paula interpolated tersely. "Packing."

"Don't know," Maggie considered, blankly. "Need to pack 'cause we're off at eleven in the morning. Could go to the Lightship for a couple of hours?"

Excluding Paula, everyone was amenable to the idea of the disco. After some discussion, they agreed that they would go around eleven o'clock, giving them an hour for washing, changing and packing, by the time they were back in their rooms.

Barba showered efficiently, anxious to create the best effect in the short preparation time, deciding that her priority was making up and dressing, hair last. Applying cosmetics, she thought about clothes, aspiring to seemingly effortless, casual glamour. A grey jersey skirt, cut on the bias so it draped and swished when she moved, a top in the same colour, sequinned around the low neckline and ruched at the hip and shoulders, seemed right. Her hair was blown impatiently with a brush and the feeble dryer in the bathroom. Hastening, she found her blue cashmere shrug, shoes with grey snakeskin-effect straps, kitten heels low enough to perform well on the dance floor. She clipped on silver chains and hoops, selected items from her handbag into a silver pouch with long straps, congratulating herself for beating the clock.

Lucy was doing well too. Dressed to slay, in a toga style tunic, that dropped alluringly off her shoulder round her plump arms, with sashes binding her abundant bosom and hips, gold jewellery and gladiator sandals, she was pinning her hair up loosely when Barba walked in.

"Wow, girlfriend!" Barba complimented her. "Not seen that look before. Gorgeous or what?"

"New outfit for new moi." Lucy blew her a kiss."Thanks. And may I say you look pretty slinky, drop-dead yourself."

"You're too kind, honey." Barba curtsied, holding out her skirt. "You ready?"

Maggie had also gone to some trouble. Barba was surprised to see her wearing a feminine top in blue floral chiffon, which fastened around her neck. Her army trousers had been exchanged for knee-length safari shorts, she was wearing mascara and brownish-pink lipstick. Jade and Leanne were identically dressed in low-cut vests and shorter shorts. The men were matching too, in t-shirts and jeans, except for Steve, whose jeans were baggy, worn with a football shirt.

Atek moved close to Barba as they left the courtyard, speaking very quietly in her ear.

"You look like a queen. A princess."

"Thank you," she mouthed.

He tipped his head to her chivalrously.

The atmosphere at the Lightship was much friendlier and less intense than she recalled. Noting the average age was older, the younger generation largely at school, there were more groups of friends and mature couples, the seasoned visitors who preferred the quiet season. Lured by the latino tune that was playing as they entered, Barba and Lucy stepped out to dance immediately. It set an exultant mood. Thereafter they would sip their drinks when one track ended and parade back like divas. Atek and Berk intermittently wove in and out of their space, sometimes holding, sometimes spinning them. Jade and Leanne were mostly fused with Musti and Mehmet when the tempo was more sultry. Sullenly nursing her beer bottle, Maggie stood at a ledge with Steve, who was looking around hopefully at the few all-female groups.

"I'm going." Maggie tapped Atek on the shoulder, after an hour or so.

His response was a sign that they should all leave together. A slight move of his head towards the door and his friends were following, which gave the others little choice but to go too.

Walking back loosely together, Atek with Barba on one side, Maggie on the other, next to Steve. Berk teased Lucy in front by tugging at her sashes and pulling her along while she protested unconvincingly. The others stopped and started in dark recesses, ancient and modern, behind them. Twice, Atek fell back, pulling his 'phone from his jeans pocket, sprinting to catch up with them.

"Fancy a nightcap?" Lucy stated rather than invited, going to a table in the bar area. "I'll get my bottle of vodka, if you get the mixers," she directed Berk, who disappeared behind the counter.

"Might as well finish mine off, first." Barba went to fetch her bottle.

"I've got some whisky I might have." Maggie called to Berk to find some cola. "Oh, get us a beer too, Steve".

Berk settled everyone with drinks and excused himself with Atek.

"Enjoy your drinks. We come back. Just need to talk with Mehmet".

Slipping past the screen that separated the garden from their rooms they went in to Musti and Mehmet's shared room. Barba heard Jade swearing loudly, Leanne's falsetto giggle, as the door opened.

"Aren't you going to have a smoke with them, Steve?" asked Maggie.

"Nah. Sticking to the beer tonight else won't get up tomorrow," her cousin replied, lighting a cigarette.

Steve told a few lewd jokes. They amused Maggie so much she had a coughing fit and had to put out her cigarette, which allowed Barba and Lucy to conceal their private disgust.

Barba had just finished emptying her vodka bottle for the second round of drinks when they were thrown into darkness.

"Christ, not another power cut," moaned Maggie.

Atek and Berk emerged from behind the screen.

"Don't worry, we get candles." Berk patted the air to reassure them.

Tealights in holders with frosted glass shades were soon lambent on the tables and the bar, casting a glow on their faces which wiped out colour and deepened the hollows of their eyes.

A strange light flickered in Atek's eyes, a puckish smile forming on his lips, when Barba said she was going to the bathroom. She thought it must be the effect of the candlelight.

Feeling her way along the corridor she found the door, which was ajar. The toilet was poorly illuminated with a bare tealight. The lack of light was not problematic. It was the tears surging up her throat, as if the contents of her heart were seeking expulsion, that scared her. The struggle inside her, a terrible desire and a profound foreboding, made her feel that if she yielded to either it would be like ripping her heart out. One way would be with her own hands, the other, out of them. Reconciling herself to the conflict, she understood what she would do, and was calm.

She passed Lucy near the stairs.

"Going to get my vodka," her friend hissed comically.

"Well, I'd better get to bed. See you before we leave tomorrow." Dredging his beer bottle, Steve picked up his 'phone and jacket.

They heard Steve close his door, then a guttural shriek, feet stamping hysterically above, alarmed them. Lucy's terrified face appeared over her balcony.

"Spider," she shouted, high-pitched with panic. "Enormous. Near my bed."

Before Barba had time to respond to her friend's fright, Berk was taking the stairs, two at a time.

121

"Ok, Lucy. Don't worry," he was calling to her heroically.

When they had stopped laughing, they began to exchange stories of phobias. Maggie shared her whisky and cola with them.

"Just going to the loo," she slurred, displacing some rattan chairs en route, zig-zagging to the hall, walking her hands along the walls like a blind woman.

When the toilet door slammed shut, Atek stared at Barba.

"Lucy and Berk have been gone a long time," she commented, to cut the binding of his eyes.

"Maybe he got caught in spider's string," Atek murmured.

"String?" she repeated. "Oh, you mean web?" she laughed.

"Yes, web." The same smile. Taking her hand, he put her bag in the other and led her to the stairs.

"Let's see if you have spiders in your room," he whispered, taking her up.

The spirals of pleasure Barba enjoyed with Atek could be likened to the lure of fast food. Never reaching a peak, just returning waves of impossible, wanton gratification. Atek was endowed with nothing outstanding, physically or technically, yet somehow never sated, she always yearned for more. Though the content was of questionable quality, the appeal was irresistible. Slick, undiscriminating, carefully packaged, cleverly marketed, and compiled with subtle additives designed to induce craving. No matter how bland the taste, or how unremarkable the substance, consumed gratefully and greedily. Superficially harmless yet ultimately degrading. The addict within her was in denial.

Waking up to a brilliant freshness, Barba saw that Atek had gone from her bed, the rain had disappeared from the sky. A benevolent sun reminded her that the morning was not too late, that this was a day to make the most of. Putting on her robe, stretching her arms high, she went out on the balcony. Hearing activity below she assumed breakfast was being prepared. Going inside to turn the shower on, she was wondering about Lucy when there was a gentle tapping on the window.

"Whoops." Lucy entered, holding her palm to her mouth in mock-contrition.

"Spider." Barba pushed her playfully. "I'll give you spider."

Lucy sniggered, reddening.

"I expect you needed protecting all night."

"I expect I did," Lucy answered, both coy and pleased with herself.

Berk had their breakfast on the table before they had descended, patting Lucy softly on the shoulders as she sat.

"Afiyet Olsun," he urged. "Enjoy."

"Sagol," they chorused.

"Got something to tell you, hun," Barba confessed quietly when Berk had brought their coffee and left them to eat.

"What's that, then?" Lucy asked distractedly, her eyes following Berk to the bar.

"I got protected too, last night," she imbued the

verb with irony.

"Noooo!" Lucy's eyes and mouth were wide-open. "Why not?" She closed them. "What happened to Maggie?"

"She went to the toilet."

Lucy almost choked at that news. "I suppose it's not funny, really," she responded, drinking some water. Her words triggered another round of giggling.

Atek's presence went unnoticed until he was in the chair next to Barba, wearing a quizzical smile.

"Just being silly." Barba touched his knee. "Where's Maggie and the others?"

"Gone," he waved towards the entrance. "Just before you came down."

"Oh, we didn't say goodbye," she said, with a tinge of guilt.

"Nor me," Atek told them chirpily. "I was in shower".

"Hi."A pink voice from a black-haired girl, with gothic-style clothes and sooty eyes, hailed them from the archway.

"Hi," they all replied in unison.

Addressing Atek with familiarity, speaking with a mild London accent. "Know where Mehmet is?" she asked. "I've tried knocking."

Without acknowledging her or answering her query, Atek walked towards Mehmet's room and let himself in.

"You on holiday?" the girl asked them in a chary tone.

"Yes, are you?" Barba enquired, with genuine curiousity.

"No, my parents live here. Mehmet's my boyfriend."

Her boyfriend approached with an irritable frown and walked out with her before they could think of a discreet response.

"Don't say anything," Atek warned the women softly and very seriously, when they were out of view.

Berk brought a tray with more coffee for all of them and sat beside Lucy. She leaned against him in welcome, then straightened up and put her hands together, beaming at them benignly.

"I've had an idea. I hope you all like it." She scanned their faces for encouragement.

Atek and Berk responded with vaguely apprehensive expressions. Barba was intrigued.

"You guys haven't got much work to do, have you?" Lucy checked before revealing more.

"Now our friends have gone we just have you to look after," Atek confirmed despondently.

"Nothing for us at the beach. That closes in two weeks also," Berk added.

"So." Lucy began to sound less confident." How about we hire a car? That is, if Berk will drive it, and we go on an adventure?"

"Adventure?" Atek moved his chair closer.

"A trip. Up the coast as far as Olu Deniz maybe? Now the weather is good. For three or four days?"

Barba shifted with excitement, watching the men turn the proposition over, their eyes gleaming as they nodded and shook hands with each other across the table. Lucy clapped her hands, seeing approval all round, pulled a map from her bag, gestured for them to move the cups, and laid it on the table.

"When did you get time to think all this up, then?" Barba began to trace the coastline with her finger, astonished and delighted at her friend's forethought.

Berk, who was the only driver, as Atek had no licence, the women professing to be too nervous, said he had a friend who ran a car rental place who would give him a good price, and called him at once. They babbled for half an hour, setting the agenda, growing more animated as they agreed each detail. Aiming to leave as soon as they could, the men went to collect the car while the women bought drinks, cheese, bread and fruit from the market.

Turning on to the harbour street they saw Musti walking towards them, holding the hand of a prim-looking girl with large, dreamy eyes and blonde hair cut in a tidy bob. Dropping her hand he yanked up the waist of his jeans, his shoulders suggesting he was bracing himself for conversation.

"Hello Musti. How are you today?" Barba extended her friendly smile to his companion.

"Hello."

"Hello," the girl answered shyly, with a strong German accent.

They paused expectantly, so Musti was obliged to introduce them. Gudrun told them she had arrived two days earlier with two female friends. Barba surmised she was about eighteen.

"I came back to see Musti, but he has been so busy. I am glad he can the time spend with me now."

"Yes, good. Well, enjoy your holiday, Gudrun." Barba took Lucy's arm.

They hurried into the market, looking straight ahead to avoid revealing even a twitch of the pity and anger they were feeling, until they were inside.

"Can you believe that poor girl has gone to all that trouble to see him, and been hanging around while he's messed around with Jade?" Lucy juggled two apples indignantly.

About to express her disbelief, Barba felt her 'phone vibrate in her shorts pocket. Opening the text from Atek, she smiled, assuming he had a request.

'Miss you. Schatz. Kisses'

Glowing, she touched letters in reply, moved by the spontaneous romance of the message, and because she was so unused to it.

'Baby, miss you already too. Schatz? Kiss'

Immediately, a text returned. 'It means darling. Be quick'

He and Berk had the car loaded already with their holdalls when they had bagged up the provisions they had bought, with ice to chill it, and thrown some of the un-packed clothes and shoes back into suitcases. Promptly wheeling them off, the men stacked them in the boot, which Berk slammed shut with a satisfied push.

Atek took Barba by the hand. He took her in the back seat of the car. He took her on a rolling, coasting, banging, bumping, shrieking, screaming, lolling, lulling trip.

Breezing through the bustle of Kemer. Climbing by the rocky drama of Kas. Twisting round the Ottoman and whitewashed charm of Kalkan. Juddering past the Greek ghost-houses of Kayakoy. Pausing at the top to sigh over the curve of the lagoon below, as white and

127

bright blue as one of the lucky beads sold everywhere.

He took her each night in a different hotel, he took her in the warm sea at sunset on the last and hottest day. He took her for a ride.

It was a foregone conclusion that the women would pay.

CHAPTER 6

The key turned stiffly, unlocking the door. Barba dragged her load into the cold space, knowing that this home-coming was no more than a going-back. The cat stalked her steps, mewling and eyeing her mournfully.

"Hello puss," she brushed his fur with her fingertips, apologetically.

Her first action was to switch the heating on fully, her second was to place the laptop on the dining table. Her third was to pull the duty-free vodka out of the bag decorated with scenes of Antalya. Her fourth was to say a silent thank you that Sean was due back a day later. Her fifth was to play her James Morrison record, humming, her head nodding and shaking; a closed-eyed expression of her own mental chariot of desire and fear.

Finding herself shivering and stiff-necked when she woke, having fallen asleep, sprawled on the sofa, her neck abnormally askew on a pillow. The wet patch around the zip of her jeans, she realised, with both relief and shame, was the spilt remains of the drink she was holding, the glass now lying on its side on the rug beside her foot. The timer on the television told her it was seven in the morning; outside it was still dark. Putting the lights out, deciding to leave the heating on, grateful that her bed was comfortable when she sloughed off her clothes and crawled straight in.

Vaguely, before it reclaimed her, she had

consciously hoped for another four hours of sleep. Later, when she came to fully, she was pleased to find that it was just after eleven in the morning. She grabbed her robe to go downstairs, pressed the restart button on the laptop and put the kettle on, while the computer woke up too. Hugging her mug of coffee she sat in front of the screen. The glowing couple on the Messenger icon, like a silent alarm, caused an internal lurch mid-body. Nervy with more than caffeine, she opened the window.

Atek says: Hi

Offline, not there anymore. The time of the message was nine in the morning. Eleven o'clock in Turkey.

Barba says: Hi. Sorry I missed u. Sleeping

Barba says: Will stay online until tonight, 10pm here. Nudge me if u come

Just to be sure, she rewrote her words in a text to him, with kisses, making sure she deleted it from the 'sent messages' folder in her 'phone.

After an economic shower, she dried herself hastily and hopped into a sweatshirt and jogging trousers. Her dirty laundry was bundled from the suitcase and the bedroom floor, the first load sorted and thrown into the machine. She made more tea, found some frozen bread to toast and set the tray on the table. Nibbling, staring at the pictures on the screen. All static. The telephone, a notepad and pen were brought to her place. Each time she wrote a line on her 'To Do' list for the weekend, she checked her Messenger and did the same as she prepared a shopping list. Her telephone calls to Bethany, her mother and Lucy were conducted from that position.

"Hi darling."

"Hi Mum," Bethany answered in a colourless voice. "When did you get back?

"Early this morning, about half-one."

"How was it?" Her daughter sounded as if no response was required.

Without pre-conception, Barba gave a summary of all the most undesirable aspects of the trip.

"Anyway, it did Lucy good to get away," she concluded, in tones of selflessness.

"Hope so," Bethany replied, doubtfully.

"How are the kids? Richard?"

She listened to Bethany's detailed account of the school week, forthcoming events and the daily challenges her solicitor son-in-law had been facing.

"What about you, honey?"

"I'm good, Mum. You know me. Same old, same old."

"Well, darling, listen. We'd love to have you all for Sunday dinner as usual," Barba adopted the altruistic voice once more. "But, I'm thinking, Sean won't be back until late tonight, and probably will be really tired tomorrow. He starts his day shift on Monday".

"Oh, that's alright, Mum." Bethany was very understanding.

"So, is it alright if I come to yours? Looking forward to seeing you all." She privately wished that was as sincere as she hoped it sounded.

"Yes, 'course," Bethany obliged. "What about Dad?"

"We'll leave it open for Sean, eh? I'll see how he feels in the morning".

The call was ended with satisfaction, she with a reason to be out on Sunday afternoon secured. Projecting solutions for the Friday to Monday period, between Sean finishing his day shift and beginning a sequence of afternoons, occupied her mind. Glancing at the laptop she put in another number and listened to it ring.

"Hello." Dot's hesitant greeting.

"Hello Mum, it's me."

"Oh hello, Barbara. You're home?"

"Yes, this morning, early."

"How did you get on?"

Barba noted that neither her mother or her daughter had enquired directly if she had enjoyed herself. Recounting the week as before, with more exaggeration about the duration of the bad weather. Her mother delivered an equally negative review of her own week.

"You want to come for tea on Monday, Mum? I'm having lunch with a friend, but I can come for you about three? You can eat with Sean and me, then" Barba was anticipating that Lucy might be the friend who had yet to be invited.

The arrangements made, Barba rang off, and sighed at the computer. She made her final call.

"Lucy, it's Barba."

"Hi, babe. How you doing?

" Not bad. Can't drag myself away from the laptop."

"Oh?"

"Msn. Missed Atek this morning. Have you spoken to Berk?"

"No, just text each. Said I'd talk online sometime

132

when the kids are out."

Barba envied Lucy's casual air.

"It was fun, hun, wasn't it?" Lucy seemed relaxed and light-hearted.

"Yes, it was Luce. Can I meet you in your lunchbreak Monday?"

"'Course. Usual? Pub at twelve-thirty? Ish."

"Great. I'll see you then. Dying to talk to you."

"Me too, hun. Got to go. Phee needs a lift. What's new?"

Another look at the computer screen, then the kettle was filled, the clothes dragged to the dryer, some biscuits bounced out of a tin on to a plate. Barba crunched thoughtfully, opening the dialogue page for Atek.

Barba says: Going shopping. Back in 1 hour

The task and the unpacking were actually completed in fifty minutes. She made more tea to drink with the sandwich she had bought, and set up the ironing board in the dining area. The laptop was turned so she could track any communication whilst ironing, and the television likewise, to view on the other side.

She got through the whole pile of clothes, one programme about a couple choosing whether to relocate to Greece or Yorkshire, another about the invasion of grey squirrels and the impact on the indigenous red. Wondering what diversions she could find next, she was supping canned mushroom soup from a bowl when Atek showed up at around six in the evening. At the sound of the three note melody that signified something was happening, she sprang on the keyboard to see the conversation box.

Atek says: Hi

Atek says: Are u there?

Barba says: Here

"At last.You are there. I'm here." Barba was talking aloud to herself.

Barba says: Hi

Atek says: How are u?

Barba says: Good, thanks. How are u?

Atek says: Ok

Atek says: I can't talk now. Friends computer. Can come in 2 hours about

Barba says: Ok. See u then

Atek says: See u

She slumped in her chair as she read the words, 'Atek appears to be offline'. Tears swelled and fell, distorting the words they had exchanged, dropping off her chin into the cupped palms on her lap. Wiping her face with the back of her hands, then drying them on the cotton of her sweatshirt, she stood and inhaled slowly. She held her breath and exhaled noisily through her mouth.

Picking up the two oyster-grey silk pieces from the top of the pressed clothes, she stepped up the stairs. The bath taps were turned on, hot streams releasing the scent of the oils she sprinkled on the base of the tub. She lay the camisole set on her bed, alongside a light robe in a deep-rose satiny fabric. Her winter gown, over-sized, taupe, thick cotton fleece, was removed from the hook on the door and put round her naked form. Brushes, perfume, creams and cosmetics were laid out like surgical instruments for an operation, on the shelf of her dressing mirror.

She soaked for as long as she could endure, lay
with the face and eye masks for the appointed time,
moisturised the entire surface area of her skin. Even
when she had pedicured, manicured, blow-dried
methodically, made-up meticulously, slipped into silk
and sprayed fragrantly, there were still thirty minutes to
wait. She put the James Morrison CD in the player,
which was replaced by the radio on after the first track,
so the babble of the DJ and the stream of pop music
could carry away the brimming in her throat. The vodka
bottle welcomed her from the kitchen worktop. She took
the orange juice and a chilled curry with rice from the
fridge. The microwave rang to tell her her food was
ready as she waited with her glass and her fork on a tray.
A sheet of paper towel was tucked into her camisole,
another in the waist of the knickers, so she could not
stain them.

Just before the hour, she threw the remains of the
meal in the bin, filled her glass and switched on the
laptop. Glossing her lips, combing then ruffling her hair
while it loaded, she opted for 'Tools' on the menu, and
going to the webcam settings, saw herself as she would
be seen. The picture was slightly out of focus, which she
did not mind because it softened her features. The
lighting was a shade unflattering. Atek had not arrived,
so she moved a lamp to the table and pushed it around
until it threw an enhancing glow on her face. She shut
the window, and waited. To encourage her to feel less
fraught, a comedy chat show she liked was selected on
the television.

Twenty minutes into the show, when a guest was
particularly entertaining, the winking in her peripheral

135

vision made her start. The short tune told her she was nudged. With her palm on her chest, she looked.

Atek says: Hi! Are u there?

Barba says: Hi. Here

Atek says: How r u?

Barba says: Good, thanks. How r u?

Atek says: Ok

She was invited to view him, he to see her. She accepted twice.

She watched, trance-like, the wheels rolling as the cameras loaded. She could see her chest rising and falling rapidly on the small screen, trying to slow it as she looked at his image, clear and sharp.

Atek says: Nice

Barba says: Thanks. Nice to see u, too

She smiled full at the camera. He did the same.

Atek says: Are you alone?

Barba says: Yes, where are you?

Atek says: Internet Cafe

Barba says: Do you have a mic?

He was wearing headphones.

Atek says: Not working

Barba says: What have you been doing today?

She read the words 'Atek is writing' above the dialogue box, then they disappeared. This repeated three times. It was more than a minute before the conversation continued.

Atek says: What are you wearing? For bed? Can you show me?

Even through her cheap lens her face could be seen darkening. She put her head down coyly then grinned at the camera. He was grinning too.

Barba says: I'm shy

She hesitated, then stood anyway, her lingerie filling the frame in the corner of the screen. Her head was still cut off even when she sat down again. She could see her nightwear and his indulged smirk frozen in their boxes. The connection is lost, she read.

Pouring another drink, the profile picture of Kerrie from Eastley popped up in her mental viewer. She felt uncomfortable then; deluded and shallow.

Nudged online, she went back. The connection was restored.

Barba says: How was your day?

Atek says: Ok. No work. No money. Not many tourists now. We close beach.

Barba: What will you do?

She was told he was writing once more, again the words did not come that time.

When they did, he told her he was going away for ten minutes and stopped the camera. To fill in the time, she shivered with a cigarette at the open back door.

Atek says: Here now, baby

Barba says: Me too

Atek says: When do you work at Tour office?

Barba says: Tuesday. How about u? What will u do?

Atek says: Hometown in 2 weeks for Bayram

Barba says: Bayram?

Atek says: End of Ramadan. Like Christmas for us

Barba says: Oh yes, I understand. We call it Eid here. That will be nice for u

Atek says: Nice if u have money for gifts for

family and friends

Barba paused to find a response that felt right. She could not.

Barba says: I work with a Muslim man. He brings us delicious food for the festival.

A miserable droop had settled around his eyes and mouth.

Atek says: Will you come again at Christmastime?

She tried to reply but the connection had failed again. She realised, with frustration prickling her like an itch, that the show that was ending meant it was nearly ten o'clock. Her hands clapped in gratitude when she saw he had signed in again.

Atek says: Sorry, bad connection

Barba says: Sorry, I have to go now

Atek says: When r u online?

Barba says: Can you come Monday? Morning or afternoon, 1 to 3pm here?

Atek says: Maybe

Barba says: Hope to see u then. Kiss u goodbye

An animated kiss through red lips smacking loudly, exploded over their conversation, surprising and delighting her. He was laughing at her response.

'Play kiss' she was instructed. She played.

The camisole was eased delicately over her head, the bottoms smoothed over her legs and feet. She replaced them with pale-blue, flannelette pyjamas her mother had bought for her last Christmas. The reading lamp next to her was left on, all main lights except the porch switched off. She was in bed before she placed the unread romance, pages splayed open as if dropped in slumber, in the hollow behind her knees. Pulling up the covers to cut out the light, she settled in. She had about two hours to find deep sleep before Sean was expected, and prayed it would be enough.

He had been offered a lift from the airport from a fellow golfer. Her first awareness of his return was a jolt out of her position, as he dropped on to his side of their bed, yanking the duvet from her shoulders as he rolled under. She could sense him looking at her before hauling himself the other way. When his back was still behind hers, she inched the sheet, a finger-full at a time, back over her arm. He began to breathe heavily.

Lifting the covers from her, painstakingly lightly, she slipped from bed the next morning, guessing it was after eight because daylight was trying to creep through the blinds. The doors of the wardrobe were slid apart slowly and gently. Underwear was guided out of the basket without having to pull it out on its runners, a jumper and jeans picked conveniently from the top of folded piles. She left the doors in place as she carried her clothes to the bathroom, so she could emerge fully-dressed after the prolonged hot shower she intended to enjoy.

A banana with wholemeal toast and copious fresh coffee was her choice of breakfast, not wanting to cook twice that morning or eating a meal too soon before her Sunday dinner at her daughter's home. Eating at the table, she was tempted to set up the laptop but realised some circumspection would be required. She listened to Gregorian chants on the radio instead, which she found both soothing and strangely disturbing at the same time.

For her next resolution, she found her purse and

took the old gardening jacket hanging under the stairs rather than find another in the bedroom. The air outside was brisk, quite pinching, as the sky was clear with no insulating clouds, which satisfied Barba. Only rain and ice would stay Sean from the golf course. Impending poor weather, the onset of winter, she knew would whet his urge to make the most of dry ground in those short days.

"Morning, Barba," the shopkeeper greeted her courteously.

"Morning, Mr. Rashiq."

"We have not seen you around. Have you and Mr. Brown been away?

"Yes, we have."

A customer stepped up to the counter, excusing Barba from further explanation. She collected Sean's two Sunday tabloids, and added her usual, taking a preview of the magazine supplement's main features. She counted out the exact cost in the queue, cheerily handing it over, whilst sweeping up the bundle, calling her thanks and goodbye as she exited.

Sean shuffled himself up against his pillows, pleased and surprised when she took the newspapers into him. It was not an errand she would normally perform, it being part of his early Sunday routine to collect them before breakfast.

"Hey thanks Barba. How was your holiday?"

She remembered to kiss him; she touched the side of his mouth with hers.

"Ok", she groaned." Weather awful. Rained solid, flippin' cold as well for first few days. Power cuts, too."

"Bad luck, eh pet? Did you enjoy it anyway?"

"When the weather got better and we got some sun. Had a bit of a trip up the coast," she summarised. "Hang on a minute. Need the loo." She ran out, averting further questions.

She enquired about his trip as she walked back through the bedroom door.

"Aye, alright. Perfect golfing weather. Sunny, not too hot, not too cold, like."

"That's good."

She listened attentively to the handicap figures which were meaningless and boring to her, wondering if he had noticed that she had not pressed for details of the sociable evenings, a source of suspicion to her before. More than a few marriages in the golf-club circuit had been casualties of the away-play; now she did not care.

"What do you want for breakfast? The full monty?" she asked.

"Aye, that'd be great. I'm starving. Didn't eat properly since the 'plane."

"Tried to stay awake, but I was worn-out, too. Anyway, I'll bring it up here."

Sean agreed with a touchingly grateful smile. She went down, happily frying, because it would keep him up there longer. It was time to tell him her plans, she decided, when she had laid the tray with the plateful of eggs, bacon, mushrooms, tomatoes and fried bread on the bed, and placed the mug of tea on the bedside table.

"I told Beth it'd be better if I went there for Sunday dinner this week. Thought you might be tired."

"Good idea." He checked his watch."What time did she say?"

"About two. What do you want to do?"

He looked at the big breakfast on his lap. "You're going in a couple of hours?"

She nodded, guessing he was thinking what she had hoped he would.

"I won't be ready to eat another meal in a few hours after this."

"No, expect not". She pulled back the curtains to reveal to him the brightness of the day. "What will you do then?"

"Might make the most of this," he pointed with his fork at the window.

"Okey-doke. I'll do you a dinner about six. That suit you?" Seeing the second, uncharacteristic blink of appreciation on his face, she took that as consensus and left him to eat.

More than an hour passed before she heard his feet thud to the bedroom floor and more lightly, make their way to the bathroom. To be heard above the rush of the shower she shouted that she was leaving. She almost skipped to the car on her way out.

Her balloon of hope, inflated by possibilities of amicable, if not joyful, partings, was needled by her daughter's ambivalent reception.

"Hi, Mum." Bethany flung open the door. She seemed pleased to have a mother to join the family for Sunday roast. There was also an air of disappointment about her, that this was not quite the one she would have liked.

"Hi, darling." She held out her arms to embrace her daughter.

"Dad not make it, then?" Bethany pulled away,

scanning Barba's attire, without comment, which was as good as approval.

"Got back late last night. Only just polished off a full English."

"Oh, bless. Did he have a good time?" The warmth and genuine interest in her query taunted Barba.

"Yes, presume so, as usual." She was looking around and listening, seeking the children, needing their innocent energy.

"They've gone to the park for a bit with Richard while I make the dinner," Bethany answered her unspoken question.

In the kitchen, preparing vegetables, the conversation moved on, from an update on the children's lives, to Turkey.

"So," Bethany peeled the top layer of an onion, " it wasn't up too much, then?"

"Well, it was quiet, you know, mainly couples and groups of friends. No children on the beach." Barba was selecting the colours to paint a scene which would seem least attractive to Bethany, who was chopping the onion, wiping her eyes with the back of her hand. No more was said about it, as the children clamoured in and around her.

This time she had bought a big jar of top-brand jelly beans from the airport shop. After dinner they were permitted to open it. They stuffed the sweets into their mouths, squabbling over and playing guessing games with the flavours. Bethany got out the ironing board and a basket of shirts, skirts and trousers in assorted sizes.

"Don't remind me. I've got loads of ironing too," complained Barba, "and told Sean I'd make him a dinner when I get in. He's on days tomorrow."

She completed a round of kissing sticky, stained mouths, her son-in-law's bristle and her daughter's cool cheek. An animated chorus of thanks and goodbyes accompanied her as she took her leave.

Sundays evenings were normally dominated by Sean's agenda of television programmes, which Barba would give most of her attention to, as she ironed in the living room. Thus there was never much reason or opportunity for conversation. It especially suited Barba that night. Sean had enjoyed the fried steak with mashed potatoes, peas and onion gravy she quickly prepared for him when he came in, and the bottle of red wine they shared. As she smoothed wrinkled material with heat, he was pacifically digesting in his armchair island. Elbows on the arms, his hands were clasped on his dome of soft belly, legs outstretched. She heard dry snores and noticed his head drifting to the arm of his chair.

"Sean," she called three times, shouting his name loudly, finally.

He jerked up, staring around disconcertedly, as if he was in strange surroundings.

"You were asleep. You need to go to bed," she advised.

To her silent relief, he raised himself and headed obediently to the stairs.

"I'll just finish these few things off." She pointed at the clothes with the iron, as he passed her.

He nodded, as to a hypnotist's instructions, and plodded up to bed.

In ten minutes, her chore complete, she waited another twenty with a glass in her hand, mindful of any activity upstairs. There was none.

Sean's day shifts began early, so when she awoke, alone, remembering it was her day off, she sprung out of bed, spreading out her arms in a gesture of liberation. Resolving to take more care of herself, she extended her grooming ritual. Deciding she needed a body brushing, she followed it with an exfoliating scrub of sea-salt in the shower, an extra minute with the electric toothbrush and a thorough application of moisturising cream all over. Rejecting the sloppy sweat-gear which was the usual at-home wear, she found a flattering, long blue jumper to wear with her jeans, reminding herself to add a long chain and bangles later, when she put on her boots. Make-up was complete and the laptop switched on before she got to the kitchen for her tea and toast.

Adding on the two hours to calculate Turkish time, she planned various distractions for the morning. She was worried that if she wavered hopefully around the computer, she could waste the morning going round in crazy circles of unrequited communication. Mentally dividing up the morning space into tasks punctuated by looking out for any signs on Messenger, she began the first round of eliminating dust and grime with vengeful swipes and strokes. Messenger remained idle all the time. Mercifully, the three hours before it was time to go to meet Lucy for lunch, passed more quickly than she had feared.

"Hey, babe," Lucy grabbed her warmly outside the pub near her office.

"Hi, honey. You're looking good," Barba remarked, cheered to see her friend looking so confident and content.

Once the sandwich and drinks had been chosen, they took off their jackets and settled in friendly tub chairs by the window.

"Am I glad to see you," Barba touched Lucy's arm earnestly, her intensity causing some concern to them both.

"Why, what's up, babe? Everything ok with Sean?"

"Oh, God, no difference there. That's the problem."

She knew the strength of her derision was unsettling Lucy, but she continued, wanting to express it first in the hope they could then converse more lightly.

"It's just that I feel I can't go on any longer this way with Sean. Like I'm slowly being suffocated to death. And even though it may be nothing with Atek, I 'd be willing to give it a try". That sounded too much like James Morrison to her. She thumped her forehead.

"Oh," was all Lucy could say.

"I can't stop thinking about him. I didn't expect this. What about you? What about you and Berk?" She was grasping for something to relate to, to share, to validate her own emotions.

Lucy made a puffing sound and brushed her hand in the air, dismissively.

"Barba, after shaking that rat off, I'm really enjoying feeling good about myself again. Berk was fun, is fun. And I intend to explore the options in that department." She scooped up her overflowing baguette with relish.

Barba ate her sandwich in desolate silence. Lucy

skilfully smoothed the conversation towards arrangements to begin the belly-dancing classes on the forthcoming Friday night, which managed to seem like a relevant and positive development of the initial discussion. Barba began to feel excited about the fun of dressing up a little, enjoying the sensuous movements, gaining new skills, and how connected it felt to pleasures Turkish. The discussion grew more creative and humourous when they talked about how they might progress to full costume.

"We can find something fabulous when we go to Turkey again." Barba was almost bouncing in the tub chair.

"Maybe." Lucy seemed pleased at the idea, but with a cautious little smile. "Which reminds me, have you thought of a costume for the Hallowe'en do at the Golf Club on Saturday?"

"No," Barba put her fingers to her mouth," that's come round so quickly."

They filled the remainder of their talk-time exploring the options of what they could be, what they possessed and what they could acquire easily.

"See you Friday at the community centre, then," Lucy reminded her as they parted. "Seven-thirty start, hun."

"Look forward to it. Have a good week, babe."

"You too." Lucy blew her a kiss before making her roly-poly way back to her office.

Driving home more serenely than through the journey there, Barba gave some forethought to the next few hours at home, before she had to leave to collect her mother and bring her back. Lucy had informed her about suitable dress for the Friday class. The teacher had suggested comfortable wear, so Barba had thought of the long-sleeved T-shirts and leggings she had, and flowing scarves to create a mood. She planned to find and experiment with some jewellery and suitable material for wafting, which could take place in the vicinity of the laptop.

It was an absorbing and delightful way to spend an hour, playing and swaying with diaphanous fabrics, her eyes lined with kohl, lips with crimson. Then the pastime seemed exhausted, Messenger had been quiet, and Barba felt the next hour present itself like a street to be walked down, with a gaping pothole to be avoided, in the middle of her path. She was glad that the Hallowe'en fancy dress had been mentioned, and gave her attention to that, including Sean's options, as she anticipated that he would suddenly expect inspiration and assistance on the day of the event. Busying herself first with a list of possible characters, then what was available to create each one, she began finding items that might be used, each task punctuated by her scurrying to the computer. Just as she had tidied away her scarves and the Hallowe'en box she had begun, she picked up the sound of the nudge from Messenger.

Atek says: Hi. U there?

Barba says: Here now. Hi!

Atek says: How are u?

Barba says: Good, thanks. How are u?

Seeing that Atek was asking her to accept set-up for their camera, but that it was also three minutes past three, she punched her thighs with frustration and declined.

Barba says: Sorry, Atek. Looked for you this morning and 2 hours this afternoon

Atek: Ok. Not easy for me to come sometimes

Barba: Sorry, I have to pick up my mother ☹

Atek says: ☹ Ok. When can u talk again?

Barba says: Friday night? About 10 here, 12 there. Or too late?

Atek says: Maybe. See u

Barba says: Hope to see u Friday night. Bye

He was gone.

Struggling with her tears, her boots and a heavy jacket, she wondered if she should have stayed to talk, but she knew after five minutes of waiting her mother would go outside to look for her, growing stiff, cold and agitated.

"Holiday didn't do you much good by the looks of it," were her mothers words when she had got herself awkwardly and painfully into the passenger seat.

"You ok, Mum? Why do you say that?"

"Well, I was expecting you to have a bit of colour, look a bit brighter for getting away."

Barba strained up to the mirror and rubbed her cheeks.

"The heavens did open for the first few days. Made the drains smell awful. And we had a few power cuts, one at night." She selected the elements most reminiscent of deprivation. She knew this would make the strongest, negative impression on her mother, as the absence of children playing had with her daughter.

"Oh," Dot's expression grew sympathetic. "So you didn't get any sun, then?"

"In the last few days. We had a good break, all in

149

all. Lucy needed it." Barba winced inwardly at the self-sacrificing manner she had adopted. Her increasing capacity for soft deception began to hit her hard.

"So she's not back with Alan yet?" There was a hard edge to her mother's question and mouth, as if it was Lucy who had had a tawdry escapade with a shameless Internet exhibitionist.

"No." Barba made it clear she had no more to say about it.

She asked about the Monday Club her mother had attended that morning, because it could be relied upon to release a stream of discontent. Dot was able then to rail at length about the tiresome habits of the elderly participants, the inadequate performance of the visiting speaker or the organisation of a planned activity, and sometimes even the free food.

In the house she found the quiz programme on the television which her mother was fond of, made her comfortable with cushions and attended to her with tea and two digestive biscuits.

"Keep you going 'til we eat in a couple of hours, when Sean comes in."

"Thanks pet." Dot's mind was clearly on the questions.

Barba decided to watch it with her, calling out the answers if she knew them, conferring with Dot or praising her for getting them right. She was glad to be engaged like that. It stopped her mind from wandering back to unsettling places. The subsequent programme was a favourite of her mother's too, an interesting documentary about the coastline of Britain. It washed away another half-hour, and led to Barba showing Dot how to search an area for more information on the Internet. Realising it was time to cook their meal, she left Dot at the computer, happily viewing a potted history of Robin Hood's Bay and the pictures which stirred poignant memories of their holidays there with Barba's father. She was still there when Sean came in. In response to Dot's enquiry about his golfing trip to Portugal, which was made with considerably more enthusiasm than she had mustered about Barba's holiday, he found the location for her. Dot listened to him like a child at bedtime, as he illustrated his story with the images on the screen.

"Sorry you two." Barba put the placemats down."Need to set the table now."

They reluctantly put the laptop aside, intending to return to it after eating, as Dot had asked Sean to show her some other websites. They talked about that as they ate, which Barba encouraged with occasional questions and expressions of interest. It satisfied her that the conversation was flowing and impersonal.

The evening soap drama series her mother followed, as if the lives of the characters were interwoven with her own reality, could not be neglected however. It lured Dot from the worldwide web until it was time for Barba to take her home. Sean switched the channels to watch the two hour detective series he was a fan of.

"Bye love." Dot stretched up to kiss him clumsily and affectionately.

"Bye Dot, pet," Sean replied, one eye on the television detective.

Barba knew he would be engrossed in the action

until it ended, which gave her time to declare an early night and be reasonably assumed to be sleeping, when he arrived in the bedroom after ten.

With forethought that surprised and dismayed her, she considered the patterns of their shared existence. She devised a path of discreet elusiveness for the days and weeks ahead, without conscious intention or projection of where it would lead her.

Preparing herself physically and mentally for work on Tuesday morning, she rehearsed the version of the holiday she would present to Nicole. She assumed that Mo would only show brief, polite interest in the events. Kash, who would be beginning his third week of fasting, might not be there, or only present in body.

Kash was at his desk when she entered, his complexion paler than usual, quietly absorbed in his work diary.

He looked up and smiled at her. No comment. She understood from the previous Ramadan, how Kash's normal exuberance was slowly taken over by a state of calm reflectiveness until Eid, when he resumed his vivacious frivolity. Nicole walked out of Mo's office. Barba leaned so Mo could see her waving. She returned the greeting warmly with her thumb and went back to her paperwork.

"Hi Barba. Where's your tan?" observed Nicole.

Barba felt mildly gloating that her colleague had so effortlessly taken just the approach she had hoped for.

"Oh, don't ask. Not a ray for three days. Couldn't get near the beach for torrential rain and bloody storms."

"God," exclaimed Nicole. "Sounds like a disaster," she concluded, conveying, by tapping

152

vigorously on her keyboard, that that was the end of that.

Barba logged on, congratulating herself for predicting that the image of a sunless holiday, without prolonged torpor on a beach, would have zero appeal to Nicole.

For the three days she spent at the office that week, she found the mood, externally, subdued and mellow. The days were increasingly truncated, less light, less bright. The early onset of decay and stagnation could be smelt in the air, even though it was still sweetly fruitful. Glorious, fiery leaves clung determinedly to branches, defying the harrying winds which would finally shake them all off the skeletons of the trees.

Internally, reason and normality seemed to have been fugged by gaseous smoke from the fire of her tormented longings. It was as if all the bonds which connected her to people, and gave her purpose in her everyday life, were like melting nylon threads. Strong as fishing line in ordinary conditions, they were loose and losing form in the furnace of her obsessive nostalgia for the outlet of her passion.

By Thursday she felt trapped and choked; needing oxygen and respite, wanting to breathe freely again. She took an early lunch-break to walk in the park by the duck-pond, which had only a flotilla of furious, hungry geese. At the stream-side she decided on her Hallowe'en costume, a relatively easy choice. No witch this year, she wanted to be a devil. With her inner hell still smouldering, but under control, she inhaled the fresh air of rationality. She spent a gratifying half-hour in the charity and discount shops looking for anything to help her create her fancy dress, and for the zombie she had thought Sean could be.

Because he had finished his shift of four days, she and Sean both had a day off on Friday. He slept in a little later than usual, and always wanted a traditional fried breakfast on the days he was not working. She usually obliged him by making it, except after night shifts, when he had eight days off, before the working pattern resumed with days.

"I've sorted out my Hallowe'en outfit," she informed him, sitting down with a bacon sandwich, while he was mopping up his egg with fried bread.

"Oh, yeah?" he munched.

"Not telling you," she teased him. "Surprise."

He looked boyishly charmed for a second, then thoughtful as he chewed on some bacon.

"What can I go as? Last year I was a vampire, again. Could do with something different."

"Same here," Barba agreed," Been a witch for three years. Got something different. Thought you could be a zombie."

"Aye. How'd I do that then?" Sean seemed willing.

"Easy to cut up and dirty old clothes. I've bought some cheap black and brown eyeshadow and white face make-up. We can get bandages to wrap round you."

"Isn't that a mummy, Mummy?" he punned, and they laughed.

"Probably. Should have watched the film, except I hate that stuff. Anyway, a few ragged bandages, I meant."

"Sounds alright," Sean conceded, taking his plate to the kitchen and throwing it into the sink.

The morning was spent in companionable activity as they found a jumper of Sean's which already had moth-holes in it and some nondescript trousers. They chopped at them with scissors then brushed them, and the bandages, with dark powder, to produce a dirty, torn effect. That kept them in child-like pre-occupation for more than two hours. They enjoyed customising his shoes most of all, having fun pulling the sole from the body until each resembled a hungry snake's mouth.

"I'm going to the Club this afternoon, while the weather's holding out," Sean told her, as they were putting his outfit into a cardboard box ready for Saturday night.

"Will you be wanting your tea, then?" Barba asked pleasantly, aware of the contrast in her attitude. Before, they would have exchanged sharp words about the time he spent on golf and his erratic attendance at mealtimes. "Lucy and I are starting belly-dancing at the Community Centre", she reminded him.

Her goodwill, and the novelty of her new interest, which the venue made more respectable to him somehow, seemed to faze Sean.

"No problem," he stammered, "enjoy yourself. I'll see you tonight." He grabbed his jacket and fumbled in the pockets.

"So, no tea, then?" She handed him his car keys.

"No, no tea, pet."

She thought of signing in to Messenger when he had gone, entertaining the temptation at various points throughout the afternoon. The sensation that she could be sucked back easily into the unbearable turmoil of the last few days prevented her. The fun of the fancy dress preparations and the anticipation of the belly-dancing had brought a breeze of playfulness which she wanted to indulge.

Wrapping their exotic scarves around their hips and waddling sensuously behind their teacher in her Romany glamour, like pubescent ducks, Barba felt as if big bubbles were rising in her, tickling her inside. She was carried away with the weaving and whirling, the undulating and the uplifting.

Perhaps that was all she needed, she thought to herself, as she and Lucy emerged into the biting night, giggling and linking arms. That is, until she and Lucy were giving a tipsy, giddy demonstration of their new skills to a delighted Atek and Berk. The intensity with which he watched her through the webcam, kindled and disturbed her. At eleven, she told Lucy to write that it was getting late and they had to go. They all played the kissing game and blew them to the camera.

Barba says: Come next Tuesday night?

Atek says: Maybe

The Hallowe'en Dance was advertised as starting at eight o'clock. She and Sean decided that nine was early enough, it allowed time for things to become enlivened before they got there.

"Bring us some wine, will you pet?" She shouted down to Sean as she got ready in the bedroom. Carefully spraying her blonde hair with streaks of orange and red hairspray, she spiked it with liberal amounts of gel to create a flaming effect. Her face was sponged uniformly pale with foundation, her eyes smoky with black powder that had a subtle silver shimmer, eyebrows thickened and arched with pencil. The eyelashes took some patience to fix, but she got them attached firmly and evenly, painting a fine black line over the join Her lips were given a thick outline before she brushed the carmine lipstick in between. The dress had been put on first, protecting it with a towel, before doing her make-up. Sean came in with her wine as she was smoothing the lace top of her hold-up stockings in place.

"Thanks." She pulled down the dress and took the wine glass from him elegantly, because she had put on black fishnet gloves.

He tugged the red, arrow-headed tail she had sewn on the back of her dress as she leaned over to put the glass on the dressing table. She caught his expression in the mirror as she straightened and her breath as he brought his hands to her hem, pushing it up as they moved over the lace to the flesh above. She leaned back on him but he gripped her forearms to steady her as he moved away, with an uncomfortable laugh that was more like a weak cough. When she looked at him directly, he indicated the bandages loosely hanging round his chest, abdomen, his hips and thighs.

"Isn't Lucy coming?" he asked.

"Not for another half-hour", she replied, thinking that would have been time enough.

It seemed strange to invite Lucy over without Alan, to have a few drinks whilst helping each other add finishing touches to their dress, as they had done for years. Any apprehension was soon pierced by Lucy's high-spirited entry, cackling and straddling her broomstick in burlesque fashion. The fishnet-clad vamp of a witch was completely clothed in black, from the

157

underwear glimpsed through the chiffon blouse to the short skirt made of strips of leather. She wore stiletto ankle boots, had sharp, black talons decorated with luminous spiders, mesmerising false lashes and heavy make-up, with glitter drifting along any exposed skin.

"Ha!" Barba called gleefully as she swept in theatrically. "What happened to the round-shouldered hag with the warts and the hooked nose?" Barba put her sequinned red horns on so she was complete.

"I killed her," Lucy declared in a menacing voice. "We have no use for the likes of her, anymore. And you, my dear evil sister," she continued, in role, "look ravishingly demonic if I may say so."

"You may say so, you sultry sorceress. Come and have a drink."

When Sean saw Lucy, the glint in his eyes told Barba that his mind had been taken off the disappointment he had expressed earlier, that things were not the same without Alan. His friend still frequented the Golf Club, but had deemed it wise to stay away when his estranged wife would be there, especially in the role of fearsome witch.

Lucy managed to enchant more males during the course of the evening, including, Barba noticed with genuine pleasure for her friend, an unattached skeleton who was in his late twenties. Barba realised she was increasingly doing this kind of mathematics with ages of couples. Another new habit was her preoccupation with media stories about celebrity relationships where the woman was much younger. Wistfully, she calculated that Lucy was ten years older than the skeleton she was skirmishing with on the dance floor, which seemed unremarkable to her. Berk was six years younger than Lucy, much less than the eighteen year difference between her and Atek, though she had led him to believe it was only fourteen. A piece of research she had found on the internet, carried out by social scientists, had come up with a formula for acceptable age differences between partners. At first she had been sceptical but the more she applied it, the more sense it seemed to make. It offered no consolation regarding Atek. To fit into the socially acceptable category, he needed to be at least thirty, half her age plus seven years. She sighed at how unthinkable and ludicrous it would have seemed a few months ago.

A cruelly-handsome vampire interrupted her thoughts.

"If you won't dance with me, I'll have to sink my teeth into your pretty neck."

Despite finding the threat rather exciting, she allowed him to swing her around to the 'Monster Rock', his cape and her tail flying behind them. Sean, even more convincing in his part for having consumed four pints of best bitter, came to claim her for 'Ghostbusters', which bored her. Miming and hopping around, as energetically as her black patent high-heels would let her, she joined in to please him.

The ambiguous behaviour he had showed in the bedroom earlier continued throughout the night. He would appear from behind her at intervals, pinching the tops of her thighs, massaging her hips through the scarlet satin or making whispered references in her ear to being' horny'. Then he would shamble off to his golfing friends, reverting to his usual habit of acting as if she was not there. She could see he was confused and yet, like others in the room, found the combined allure of her new inner confidence, her purpose of having a pleasurable time as she could, and her seductive dress, irresistible. He was also dousing himself with large quantities of beer. By the time the taxi driver had arrived to take them home, with Lucy staggering out first with her broken broomstick, his eyes were starting to belong his costume.

"It was a good do, wasn't it, pet?" He pulled her to him when she had thrown off her coat with the intention of getting to the bathroom as quickly as she could.

Having been in a state of resting arousal for most of the night, the hardness under his bandages fevered her. Finding it with her hands, and his inner lips with her tongue, she encouraged him.

"Just need the loo." She pulled at his bindings, and away, gently.

Fast asleep and dribbling, in the foetus position, he was lying on the sofa when she came down. Covering him with a fleece throw because the heating had switched off, she left him there.

He was in the same position when she came down late on Sunday morning. She drank two pints of water and ate fresh fruit and live yogurt in the kitchen, hoping the lead-headed nausea of her hangover would wear off. Brushing her skin with the dry bristles before her shower made her tingle a little, she began to feel as if she would revive. The lashes having fallen off in bed, the last streaks of her devil make-up mingled with the rivulets of flame colours from her hair, in the shower. Cleansed, feeling more alert, she moisturised and applied

160

new make-up to brighten her face, choosing a turquoise jumper to wear with her jeans because the colour emphasised her eyes and softened her features, which she felt was especially needed. Ready to go, she wrote Sean a note and stuck it to the fridge with a magnet.

'Gone to Beth's for early (cold) lunch. Thought best not to wake you. Kids going to Halloween party at 4. Be back around then. x'

Lunch was a buffet of salads, sandwiches and fruits which Barba was glad to pick at. She ate some wholegrain rolls for the carbohydrate content, hoping it would absorb any excess alcohol still coursing through her body. The children were straining to get to the business of making food to take to the party. She was soon as happily absorbed as they were, cutting out shapes of cats, bats, witches hats and ghosts from shortbread mixture. There was black and orange icing sugar in tubes to decorate tiny sponge cakes, ghoulish eyes to make from radishes to place in salads. They thought up gruesome names to give to drinks, such as 'Bug Blood' for blackcurrant cordial and 'Ogre's snot' for limeade. The latter was her idea, which particularly impressed Ky.

She described the Hallowe'en party at the Golf Club to them as they got into their own costumes for the party.

"I'll bring you some photos of me and Auntie Lucy, and granddad and his friends next time, so make sure you bring some of your party for me to see," she told them, which prompted Richard to look for his camera.

They lined up for a first shot. Barba told them

how wonderful they looked. Ky was unidentifiable, with a horrific 'Scream' mask, robed in black from his neck to feet. Barba shrieked and hid behind the sofa so he could stalk her, squeezing the sac which ejected blood through tubes down his face until Barba screamed and escaped. She led Laura to pirouette around him . As a radiant white witch, she could wear her beloved fairy costume again, this time with a white pointed hat she and her mother had made, and a silver-sprayed broomstick.

"You are so plump and juicy I could eat you." She pretended to gnaw the plump, bare arms of the twins, who wriggled and giggled in their orange and green pumpkin outfits.

She purred and rubbed Lou's neck with her nose. He chuckled and copied the sound, dressed as a little black kitten-cat, with a woollen hat with sewn-on ears and pencilled in nose and whiskers.

"Remember, we've got another treat on Friday," she reminded them through the car window before they set off for their party. "Bonfire Night Party at the Golf Club on Friday. Starts at seven. See you. have fun." She kissed her hand and waved it to them as they drove off.

The smile stayed on her face until theirs were indistinguishable, in the distance. On occasions like this she felt as if a draft of oxygen and pure, cool water had firmed the connections of her life again. She could be lost in the flow of joy, yet found in the very peace of losing, because it also meant she felt present, content in the moment. The problem was that it was too occasional, not enough to quell the gnawings of discontent and restlessness that threatened to consume her. She thought about the evening ahead and her day off shared with

Sean, calibrating the hours into distracting activities, his and hers, as she drove home.

Atek did not come on Tuesday evening. She was alone. Sean had already left for his first evening shift of four. She put on more make-up before turning on the laptop. For five hours she moved as if there was an invisible elastic thread attaching her to it, so she moved within its radius. At eleven, she was on her third vodka, almost reckless and abject enough to call him. What stopped her was the knowledge that even if he responded, past midnight there, it would be too little, too late, for that night, anyway.

Wednesday night was like a repeat of a mediocre soap drama, in which she had the leading role, except that just before ten, she heard the signal from Messenger. Clutching her stomach, rejoicing and restive at the same time, seeing that it was him. More vodka and orange juice was poured before she was ready to be online.

The usual greetings and polite enquiries were exchanged, they both said they missed the other. She said she had been looking for him yesterday.

Atek says: Sorry. Not feeling really good

Barba says: ?

Atek says: U know Bayram soon. On Friday I go to my hometown for celebration.

Barba says: But that's good?

Atek says: Good if I have money for gifts for family

Barba says: Tell me about your family

Atek says: My mother is dead. My brother who is like father to me. He is divorced, but has two daughters. My sister is married. She has son, like brother to me.

Barba says: Where is your father?

Atek says: He is in prison

Barba was shocked. She looked at the camera. His eyes appeared hooded. She typed in a question mark.

Atek says: My father is an angry man

He asked her about her family then. Omitting Sean, she told him about Bethany's early marriage and the children. It was his turn to register surprise.

Atek says: Soon it will be Christmas for them. Like Bayram for us

He had not smiled through any of the conversation. He said he had to go but she did not want him to. At least, not until something was shared between them which felt good and right, an antidote to the discrepancies of their realities.

Atek says: Bye.

Barba says: Goodnight kiss

Atek says: Kiss

Barba says: Will you be here tomorrow night?

He appeared to be offline. She thought she would have felt reassured if they had played the kissing game first.

In preparation for the celebrations beginning at the weekend, Kash had arranged to take Tuesday morning off to shop for gifts. Nicole was taking the early lunch break, Barba an hour later. Kash jostled in with paper and plastic carrier bags on each arm, balancing a cake box. Barba jumped up to help him with the door.

"Hey, Kash, you shouldn't have bothered," she joked, taking the cake box and a gold and cerise gift bag from him.

"Glad that's over." Kash put his load on his

desktop and wiped his palms on his forehead.

"Eid pressies," he indicated proudly to Barba.

She asked who they were for. He showed her his purchases, telling her a little about the intended recipient, so she began to feel somehow included in the gift. Nicole came in and joined them, peeping in the bags to see the presents.

The Post Office was on the adjacent street. She joined the lunchtime queue, coming away with a Moneygram form and some instructions. In the corner behind a screen advertising a new credit card, she sent a text to Atek:

'Need your address, date of birth for small Bayram gift. Kisses'

In one minute she had the information. She stared and re-read the figures in front of her. He had said he was twenty-eight years old. His birth date was the same month and year that her son would have been born, twenty-four years before. In a suspended swoon she rejoined the line of people shuffling forward to the counter, where she pushed her fifty pounds through the mouth in the glass screen. She was asked if she wanted to write a message with the transfer. She wrote 'Happy Bayram'. The clerk gave her a copy of her form and a receipt with a reference number which she texted to Atek. A few seconds later there was a response. He needed her details. So Barba, who prided herself on being truthful and open, she chided herself ironically, had to reveal that she was four years older than the age she had told Atek, who was four years younger than he had said he was.

His next message told her the money had been

165

received, and thanked her, but the giving had seemed more like a transaction in the end, than a mutual blessing.

She did not see or hear from him for eighteen days. That Thursday night she resumed her vigil, though when she accepted that he was not there, she excused his absence by imagining his homeward journey. Envisaging him packing a small case, waiting at the bus station and embarking on the tiresome, overnight journey to his hometown. He would take another bus to his village, to be delivered into the arms and welcoming chatter of his family. Finally, after a wholesome meal and a chain of conversations, she pictured him finding his bed wearily, to sleep soundly until early the next day.

With his story sealed in her mind, and Sean working a final evening shift, she could allow herself to share the childish excitement of her grandchildren at the Bonfire Night Supper at the Golf Club. They warmed their hands on the polystyrene bowls containing hotpot, watching the blaze, a dragon in constant metamorphosis, spitting and sparking against the black night. Barba whooped and gasped with them, at times holding Lou. He was spellbound by the golden rains, the rainbow fountains and the puttering bursts of incandescent coloured flames and gases. When the rockets arched like spears of warrior gods shooting up to the sky, his bottom lip quivered as they exploded with violent light and sound. With the other children, she drew hearts in the air with sparklers, knowing they were some magical illusion. To eat with her chunk of parkin cake, she ordered ginger wine fizzed up with ginger ale, so even the textures and tastes of the evening were fiery, stimulating and spiced.

For the week that began with Bayram, she
pardoned Atek's disappearance by extending his saga to
include several socially hectic days like those between
Christmas Day and New Year. She visualised him
visiting relatives, eating, talking and travelling to the
next uncle or cousin. It was hard not to feel especially
bereft when Sean was out for four nights work, because
of the missed opportunity for communication. The end
of the night shifts in Sean's working sequence meant he
would have eight long days and nights off.

The Belly-Dancing classes offered some respite.
Each abandoned sweep of her arms felt like flinging
away the reins of her ill-considered conventions; every
flick of her hip shaking off the rags of her
disenchantment, freeing a wild and beautiful spirit within
her.

Her daily life began to seem like a little rock
pool, which she inhabited, a tiny translucent, grey-brown
fish. Most of the time, she would seek camouflage and
dull safety, in the pockets of water under rocks and in
concealed crevices. There were attractive, colourful ferns
and anemones she would make forays around, darting
above the dangerously lovely tendrils or weaving in and
out of the feathers of the weeds, playful and ticklish.
When Sean was around, he became the inquisitive boy
who up-turns, prods, probes and attempts to grasp the
creatures who evade him resentfully, desiring only to be
unnoticed. The more elusive she became, the more
determined he seemed to seek and prise her out.

Towards the end of the second week, weariness

overwhelmed her. Conflicts had been raging inside her, like internalised scenes from ancient Greek myths. The revelation of their ages, the coincidence of Atek and her son who should have been; the wanting, the resisting, the fear of rejection, the strain of hiding, the frustration and the guilt, had exhausted her. She felt as if she was steering a chariot pulled by two horses, veering in opposite directions.

She waited until they were seated at the dining table with their Sunday breakfast and a pot of tea, although she had been contemplating the confrontation for days.

"Sean," she began tentatively." I think we really need to talk."

His shoulders contracted, though he did not let the tension show on his face.

"What about, pet?" he asked warily.

"It's just that we never seem to have sex these days. I think it's been about three times so far this year." She hurried her speech, unwisely she thought, but she was compelled to say what she had to all at once. Pausing for his response, she noticed his back relax again, which surprised her, as it implied he had expected something worse.

"I thought it would be a good idea if we went to Relate or something like that," she went on hopefully, when he did not say anything.

"Aw, Barba, pet, it's just the way we are." He patted her arm and stretched to the sideboard for a Sunday paper.

It's not just the way I am, her rebel repeated in her head throughout the rest of their meal, which was eaten in silence. It's not just the way I am, it insisted, as she did the laundry and cooked a roast dinner for four adults and five children. It's not just the way I am, it whined, while she was ironing, and again, more pitifully, when she went to bed early so she could avoid the embarrassment of sharing a bed without intimacy.

She had noticed her days getting shorter. When she woke on Monday morning it seemed at first as if dawn had failed to arrive, but she was alone, and realised that Sean had started his day shift. Pushing back the curtains she unveiled the grey November morning, seeped in a morose fog which blurred the bare landscape and muffled everything, except the cold.

Needing a goal to tie up her free day and thoughts, she recalled the conversation at Sunday dinner. The subject of Christmas had wrapped around it and hung in the air, like the tinsel and lametta already for sale in the shops.

"What I want for Christmas," each one of the children had begun, apart from Lou, who was more interested in his dessert.

"What I want for Christmas is a good night's sleep," Bethany had responded, smiling.

"What I want for Christmas is, mmmm, let me think." Richard rubbed his chin and squeezed Bethany under the table. She squealed and slapped his arm, then nuzzled his neck.

The children laughed, bemused.

"All I want for Christmas is me two front teeth," sang Sean, tucking his lips inside his mouth, making a smacking noise which the children copied, between giggling.

It was not really a joke, thought Barba, and disliked herself for it, because he had dentures there.

She did not say what she wanted.

The talk had made her aware that the season would begin in earnest soon. She would find Advent calendars for the children to give them the following Sunday, ready for the first day of December. Dressing quickly, to feel warmer and also more purposeful, she decided to eat breakfast at the supermarket cafe, wanting to get out of the house as soon as she could.

Temptation was deliberately ignored; she had put the laptop out of sight in the cabinet the night before Sean had his eight days break. It had remained there since.

Two hours later she was taking it out of its cell, struggling with her breathing like a fish in air.

Atek stared at the fish in the keep-net, its futile thrashing around for a gap or a way over, to escape its trap. The closer it got to the net, the mesh, which was deceptively fine, was found to be strong and containing when pushed against. It let light in, allowed a meagre kind of survival, but freedom, opportunity and abundance lay outside. Not unlike his own situation, he reflected banefully.

Hearing shouts from further along the bank, he saw that other friends, who fished for their livelihood, had drawn in their morning's haul and were loading the truck to take to the Saturday market. He threw down his line, called to his more patient cousin that he was going, and raced to catch a lift into the town.

With a few lira rattling in his pocket and

boredom in his head, he opened the door of the Online
Guys cafe. He occupied a vacant unit, determined to cast
his inter-net as widely and effectively as he could.
Scrolling down his network list, he speculated about who
might enter his pool and take the bait. It was a promising
start because both Oda from Dusseldorf and Hulda from
Oslo were online, apart from a few Turkish male friends
he might talk to later.

As Barba was offline, he chose the next most
generous donor at Bayram. Oda was attractive, in a
tough kind of way; voracious if not alluring. German life
really did not appeal to him but she seemed keen on him
and was financially in excellent condition.

'Oda schatz,' he began.
Oda says: Hi! How are you?
Atek says: Not really good.
Oda says: Why?
Atek says: Winter here is hard. No money, no
work
Oda says: I am sorry
Atek says: I miss you schatz
Oda says: Darling, I miss you too
Atek says: Will you come again at
Christmastime?
Oda says: Not this year, baby. Maybe in May
He closed the box peevishly, cursing her openly,
calling her a German bitch in his own language. Hulda's
window was opened. At least she too had sent some
money for his celebration. He had an uncle in Sweden,
so there were interesting possibilities there. Hulda
though, was intensely dull and narcissistic. Everything
she did; her values, even sex, seemed to have been learnt

171

from a text book and practised to technical perfection.

Atek says: Hulda raring. Are you there?

The script digressed little from his dialogue with Oda, except that Hulda said she did not know when she would come again. He almost spat at her profile picture but was diverted when he noticed that Barba had just signed in. Hesitating, remembering her grandchildren. She was older, though sexy, and he liked the English and their humour. Several of his friends from the beach had married English women and settled there, in different cities. Some of them were doing very well for themselves.

Atek says: Barba darling. Where have you been?

He asked the rote questions, gave similar answers and paused expectantly. Jumping up with a triumphant yell, grinning and reeling in an imaginary line, he read the words:

Barba says: Yes, baby I will come again at Christmastime

Hooked.

CHAPTER 7

Specifically, it was a few hours after midnight on the second day after Christmas when they stepped out again into the Antalya air, accustomed now to the surroundings, though not with the enveloping chill of winter.

Lucy spotted Atek jogging towards them. He swung Barba round, kissed her and hugged Lucy quickly, prompting them to get to the car before the airport police moved Berk on. Berk was waiting at the driver door of the hire car which Barba had sent money for, with extra for their expenses, before the Christmas shutdown. Opening his mouth and his arms widely in welcome as they reached him, laughing, he rocked her, as Lucy filled the spaces comfortably. This time there was an ease about their meeting, as much because it was needed, when they had only a short time to enjoy together, as it was to do with familiarity.

Bundling everything and themselves in, Barba gave Atek the directions for the cottage in Ilica, an old fishing village several miles down the coast, west of Side. Appearing to have done his research, he directed Berk confidently. They found the car park easily, tucked behind a sprawling all-inclusive hotel which catered almost exclusively for Germans, according to Atek.

The security man in the booth asked them officiously for their passports, which irritated Barba.

When he opened hers, then Atek's, and looked up at them, she wanted to snatch it off him, tell him he did not understand anything.

Her mood changed to pleasant anticipation as the guard led the way down an alley flanked closely by terraces of whitewashed cottages which climbed up the hillside. Theirs was only a minute or so walk from the beach, they noted with delight. They were shown a small iron gate in a wall bordered with plants and fruit trees.

"Tell him the key is under the flowerpot," Barba instructed Atek, when they were all stood in the little square yard.

The wrought iron grille was unlocked and they entered through the kitchen, which was well equipped, with worktops and appliances fitted round a large square wooden dining table in the centre. In the small hall was a door to the bathroom and a storage room. The narrow, wooden staircase rose up through the living area and turned at the entrance to a double bedroom. A few more steps led to a small dressing room with a tiny single bunk through which the access to the roof balcony was made. Two archways separated the kitchen from the lounge which had an open fireplace and just enough space for a sofa. There was a small television and music system on a table. Another double bedroom led off from there. Its dark wood fittings, the shutters and the floors, its quaint traditional feel appealed to Barba's taste. The layout, though small, seemed perfect for their needs for the next four nights and days. Watching the faces of the others, she was gratified to see they appeared to feel the same.

"What do you think?" she asked them.

"It's perfect, hun," Lucy affirmed. "Mind if we take the ground floor?" She pushed Berk back into the bedroom he was emerging from, smiling his approval.

"Nice, Barba. Shall we go upstairs?" Atek picked up her suitcase.

She could see why Lucy did not want the stairs. They were awkward and creaked, not wide enough for comfort, but she liked being near to the rooftop.

Both bedrooms had two single beds with heavy iron frames which they pushed together. They discovered a short time later that the base lifted and clanged noisily, the legs bounced and scraped along the marble floor like a chained spectre, while Barba howled. The few residents in earshot must have considered a haunting if they were disturbed in the middle of the night.

In the morning, Atek and Barba drank orange juice and coffee with biscuits she had bought with her. Someone had thoughtfully put bottled water and milk in the fridge. From the leaflets and notes in a wallet left out for them, they discovered that there was a little market at the end of their row, up the steps and left. It generally opened in all seasons, for the Turkish and European residents, permanent and transient. Atek went to see if he could buy some pastries, something like croissants, or at least fresh bread.

"Get butter and honey, darling, please." She handed him a ten lira note.

"We need to go to a supermarket, though, don't we, Atek?" she suggested when he returned.

They made a list of what they needed while they waited for their friends, chewing slices of the soft, warm loaf smeared with honey.

"Berk." Atek tapped on the door in the living area.

There was a grinding of metal and a slapping sound on the floor. Berk answered, grouchily, in Turkish. Atek replied, also in their language.

Lucy sailed through to the bathroom first, with an aura of dishevelled radiance. Barba handed her juice and coffee when she joined them in the kitchen. Berk came in and sat close to Lucy, who stroked his face and called him 'baby' after every sentence from that moment on. That was when Barba first noticed that every time they were together, they were physically joined somewhere.

"We thought we had better go shopping first. Atek said we could have a grill for lunch. There's one outside."

Lucy hugged Berk to show that she liked the idea. While they ate, Atek went to clean the barbecue. Barba found a vase, some small glasses in which she put tealights fragranced with essential oils which she had fetched in her luggage. First she placed some on the bedside table in the room she was sharing with Atek, then downstairs, on the side table and around the fireplace.

They returned from the supermarket laden with fresh meat, salads, fruits, olives, cheeses, beer, more bread, wine, water, juices, flowers, logs and charcoal for the grill. Two trips had to be made to the car park, joking about the amount they had bought for a few days.

The intention was to milk each moment for creamy pleasure. As soon as places were found to store their purchases, Berk was ordered to get the barbecue going. Atek chopped and marinated chicken and lamb while Barba began preparing the salad. Lucy sliced some bread and watermelon, then opened a bottle of cooled white wine for her and Barba. She took out a beer for each of the men, as wisps of charcoal, spices and sizzling meat drifted inside, teasing their hunger. Berk received his beer with a kiss and another 'baby', which made Barba smile. Was this the inner Lucy re-born, after being pummelled with Alan's contempt for so long?

The sun blessed their late lunch by appearing and staying for the duration, creating a spring afternoon in December for them, as they feasted in the walled courtyard and rambled along the beach, westward, to honour it as it set. The pebbles looked precious when the tide washed over them. Barba began searching for one that would seem right to keep as a memento.

"Look, Barba." Atek straightened up and beckoned her over to the water's edge.

In the hand he was holding out were two identical grey-black stones. Barba picked them up and smoothed them between her fingers and thumbs. Shaped like distorted hearts, small and hard. As she offered them back to him, he took her fingers and closed her hand over them.

"Maybe we could keep one each," she suggested, reading his gesture.

"No. Together. You keep," he said, with a tenderness she had not heard in him before.

"Thank you. I will keep them together," she smiled, wrapping the twin stones carefully in a tissue and putting them her pocket.

Dark fell quickly, bringing with it a biting wind.

Lucy and Berk hurried ahead, clutching their jackets and each other to keep warm. Atek pulled Barba back and took her in the back of the wooden-framed shelter of the summertime water sports business. They did not feel the cold until later.

Berk had stacked the log fire, Lucy had lit it then the candles, and had bowls of pistachios and drinks waiting for them on the big table. Atek chopped vegetables, throwing them into the large pan where the chicken he had put aside from lunch was simmering in stock. He added spices which Barba recognised, not from the Turkish labels on the sachets but their colour, texture and the aromas which seeped through the pan lid and met pine smoke, frankincense and sandalwood. A recording of Turkish guitar music was selected from amongst the pile left for guests. It serenaded them as they ate stew with bread and wine by candle light, in front of the fire, the men on the rug at the feet of the women on the sofa.

The only variation in the events of the second day was the lamb they ate for dinner and the exchange of childhood stories, the most entertaining being Berk's account of the bus he used to have to catch at dawn, riding to school with chickens and goats.

Fortunate to have enjoyed two full days of sunshine, when they awoke to a dull sky and a troublesome wind, they discussed over their Turkish breakfast how to spend the day. Barba and Lucy asked for a stroll on the beach before lunch, in case it rained later in the day. It was late morning still when they drove to Manavgat, so the men led them to a row of shops where they hoped to find outfits for their belly-dancing outfits. With Atek and Berk less involved than they would have found flattering, the friends took delight nonetheless in choosing. Harem pants, sequinned and coin-fringed bra-tops and headbands were bought, while the men stood by, smoking and chatting with each other. For lunch, they ate a delicious casserole with chickpeas, vegetables and bulgur wheat, in a traditional, simple restaurant busy with Turkish diners, which indicated the quality of the food.

The rain began sneakily, tapping them lightly when they were not looking, then opening up like a booby trap as soon as they were in the open street, running to the cinema. They crowded in the foyer just as the deluge began outside.

"We can watch a Turkish one if you like," suggested Barba, noticing that Atek and Berk seemed drawn to a particular poster amongst the advertisements. "If the story and the acting is good we'll be able to enjoy it, won't we, Luce?"

"Sure. Choose the one you want, baby," Lucy told Berk, who squeezed her in thanks and pointed to the film they wanted to see.

"It's just that he is our favourite actor." Atek grinned apologetically.

"Decided then. Let me get the tickets." Barba went to the booth, followed by Atek, to translate for her, if needed.

The uncomplicated plot was easy for them to follow, about an excruciatingly handsome, but emotionally damaged, son of a gangster who turns into a vengeful psychotic. The violence was too gratuitous for Barba's taste but rewarding in that it gave her an excuse to move closer to Atek, who held her hand when she started in horror.

Berk had a surprise for them after dinner. They were resting contentedly, with the glow inside of warm food, and outside, of the flames in the hearth and the candles. The sensuous, smoky scents curled around them. As Berk held a lighter flame to a large, hand-rolled cigarette, a sharper aroma, earthily fragrant, hit their nostrils.

"Hashish," Berk announced proudly, holding it up like a kind uncle with a lollipop.

Lucy took it out of his hand and drew on it like an old hippie. Barba copied her nervously when it was her turn, twitching because she was scared, and a little thrilled, by their naughtiness.

Jumping up suddenly like a boy with a brainwave, calling in Turkish to Atek excitedly, Berk ran into the bedroom he shared with Lucy. He emerged holding something behind his back, then the music Atek had put on gave them a clue. Lucy squealed girlishly, grabbing Berk to see what he was holding behind him. Dodging her playfully, he waved the belly-dancing outfit she had bought in the air.

"Put yours on," Atek ordered Barba, lifting his eyes up to the bedroom.

In an obedient haze she went to dress up, reddening her lips and darkening her eyes before padding downstairs in bare feet, jingling exotically as she descended. Lucy was ready too.

Smoking some more, they swayed to the Turkish tunes until the desire to move was greater than any vestiges of inhibition. The men leaned back on the sofa for the hilarious though undoubtedly seductive performance. When the women moved in to them, shaking their shoulders until the coins chinked furiously in their faces, they rose to sense the rhythms through their touches, as well as their eyes and ears. Round the living room they all undulated, into the bedroom, around the joined beds, Barba leading, Atek holding on to her hips, back into the living area. They looked around when they heard the door click shut behind them and the key turn in the hole.

"They stopped dancing," Barba yelled mock-tragically.

"No, they make their own dance," Atek corrected her.

Their bursts of laughter continued as Atek grabbed the bottle of wine from the table and guided Barba, still gyrating and moving her pelvis from side to side, up the stairs.

The following, and their last day, they were up at eight in the morning, having had a relatively early night. Barba was relieved to find herself feeling unexpectedly lively, not too hung-over. They had already planned to pack and tidy the house first, then do something special depending on the weather conditions. They had to leave the house at midnight for their flight which departed three hours later.

"I think it's really going to be a nice day." Atek pointed at the sky with his cigarette, from the kitchen door way. "We could go to Green Lake with picnic."

His idea was met with such enthusiasm that they finished their coffee, packed some plastic cups, plates and cutlery into bags, grabbed blankets and towels and headed for the car. Berk stopped at a shop just outside Manavgat where they bought cake, loaves, cheese, olives, tomatoes and different fruits, with fruit juices and water to drink. The route was familiar to Barba and Lucy from her Truck Safari, and the lake the same one they had visited, though this time they parked near a different, unspoilt, more picturesque side of the shore. They spread their blankets close to the edge of the water, and together unloaded and prepared their last breakfast for an unknown time.

When it was cleared away, Barba asked Atek if he wanted to go for a walk.

The sun was climbing and gaining strength as they picked their way through young olive saplings, the fallen needles of the pines and the furrowed clods of clay. Resting on two boulders on the bank, silently gazing at the pool of liquid jade before them. Barba lifted her head to discern the source of a hushing sound which started soft, reached a crescendo, faded and repeated.

"Oh, it's the wind through the pine trees," she exclaimed reverently, after a few minutes.

She turned to Atek, who was sitting with his eyes closed.

"Did you mean what you said last night?" she asked.

"About?"

"About me coming to live here."

"Yes, I told you. You are English. You can do anything here. I am Turkish. I can't do anything."

Barba thought it was a strange assertion. She got up to follow him as he started to walk away. Coming

182

back towards her when she stopped, beckoning him to join her. A small tortoise was floundering on its back in the scrubby grass, its stumpy legs flailing helplessly in slow motion. He watched as she picked it up by the shell and righted it. It scuttled away as fast as it was able, without looking back.

"You want us to be together?" she continued, as if there had been no interruption.

"You want to talk on msn for ten years or something?" he replied.

She laughed. "No, 'course not."

"Do you know?" she said, changing the subject because they were in earshot of their friends again."It's so hot, it's making me want to swim."

"No." Atek shook his head seriously. "It's colder than you think. And very deep."

When the sun began to sink towards the mountains not long after four o'clock, they began their return journey. Barba, in the back with her head on Atek's shoulder, silently prayed when she heard the call from the mosque, as they drove through the town in the disappearing light.

"Berk, make us a fire for our last evening, baby," cajoled Lucy, as they entered the cottage. "You guys will clean it out in the morning before they come for the keys, won't you?"

"Of course, baby," Berk assured her and began clearing the ashes.

Barba took the wine and beer bottles from the fridge while Atek ordered kebabs from the unpretentious little restaurant on the main road, with the lovingly-prepared food. The CD player and the fire crackled to life, as the waiter arrived on his motorbike and handed the warm paper packages through the kitchen door. Lucy lit the last of the candles.

"Bit different from last night," Barba recalled, as they ate, and listened to the guitar in subdued intimacy.

Laying out some playing cards, Berk began to show them some tricks. Atek knew some too, then they took turns to show each other games to play.

"I'm going for a shower," Barba announced. "Only a couple of hours left". She looked at Atek, who had his mobile 'phone in his hand.

He was undressed and waiting for her on the bed when she came up from the bathroom.

The fire was extinguished, the door closed, at midnight.

They told them to say goodbye outside the departure entrance, so as not to protract the pain of parting.

"When will you come again?" he asked.

Lucy asked her the same question when they had taken off.

"As soon as I can fix everything."

"Fix everything?" Lucy repeated, her voice high with concern.

"Yes, I've decided to escape my dull and dingy life," declared Barba.

"Move there, you mean?" Lucy was open-mouthed at the unexpected response.

"Yes, move there." Barba's inflections lifted with excitement as she heard herself say her intent.

"Does Atek know?"

"We've discussed it."

"What about Sean?"

"Do you think he'll notice, Lucy?" she asked her wryly.

Her friend looked out at the sunrise above the clouds. She was silent.

Barba rubbed Lucy's knee.

"Would you come too, babe?" she coaxed.

"Listen, hun," Lucy said, with a firmness that took Barba by surprise," I know where you're coming from. But, first, Wayne and Phee are the wrong age and have had enough instability in the past few months. Second," she paused, "I don't intend to fry just one fish, after Alan."

Barba remembered that the skeleton from the Hallowe'en Party was being kept dangling. She thought of a fish jumping from a frying pan into a fire.

"Third," Lucy continued, "I'm not throwing caution to the wind for a Turkish twerp like him just yet, much as he floats my boat," she smiled fondly, recollecting him. "Somehow feel I'm not getting the full picture with him. Haven't worked it out, yet."

Barba was as impressed with her friend's use of idioms as with her prudence.

"I just need to go," she stated, her voice thin.

Lucy nodded to show she understood, and put her arm around her.

"You will visit often, won't you, hun?"

"Oh yes," Lucy squeezed her shoulder reassuringly. "That I will do, honey."

She pulled down the blind to help them sleep, which they did until the stewardesses rattled around with packaged breakfasts.

185

They were still sleepy on the metro to Newcastle city centre, where they separated. Lucy was travelling home by bus while Barba caught the six o'clock morning train to Edinburgh. She then had another rail ride to the village where she had promised to join Sean at the hotel where his family congregated for their traditional Hogmanay celebration. Waiting for the connection, she pushed her hands deep into her jacket pocket, hunching herself against the frost and fatigue. The fingers of her left hand touched something small, hard and cold. They closed around the misshaped hearts of stone.

Having dozed for most of the two hour journey into Edinburgh, she bought a large coffee from one of the espresso booths to sharpen her senses for the final part of her journey.

Twenty-five minutes after boarding she was wheeling her suitcase over the floral Wilton carpet of the hotel reception area. The receptionist handed her the key as she wished her a good morning, recognising Barba, who had stayed there every New Year for twelve of the eighteen she had worked there.

The door was opened as surreptitiously as she could manage, squeezing to stop daylight invading and waking the sleeping. She was relieved to see twin beds, one occupied by Sean, a faceless mound under a frilled tartan quilt. The manager would have apologised for the absence of a double suite, she thought. Glad not to have been present, so he did not see how perfect that was for her. Putting her case down gingerly, slipping her coat over the upholstered chair, she guessed, from Sean's position, and because her entry had not caused him to stir at all, that he had already begun the festivities the night before. Knowing his other relatives, particularly the male ones, shared his penchant for a good scotch and his opportunism to indulge imbibing it.

Calculating that, as most of the party would come down for breakfast later, it was a good time for her to eat hers in solitude. Intending to use her travel fatigue as an excuse to sleep until at least midday, she crept out, back down to the breakfast room.

There was only one other table occupied, by a young couple, keeping eye and hand contact as they talked and ate toast with their free hand. Barba sat by the window, attended immediately by a rotund waitress with a ruddy face and apricot-coloured hair sticking out of her cap like straw. She placed cutlery wrapped in red napkins on the tartan tablecloth in seasonal colours, and took Barba's order for fruit, yogurt and toast with coffee. When she bustled away, Barba gazed out at the misted peaks, seeing the Taurus mountains again, through fog.

On her way up to her room, hearing the dining room filling up with voices and chairs being moved, she realised that her timing had been just right. Sean was in the same position when she crept in. The note was propped up in front of the television.

'Didn't want to wake you – fast asleep! Had breakfast – see you at lunch? X'

Preferring to avoid making any noise which might rouse him, she left her make-up on and, wearing a robe for insulation, smoothed herself under the covers of her single bed.

Opening one eye to squint around the room, she confirmed that she was alone, before she got out of bed

187

and into the bathroom. Prolonging her shower, the hot water was uplifting and helped her to rehearse in her mind her demeanour throughout lunch, the rest of the day and night ahead.

She found Sean at the bar just outside the dining room. He had his back to her, turning when one of the cousins he was drinking with waved at her.

"Hello pet." He extended a hand to guide her to them. "Do you want a drink?"

First things, first, she thought dryly.

"Not sure," she hesitated," I'll have some wine with lunch though."

Sean ordered a glass of white wine and some mineral water, anyway, as if he merely wanted something to do.

"How was Turkey?" he enquired tightly. "Any luck?"

Barba stared at him for a moment, then relaxed, realising what he was referring to.

"With property, you mean? Well, we looked at a few. Lucy liked one or two, but nothing definite, like." Technically, she was telling the truth, although the houses had only been viewed on the brochures they had picked up from the estate agents in Manavgat.

"You thinking of buying a place in Turkey?" One of the wives of the cousins had joined them and overheard some of the conversation.

"My friend is." Barba was not about to tell anyone what she was thinking. "She wants to invest, and was told that winter is a good time to get bargains in property over there. And of course, there's a good exchange rate." She picked up her wine glass.

The wife began talking about her friends who had homes abroad, mainly Spain, so Barba asked her as many questions as she could think of, to convey interest so she would keep talking. This had the effect of encouraging the men to find topics which interested them more and converse among themselves for the duration of lunch.

Smoking outside after the meal, Sean asked what she was thinking of doing that afternoon.

"I'm a bit tired, still," she yawned. "I think I'll read in the room and see if I can have a nap before the party. How about you?"

"We'll chill out, I think, in the television lounge."

Before she settled on the bed with her novel, she found the case she had packed for Sean to bring with him, which contained some clean clothes and her party dress which she hung on the shower rail to de-crease. After one chapter, the words slid off the page and the book out of her hand. It was dark when she came to, with a momentary sense of panic, until she recognised her surroundings.

She had dreamt that she was due to catch a flight. Atek was waiting, but she had become lost, finding herself amongst ancient, deserted buildings. They were flat-roofed, middle-eastern style, separated by shadowy alleys and steps leading down, which she descended. Then a hillside, strewn with white pillars. On the top of the hill was an arch like the Apollo temple remains at Side. She, dressed in a white, flowing dress, and Atek were converging from either side of the hill until they met face-to-face at the temple and were about to kiss. Their lips had not touched when she awoke.

Disturbed, more deeply than she could analyse, by the dream, she turned the television on, and the taps of the bath. There were some tea-lights left in her suitcase which she found and placed on the bathroom windowsill. She praised herself for thinking to chill some wine in the miniature fridge in the room, removing cans of soft drinks and bottled water, leaving some beer and mixers. The tooth mug was rinsed in the sink and filled with Chardonnay. She hoped Sean would allow his usual hour to shower, shave and change for the celebration, giving her an hour and a half to pamper and prepare. Preparation included practising her lines for the event.

With memories of Hallowe'en in her thoughts, she had brought a fitted, long, black dress, sleeveless, with a flattering, but not low, scooped neckline and a purple pashmina to please Sean's mother, because it had been a gift from her. She had purple shoes with high heels and coordinating jewellery. Pinning her hair up in a French pleat to complete the classic, lady-like look she was effecting, she heard Sean come in and stand behind her, looking at her reflection in the mirror. He bent down and kissed the back of her neck. The uncharacteristic spontaneity startled her, she felt her shoulder blades lock automatically, feeling guilty, knowing he must have sensed that too.

"Oooh. You made me jump." Smiling with her cheek muscles, the amateur actress.

He started taking off his clothes. Picking up her tube of foundation, she squeezed out a blob of cream on her palm and began dabbing and smoothing busily on her face. In the corner of the mirror, she saw him put his robe on and walk, with an air of resignation, to the bathroom.

"I'll go down when I've finished my make-up, pet," she called in a cheerful voice, "I've not seen your parents yet."

Either he did not hear her, or did not see the point of answering.

Her performance improved when the characters remained faithful to their script.

"Barba darling. You made it," Sean's mother chirped when she walked into the lounge, where she and Sean's father were greeting people with liqueur glasses of good scotch as they drifted in.

"Hello Maeve. Hello Ruary." She kissed them in turn."Sean will be down soon. How are you?"

"Very well, thank you. And so are you, by the look of you." Maeve scanned her from head to foot with her falcon's eye. "Must be all those holidays," she peeped.

"Yes, thank you," Barba replied, as if she had heard only the compliment. "Sean and I enjoyed our holiday in Turkey. I went back, you know with a friend, when he went to Portugal, to play golf again."

"Yes, and you've just been again with your friend, haven't you?"

Barba knew the reference to Sean's golfing trips had not been lost on his mother. Given the cue she was looking for, she was able to steer the conversation on a different course.

"Yes, Lucy has had a tough time lately, and she's looking for a holiday home there? How is Sue's house in Spain coming along?" She paused to allow the gushing description of Sean's sister's renovation of a Spanish villa, her husband's successful business expansion, and how well her grandchildren were doing at ballet and trumpet-playing.

Listening intently to keep her on track, making interested exclamations during the pauses, until Sean and his sister, with her husband Simon, joined their table in the dining hall. Barba was able to use all the information Maeve had offered, to fuel the conversation with Sue and Simon, as long as it took for the hors d'oeuvre to arrive.

After dessert, pencils and post-its were placed on the table with the cheeseboard, the mints and the coffee. Family tradition required them to anonymously write down their New Year resolution, fold it and put it in the box the waitress was holding out at each table, so the most entertaining or commendable ones could be read out in the build-up to midnight. Scribbling hers down quickly, she kept her hand over the paper like a clever pupil hiding answers from cheats, folded it and threw it in with the others.

Rising from the table she told them she was going to freshen up in her room. That much was true. When she got there she found her 'phone and sent the text, just before ten o'clock, two hours ahead in Turkey.

'Kisses for a Happy New Year, Atek'

She did not have to wait for a reply. The signal vibrated in her hand.

'Happy New Year, together I hope so. Kisses'

She had to apply mascara again before she rejoined the party.

The band were assembling, the drinking had begun to gain a fluency now that the eating had stopped, gradually more kilts and gowns were swishing on the dance floor. When there was a concentration of bodies, laughter and music in the centre, the rounds and reels began, the more accomplished competing flamboyantly with the more drunken.

At twenty minutes to twelve, the appointed master of the ceremony, Sean's husky uncle Bry, dipped his hand into the box to share their aspirations, the tongue-in-cheek with the tongue-between-teeth.

She recognised hers, towards the end of the readings.

"To live my life to the full." Amen

It was the evening before Burns Night in the third week of January that she shared her resolution with Sean. It had taken three weeks to get confirmation from her organisation, Douglas Scott, that they would employ her as one of their holiday representatives in Side the first of April. With a dazzling reference from her manageress, Mo, and the testimony of her experience with them, it had been a relatively straightforward process. Telling the people in her life of her plans was not.

"Do you know what I did with my tartan tie after New Year?" Sean called from the bedroom where he was packing for his two nights stay back in Scotland, where he always celebrated the poet's birthday with a few male friends.

Barba found it hung up in the wardrobe and handed it to him. He wrapped it round his neck.

"I've got a new job with Douglas Scott, Sean," she announced loudly, because she had to force the words out.

He paused the tying, puzzled by her outburst. Her innocuous words sounded threatening.

"It's as a rep in Side in Turkey. I'm in a rut. We're in a rut."

He sat down on the bed next to her.

"So I'm starting at the beginning of April. I'm going out there in a few weeks to settle in. I've booked the cottage Lucy and I stayed in until the company give me an apartment."

His silence she knew was because he was stunned by the completeness of her plans, but also she had a sense that he expected it, some foresight on his part.

"What about the house?" he asked.

That is what concerns him, she thought. She surprised herself by feeling rejected because there was no declaration of love, of pain, remorse; no plea to stay.

"I'll put it on the market," she told him, matter-of-factly. "You can stay until it sells, which probably won't be at least for a few months."

He flinched at that information. The house was hers.

"You seem to have thought of everything," he said flatly, standing up and finishing the knot in his tie. He took his overcoat from the hanger, zipped up his case and left, wordlessly.

Bethany accused her repeatedly of being selfish.

"What about me?" she jabbed her chest violently.

Barba thought about the seamless transition as carer of a teenage girl to pregnant woman to young mother, all the hours spent in service to her. Housing them, looking after her children so she and Richard could establish themselves, get a mortgage, enjoy each other's company; anything that was required of her, actually.

"You can have my car," she offered.

"What about the children?" Bethany opened her hands to indicate the absent offspring, while Lou banged on the floor with a plastic hammer.

"They can come out in the school holidays. It'll be great for them."

Bethany snorted hopelessly.

"What about Dad?" she wailed.

"Sean and I have come to the end of the road," she declared, without emotion.

Bethany wept.

Telling Dot that she felt it was about time she had a life, she gave her the facts as delivered to Sean and Bethany. Observing the impact on her sixty-four year old mother's face, thinking, as she often did, that she was not an old woman, just a person who believed she had to be, the day she retired.

"It's who I am," Dot had asserted plaintively, a few weeks before she finished at Woolworths. Her whole identity was inseparable from the job she had started as a Saturday girl when she was fifteen, the only continuum in her life to date.

"What about Sean?" she too had asked.

"You can still see him," Barba consoled her, realising that, for her mother, her relocation meant filling Friday afternoons with another activity. Now she could go to the craft workshops, Barba thought. It was her father who would have missed her terribly, for herself.

Perhaps she had not credited the people close to

her with some insight into the shortcomings she felt in the quality of her life, she thought, when the ordeal of telling them her news was over. There was a level of foresight and acceptance on their part, which she had not expected. The drama was reserved for her workplace.

"No way," Nicole spluttered, and regaled her with questions, about the job, the pay, the apartment. "Have you got a fella? she asked her slyly, when all the other answers had been given.

"I'm leaving Sean because it's over, not for anyone else," she answered obliquely, standing up to welcome a client so effusively he wished her a good morning with suspicious reticence.

Kash was looking at her thoughtfully, having listened without reaction to her announcement.

During the lunch break, they told each other how much they would miss being together, talked about visiting her for a holiday, wondered if she would be replaced and arranged to go out for a meal and drinks to say goodbye.

Atek was not mentioned, and no-one enquired again whether she had a lover, which at times she construed as mildly insulting. Not as much, however, as the 'Turkish Tales', as she referred to them when confiding in Lucy, which made her head ache. A weekly magazine left in the kitchen by Nicole, with the headline 'Turkish Love Rat' scrawled across the front page. There was the Talkbook group dedicated to the same theme which Nicole casually brought into a conversation. She did the same with the story of her friend's grandmother, who had white hair, was in her sixties and had married a thirty year-old Kurd she met in Marmaris. He apparently stayed with her for two years, then drove off with his visa secured and her savings, in the car she had sweetly provided him with. There was the article in the local newspaper, about the plight of Mustafa and his hairdresser wife, Noleen, who had been waiting for permission for him to enter the country for ten months. Noleen was in despair that the permit was delayed, because the authorities had concerns about their twenty year age difference, and the fact that they had wed after a two week whirlwind romance when she was holidaying in Izmir. It was reported that she had become a Muslim, using up all her leave and spare income to visit her husband in Turkey.

Barba did not know what she was supposed to say. She said nothing, even when Kash broached the subject more sensitively in the kitchen, when they were making tea one afternoon.

"Be careful, won't you, Barba?" he urged her gently. "They are lovely people, but a lot of them are piss-poor. I know. And they want your money."

Sighing, she patted his hands, moved by his concern, his compassion and his insight, because of his own culture.

"Thank you for caring, Kash. I have to go, though. I can't explain the pull to anyone properly. Just feel it." She pushed her fist into her abdomen. "I'll remember what you are saying."

The night Sean had returned to Edinburgh for Robert Burn's birthday, she told Atek her plans on Messenger. She had received a text message from Sean telling her he was going to stay on for a week, as he had his eight days off work. That was all, which was appropriate, she had thought. Barba had given the date she would arrive to Atek, told him she had arranged for transport to the cottage through the owner, and asked when he would join her. He asked her to call him when she arrived in Turkey and he would join her two days later, on the twenty-third of February.

It was more difficult for Atek to get to an internet cafe when he was staying in his village, requiring him to catch a bus to the centre and leave in time for the last bus back. Because of this, talking online had been infrequent and haphazard since he left Side at the end of October. Partly for this reason, and mostly because it gave her a strange sense of integrity, Barba asked if he would mind if they did not have contact until they were together. He said he understood.

Taking advantage of Sean's absence she began to clear out every useless and unwanted item that was not his, moving herself into the spare bedroom with the things she would be taking to Turkey. When he arrived back late at night, with only two weeks remaining before she left, he slept in the bed they once shared. He went to work the day shift the next day, without reaction or comment. Her decision was never questioned by him. Any discussion was kept to practical matters, which were minimal, as he only had to pay for his food and utilities. Conducting his life as before, with a manner of stoic resignation, Barba wondered whether he did not feel anything except puzzlement.

"The children will have to get used to not seeing you," Bethany had argued, when she called Barba to cancel the remaining two Sunday dinners as a family.

She spoke as if she was preparing them for death.

Barba felt the cut. Managing to murmur abject assent she ended the call and wept with the pain.

"Nan's going to live in a holiday place and you can come and see me. One day I'll get a house with a pool, just for you to play in," she told her grandchildren when she visited the evening before she was flying out.

Bethany had glared at her when the children received this news with delight. Richard was tactfully hiding behind his newspaper. Taking her daughter's hand, holding on despite her resistance, she placed the car keys in her palm.

"Please will you drive me back? I've left the registration document and the other paperwork in that envelope on the sideboard."

She allowed herself to hold the children closely for a few seconds, and left Richard with an affectionate hug.

"See you soon," she promised as she followed Bethany out.

"What did Grandma say?" Bethany asked, once she had stopped grinding the gears and moved off.

Barba had said goodbye to her mother first.

"She talked about the Friday Tea-Dances she is going to, now she's not obliged to see me." Barba laughed, but Bethany was determinedly icy.

"And very excited about the holiday she's booked for May," she added, in a confidential tone.

"Oh?" Her daughter could not hide her curiosity.

"She and Elsie are going on one of those singles packages for older people."

Bethany looked dismayed. "Where?"

"To Side. To visit me. Great, isn't it?"

There was no indication of thawing on her daughter's part.

"We'll still be seeing Dad, you know," she told her, as Barba opened the passenger door.

"On Sundays, he'll be coming to us for dinner."

"Good," Barba responded with genuine warmth, "I'll call you when I get there."

The goodbye kiss felt like a handshake.

Lucy understood. Even though she had not taken such drastic measures as Barba, her separation from Alan had been the loss of an encumbrance. She came for her friend at midnight, as buoyant and helpful as if they were going on a day outing. Sean's evening shift finished at that time so she had left him a note on the microwave.

'Take care. Will send addresses etc. soon. Thanks for being so understanding. Barba X'

Had he really understood? she questioned herself.

Not knowing how she would feel as she took the first steps to a new life, she became aware of growing sensation of lightness lifting inside her, increasing with the physical distance. Lucy chattered on about the times they could meet online and when she would come out. She hoped to visit alone and in the school holidays, with the children, and perhaps Ky and Laura, if Bethany approved.

"I'll teach you the belly-dancing moves every weekend," she vowed.

"Promise," giggled Barba."I'll be ready in my outfit. I'll teach you Turkish."

She was ready for her flight.

CHAPTER 8

The light was thin, the temperature low and unwelcoming, as she stepped through the doors alone for the first time. Amongst the group holding cards behind the barrier, she saw her name, in large black capitals. Barba Ford. The dark man waiting for the woman who was burning her bridges. They recognised each other instantly. He was the agent of the owner of the cottage, whom she referred to as her friend. Barba had wondered what their relationship was when he had called to check everything was satisfactory, the first time they stayed at the cottage. With an air of kindly efficiency he wheeled her bag, walking at a challenging pace to his car.

During the drive he asked her with interest about her job with Douglas Scott and learning Turkish. He spoke affectionately about his wife and his two children. Atek was not discussed, although Barba had intimated that she would be sharing the cottage. It was a discretion she was content to observe. This time he had the keys to the door, and caused her more gratitude for practical help. He showed her how to set the air-conditioning units for heating, which, in the shady cottage on a February morning, was much needed.

"Thank you so much," she shook his hand again when she had paid him, "and so kind of you to remember the milk and everything".

"No problem," he replied warmly. "Good luck

with everything, and let me know if you need anything, Barba. "You have my number."

When he left, she felt the pangs of a lone sleeper, even as she acknowledged her weariness. She made a warming cocktail of duty-free brandy, milk and some Turkish honey she had found. Eating chunks of the fresh, aromatic loaf left thoughtfully on the table, tearing it indulgently with her hands. When her physical emptiness was assuaged, she thought of using the bed downstairs, but went up instead. In the small room she took three thick blankets from the closet, which she cocooned herself in, still clothed. She slept for several hours on one of the single beds she and Atek had put together.

It may have been his text message which disturbed her, though not consciously.

'Hi baby. Glad you are here now. Cant wait to see u. Need money to come. Kisses'

Awake at once, she checked the time, wondering how soon she could get to the nearest post office, assuming he would either buy a ticket for the bus leaving that night, to arrive early the next day, or wait until the following night. Carelessly, she splashed her face, stroked in her cream, cleaned her teeth and ventilated her hair with a brush. The milky coffee she made was drunk with drying bread, as she read the dolmus information from the guest's folder.

Her spirits were racing ahead of her as she went down the alley, overjoyed to see the sea again. Remembering she would need her passport, she sprinted back to unlock the grille and the kitchen door, to find it. It was an hour before the post office closed at four in the afternoon when she finally alighted the bus in the town centre. In her jumper and jeans, she was prickling with the heat of the sun, excelling itself for the time of year, and her own exertions. Anxious to have a temporal margin so Atek would get the money that day, she thought of asking him how much his bus fare was, but it felt awkward and too motherly. As before, she overrode her good instincts to be in control of her finances. Instead she chose to defer to Atek's dignity and his sense of being regarded by her as trustworthy.

When he confirmed that he had the money fifteen minutes before the post office shut its doors, she sat under a tree searching for a purpose since that mission was accomplished. Feeling like she had jumped off a rock, buoyed up with elation, only to find that she had not considered what might lie beneath the waters, that she had not equipped herself for.

The vibration in her jeans pocket alarmed her momentarily, for no reason, except that it was unexpected. It was Atek, telling her he was going to travel the following evening, which meant he would arrive at the cottage about eight in the morning. Questioning herself as to whether she was disappointed that he had not been ready to come at the first opportunity, in reality she welcomed a space in which to prepare, mentally and physically, for his joining her. That intention gave her the motivation to plan her evening and day ahead. She could rely on the small local shops for food and her immediate needs. There were enough cleaning products in the cottage for that purpose. Cheering herself by buying fresh flowers to arrange when she had finished putting their new home in order, she made her way to the bus stop.

There were still logs for the fire that they had left previously. Unpacking the oils, candles, bottles of spirits, music, several novels, her laptop and the mobile broadband device Kash had advised her to buy, helped her to feel resourceful and competent. Finding places for them, she prayed that Lucy could come online that night, that they could connect so she could see and hear her friend again.

The external scrubbing, polishing, washing and oiling of herself and her surroundings enabled her to ward off doubt and melancholia in the waking hours until he came. It also served as a ritual, reflecting her own internal process of readiness. Pampering herself with fragrant oils after bathing, in the glow of the candles and the fire. Humming to her favourite love songs, sipping wine. Smiling at the recall of brief but light-hearted exchanges with Lucy online. Feeling in touch again, with herself and those she most desired to love well.

When he entered, trundling a case she would have used for a short stay, through the door, she was ready for him. Extending his free arm to sweep her to him, he met her mouth with an ebullient kiss. Bouts of urgent and boisterous intimacy ensued, followed by periods of shy familiarising. It was like a ball being thrown about and lobbed into a net to score a goal, then resting there until it was able to be retrieved so the game could continue. Lasting for five days, this early phase seemed to dissipate into something more natural on his birthday, perhaps because it was their first important occasion to share. It was recorded on his identity card as the twenty-eighth of February.

"Really I was born on twenty-ninth, but normally I can't use that, you know."

"So really you have had only six birthdays?" she joked, then felt foolish at the implication of childishness. They continued to laugh at the absurdity of leap years and she began to explain the tradition allowing a woman to propose.

"So, last year I could have asked you to marry me," she teased.

"Maybe I can be your husband?" he answered intently, studying her face.

"Maybe you are too young to be my husband," she blurted, wishing to sound whimsical rather than hopeless.

His expression was set, not offended, as if her response was unimportant.

"Anyway, my darling, it must be nearly time for you to collect your birthday gift?"

The idea of buying a motorbike had arisen from the problem they had of getting around freely and conveniently. Barba had talked about waiting to buy a car until her house had been sold, when Atek had said she needed one, then he suggested the motorbike. That day, their second together, he had also casually reminded her of his birthday. The third day he told her a friend of his was selling a bike for a good price. On the fourth day she told him he could have it as a gift from her, and withdrew the amount he had told her from her account.

"To take me for rides, baby," she crooned, kissing his neck.

"Soon." He pulled her to him for the second time that day.

The first time had been in the morning when they were in bed.

"Happy Birthday, darling," she had said, as soon as he woke.

"So I get my first present now," was his reply.

An effervescent energy stayed with him throughout the day. The third time was in the wooden shelter on the beach front, which housed the life guard for the guests of the exclusive, all-inclusive German hotel. Riding to Side beach on the gleaming red bike at dusk, breathing in the wind like a stimulant drug, her chest pressed to his back, her thighs gripping his, her arms round his waist. They parked on the edge of the sand and walked in the surf to the area where the pine woods began. No-one else could be seen in any direction. Kneeling on the wooden decking below the lookout openings, they giggled because they were high from the ride and their daring, with clothes undone, but still on.

"Thank you for my best birthday, baby," he said, when they returned from dinner at the Pide restaurant.

Telling him to make a wish, she lit two candles on the small cake she had bought for him when they went for their first motorbike ride to the town in the afternoon. When he blew them out, after she had sung 'Happy Birthday,' she told him to keep it a secret.

The following day Atek took her to a store in Manavgat which he told her catered for shops and hotels mainly, but would deliver anything if it was bought in enough quantity. She agreed with his idea that they should make a list of all the dried goods they would use regularly and buy in some bulk. It would save money and solve the problem of shopping for groceries with only the motorbike to carry them.

Atek gave the list to one of the two Turkish girls who looked alike and bore a resemblance to the owner who greeted them at the door. Barba presumed they were a family business. After wandering down the aisle of goods with an attitude of a solitary shopper, Atek went outside to wait so she decided to join him. Smoking in sullen silence, it was as if he was deliberately avoiding looking at her, conversing with her. Simulating interest in the contents of the furniture shop next door to mask her inner misgivings, she heard a female speak laughingly in Turkish. Turning, she saw the girl pull the cigarette from Atek's smiling lips, her eyes in contact with his, stamp it out with her shoe and put it in a bin. The leaden rising in her chest constricted her breath and her ability to say anything, as she watched him go back inside with the girl.

Standing behind him at the checkout, his hands resting apart on the counter, perfectly mirrored by the girl who was facing him, she waited for the bill to print out, to pay, aware that the shop assistant had presumed they were not attached. Invisible poison darts fired out of her eyes into the sycophantic skull of the girl. As if she suddenly felt their impact, she looked sideways at Barba and recoiled, adjusting her position at the cash register. Stepping forward, frosty and aloof, between her and Atek, Barba pushed her credit card into the machine, entered her secret code and signed the receipt.

"Next time we can order by telephone," he said, a few minutes after leaving the shop, which stung her more, as it showed he was aware of her feelings about his behaviour.

"If we get bigger one you can see from the kitchen, too," he pointed out as they compared televisions in the electrical goods store.

During their lunch by the riverside he had chatted incessantly, flattering and amusing her until she relaxed. When he suggested going to look at televisions, she knew he thought he had compensated for the insult in the grocery.

Atek liked to watch television in bed at night and had taken the small set upstairs on the second night after he arrived. Not many programmes appealed to her, even in England, but she sometimes liked the television on in the background. It was too troublesome to carry it up and down the narrow stairs.

"Will be good for you, Barba, you know. You learn more Turkish with the programmes. We can get satellite so you can watch all the English ones you like, film too."

Atek asked the proprietor if they could deliver the larger set to the cottage. They could and did, one hour after they arrived back home.

Her laptop was also occupied more by him than her. He would sign in to Messenger and talk to the many friends who had married and moved to European countries. Most evenings she wanted to speak to Lucy online for a short time, and with her mother at the weekend. If he was using it he would be irritable, handing it over to her as if she was selfish and unreasonable. Once she went into the spare room, where he often liked to sit with the laptop on one of the beds, to ask for it. As she entered he glanced up at her, moving the mouse forward, clicking and closing, she could tell, even though she could not see the screen, a window he had open. Catching her eye as she looked questioningly into his, he blushed.

"I want to use the laptop in ten minutes, Atek, if that's alright," she asked him politely, quietly, before leaving the room, the lead weight gaining mass in her core.

The first week in March, their second together, was when the friends began to arrive. Sometimes she was introduced, sometimes not. Atek would prepare Turkish tea and they would talk together at the table in the kitchen, or if it was fine, outside in the front yard area, where they smoked. Listening intently, mentally making notes of words to remember and learn, she wrote these in the notebook she was using as she learnt the language from text books. Relying on Atek to correct the pronunciation was frequently a source of amusement, as she often distorted words and phrases, sometimes shockingly.

Occasionally, if the friend had a car, Atek would disappear and reappear up to two hours later, without explanation.

"You don't need to understand everything," he would tell her, exasperated, if she challenged him.

"It's about building trust, Atek." It seemed that she was repeating those words frequently since the friends began to drop in.

His voice would grow strained and high as he protested. "This is not trust."

Aslan and Kunt were the first to stay overnight in

209

the spare bedroom, to be transported by Atek with petrol she paid for, sharing their meals with food she had bought.

"Before season starts, friends must come to look for work, Barba. Just for one night, okay?" he cajoled, every time.

It was always for more than one night, on average three, though Erol the photographer stayed for five, because he had the excuse that he was waiting for his German holiday rep girlfriend to arrive, so he could move into her apartment.

"We could make film in bedroom, just for me and you to see," Atek had proposed one afternoon when he was looking at Erol's cameras.

Barba tried to laugh away the suggestion, which at first confused, then disturbed her.

Erol was succeeded by Necat, who moved out when he was employed by the hamam, then Haki and Fikrat, who were taken on as kitchen boys at Sultan's. It was Fikrat who revealed that Berk was in Sweden to see his daughter, when Barba commented that she had not seen him since she had arrived. Lucy had asked if she had seen him, because he had not been online for three weeks.

"Sweden? Daughter?" Barba had repeated, uncomprehending.

Neither answered her. Atek glared at Fikrat, who reddened and tightened his mouth. The mass of lead shifted in her stomach.

"He has daughter, she is five. He goes to see her in Sweden," was all he would tell her when she asked him about Berk when he came to bed that night, in a mood sedated by hashish.

"You don't have to say anything." His tone grew more hostile. "No need to cause stress, Barba," he warned her.

After their evening meals she looked forward to walking with Atek on the beach, when the light was enough to guide them, yet dim enough to feel private and anonymous. Sometimes he would put his arm around her, or hold her hand, but often he would walk separately, with an aura of distance. The weight would press against her heart, and she wished he was more consistent.

As March progressed and activity on the beach grew, the bars began to be repaired and refurbished. Each evening a few of the workers remained there; the more there were, the less willing he seemed to accompany her.

"It's just that I feel we need to enjoy time with each other if we are to have a good relationship," she argued, when he told her one evening that he did not really like the beach at night.

"We could swim in the sea in the morning," he suggested. "I like that".

March had been unusually warm already, the sea comfortable when she had swum in the daytime. When they were woken earlier than they normally did, by bright sunshine infiltrating the curtains two mornings later, she proposed that they do it then. He agreed sleepily. Putting on her bikini like a child getting ready to go out to play, happily, because the intimacy they had first enjoyed had quickly seemed intruded upon, by the ever-present friends. Sensing his presence behind her she glanced back at him. Seeing the savage scowl that could only have been directed at her, she froze, raising an eyebrow in question at him.

"What?" he grinned, disingenuously, immediately relaxing his face.

Haki was slumped on the sofa with his head in his hands when she wished him good morning in Turkish and went to make coffee before their swim. Atek exchanged a few quiet words with him then followed her to the kitchen, taking her aside so they could not be seen from the living area.

"I didn't say anything to him," he whispered in her ear," but is it ok if Haki comes with us?"

Speechless with disbelief and hurt, she slammed her coffee cup on the table, grabbed her towel and opened the door.

"Thanks. You've spoilt it for me, now," she hissed at him, before walking out, her jaw clenched, her eyes burning.

She was removing her kaftan near the bench, where excited holidaymakers waited for water sports, when he caught up with her.

"What's wrong? He is not good today. Father is ill."

"Yes, I am sorry, Atek, but you don't get the point. Why I ask you to spend time alone with me."

Ignoring him determinedly, she played in the waves which were strong and so vigorous they knocked her over twice. Emerging, chuckling and spluttering like an infant, while he stood at the edge, a solitary observer.

"That was great," she told him as she towelled

herself. "I would have liked to have played with you even more."

"Anytime. I am here," he replied with a wry, remorseless smile.

Haki had left the cottage when they returned. They met him later at the beach bar in Side that afternoon. Atek was meeting the owner and some of the other waiters to discuss the date of opening and the work that had to be done. Haki was alone at one of the tables which were already in place for the first trickle of tourists. Buying three coffees at the bar, he handed Barba one and took the other two to join Haki. Putting the drinks down, he sat himself next to Haki on the bench. Carrying her coffee behind him, Barba took the chair opposite, looking out to sea so she did not have to look at Atek, with his arm round his friend's shoulders and his body turned away from hers.

"His father is good friend of my family. I must go because he is very sick".

When he had convinced her of the need to return to his hometown for a few days, he then embarked on a new course of persuasion.

"His family need to pay for medicines and hospital. It is not same in Turkey, you know. It is hard for us."

This discourse was replayed so many times during the night and the next morning whenever they were alone, she reached a point where she felt she was being flattened to the ground with a hammer of guilt and approbation. She asked him to take her on the bike to the cash machine so she could withdraw the two hundred

213

lira he insisted was the minimum needed to help.

"We have to be more careful with money, Atek. We won't get paid for another four weeks or so," she cautioned him as he almost snatched the notes from her hand.

"Maybe your house will be sold soon," he said with an optimistic lilt in his voice.

"It takes time, Atek." In her mind she committed herself more firmly to her resolution not to tell him the amount of potential equity in her house. So far she had been convincingly vague, giving the forecast of an economic recession, and a slump in the property market, as a reason.

That night he caught the bus to their hometown with Haki. He was away for seven days.

CHAPTER 9

The notice that the apartment allocated to her in Side would be available in five days came the day after Atek went home. Unsure of his exact return, she had everything packed ready to move, as it conveniently came at the end of the month and she wanted to avoid paying more rent for the cottage. She called him the day before she went. He told her he missed her, was sorry but Haki needed him there. That he would come back to their new home the day after the relocation.

That same afternoon she caught the bus to Side to collect the keys and get her first view of the place. It had two bedrooms, which she thought would be useful for friends from home visiting, if she could guarantee a vacant bed. The rooms were light and spacious, with a huge living space which included a kitchen and dining area. It opened on to a wide balcony overlooking the pool, which compensated somewhat for missing the proximity of the sea. In contrast to the cosiness of the cottage, the apartment was cautiously furnished in pastels, the features modern, tiles everywhere. Appreciating the clean lines of the place, she noted the dishwasher, seeing herself loading it smugly after meals.

The walk to the beach took her about ten minutes, where she found Berk, leisurely planting bamboos by the entrance to the bar area.

"Merhaba, Berk," she called

brightly."Gardening?"

He responded in his usual friendly way. Sweden was not mentioned, as she was there to ask him a favour. She told him about the move, guessing he would have more information than she about Atek's agenda.

"Please could you use the beach bus to bring our stuff over?" she asked him sweetly. "I could get a taxi but the television box is quite big."

"No problem, Barba," he assured her without hesitation, promising to be there early.

Good as his word, he arrived at the cottage the next morning with one of the new, young beach boys to help.

It took just over an hour to move in. Glad that she and Atek had relatively few belongings between them, she began unpacking clothes when her helpers had gone back to the beach. Putting them in the new wardrobes in their bedroom, which also had a balcony overlooking the pool, she heard knocking. It was followed by the door opening and Carol stepping in with Fern, calling her name. Answering happily, realising that she was now in the heart of the British community who resided there most of the time, already feeling amongst friends.

Carol introduced Fern again. Barba remembered meeting her in the Korner Bar one night on their first visit, which seemed so long ago. In less than six months her life had undergone a transition she would not have dreamed of, she thought. She told them to sit and took a bottle of white wine from the fridge.

Fern, who she had liked at the first meeting, and her Turkish husband of fifteen years, were hard-working businesspeople. They had owned bars, a restaurant and were now doing well in real estate. Their two children, a son and a daughter, aged ten and twelve respectively were bi-lingual. Fern was fluent in Turkish and spoke fondly of her husband, who everyone said was a good man, Carol had told her.

"Actually we came to see if you needed any help as well as an English welcome," Carol explained.

"That is just so thoughtful of you, but there's not really anything to do. The apartment has been left in an immaculate state," Barba replied appreciatively. "But it's so nice to have your company."

"Let's have a kind of house-warming, instead then," Fern said.

Her idea was keenly taken up. Two more properly chilled bottles of white wine were purchased from the nearest mini-market, with the intention of spending a convivial afternoon getting acquainted. Pistachios, cashews and dried fruits were put out on the table.

Exchanging news and stories like old school friends, the only lull in the conversation occurred when Barba was giving them a summary of the sequence of events which had led her there. It seemed to impress them, until the cohabitation with Atek was discussed.

"So when do you start your repping?" Fern enquired, breaking the pause which hung around Atek's name.

When Barba had told them as much as she knew about her forthcoming work, she asked Fern how she and her husband, Cem, had met. Fern gave a hilarious recount of her mildly racy days as an air stewardess, their courtship. She also made a comment which resonated too strongly with Barba for comfort, recalling it many times afterwards.

"I knew that he loved me because he never once asked me for money," she said, with affection and pride.

Barba offered to fill their glasses.

She was still in bed when the security doorbell chimed the next morning. Taking in the new surroundings hazily, she picked up her 'phone to see the time. There was a text from Atek and three missed calls. Suddenly alert and guilty, she rushed to press the button to let him through downstairs and opened the door. He was striding jauntily up the stairs. She stepped forward, holding out her arms to him. Keeping his by his side, he turned stiffly to indicate a young man coming up hesitantly behind him.

"Hi. This is my nephew, Alev," he introduced the bashful teenager now at his side.

"Merhaba, Alev," she welcomed him.

He put out his hand to shake hers. Looking at his young-lion face, she instantly and instinctively trusted and liked him. Understanding that he had come to live with them, that she was expected to regard him as family, before Atek specifically asked her if she minded. Suppressing her concerns that she would have nowhere for her own family and friends to visit, she showed him to the spare room. Taking in his new surroundings, he put his bag down tentatively and thanked her quietly in Turkish, twice, which made her feel a pleasure in sharing with him.

Atek wandered through the place, expressing his appreciation by the satisfied smile on his face. Exploring the kitchen cupboards, he asked Barba if they had the

Turkish leaves for tea and told Alev to get some fresh bread. He had already found the cheese, olives and tomatoes in the fridge. Neither of them were talkative over their breakfast. When Alev went to catch up on sleep they went too. Except Atek told her and showed her how much he had missed her first.

Early in the afternoon, Barba showered, thankful that there was an en-suite, anticipating that the spare bed in Alev's room would not remain unoccupied for long. As she dressed, Atek woke and they had the delayed discussion about his nephew staying with them.

"He is good person. Quiet. He will help you," Atek testified.

"Yes, I can see that," she conceded. "Just that I thought the spare room would be for my family and friends too."

"We can find places for them here, not expensive. Your English friends have apartments."

That was true. Fern and Cem, for example, had several they rented to tourists. It would be better for space and privacy if visitors had their own place, she agreed.

"Alev will work at the beach too. And maybe he is out a lot," Atek added.

While Alev was already demonstrating his worth by preparing some soup for their lunch, Barba and Atek took some rubbish to the communal bins behind the building. There was a mongrel, dusty and thin, snuffling around the containers.

"It looks like Gee-Gee," Barba exclaimed, thinking she recognised the sandy-coloured, short-haired dog, with alert ears and the build of an under-grown

Labrador.

"It is Gee-Gee!" she shouted, as it noticed them and scampered over, its tail wagging, its eyes friendly behind the two chocolate brown patches which identified it as the now adult puppy from the beach.

"What is he doing here?" she enquired of Atek, who was standing back, with an expression of distaste as she scratched the dog's forehead.

"Owner went to Istanbul at the end of the season," he told her, "he will get new. Tourists like puppy," he shrugged dispassionately.

"You mean he just leaves them behind when they're not cute pups anymore?" Barba asked angrily.

Atek appeared to be thinking about the meaning of her words, linguistically rather than emotionally. Too outraged to care about his principles at that moment; the problem of how to take care of the dog, without being allowed to have it in the apartment, engaged her. It was possible to feed it, monitor its health, and enlist the help of Fern or Carol, who both had houses, if they were agreeable. She thought she would call on Carol first that afternoon, after she had collected her uniform and her instructions from the Douglas Scott office.

Atek told her that he and Alev would go to the beach bar for the afternoon, where they would help with the preparations for the summer tourist season. They were hoping for a marked rise in visitors during the Easter holidays, in a fortnight. Barba was also expected to be fully-fledged as a rep by then, with four days of meetings and inductions that week, ready for her list of allocated hotels with guests the following week.

Walking up to the building which she

remembered as pinkish, the colour of beef paste, she reflected on the new life that was beginning to form more tangibly. She was greeted by a friendly, plump woman in the same suit and shirt that she had worn in the travel agency. Introducing herself as Karen, she knocked on the open door of an adjoining office to make known her manager. Stuart, an energetic Scotsman in his thirties, jumped up to shake her hand.

"Welcome to the crew, Barba," he welcomed her. "Sit here and tell me a wee bit about yourself while we get a drink. Karen will get your togs and talk you through the schedule for training, then your work starting next week."

Breathing in, to start at a beginning, she thanked him and gave a summary of her time at the travel agency in England. Explaining how she had wanted a change following the separation from her long-term partner, had felt attracted to the nature of the work and the place. Atek was again omitted, although they were aware that she had opted for her own subsidised place, rather than sharing with another rep for free. That personal side of her life could unfold in its own time, she resolved. Stuart was distracted anyway, apologetically answering two telephone calls as she talked. He managed a quick précis of the company history, named a few of the best places for a night out in Side, before Karen came in with the water they had asked for and took Barba back into the main office.

Barba's nervous excitement was like a brush with gentle nettles as Karen read through the list of inductions she was required to attend. They consisted of four two-hour sessions covering company policy, interpersonal skills, professionalism, nature of roles and duties and targets. Her neck prickled as Karen moved on to the timetable and shift patterns. The schedule included some early starts in the morning and late nights when she would be on airport duty, meeting new arrivals and accompanying departing guests. There were welcome talks for each fresh group which Karen described in a more serious tone and expression. Ensuring that the importance of meeting targets, by selling as many tours and trips to her guests as possible, was impressed upon her.

"Alright so far?" Karen took a sip of water and stared at her. "Obviously you will get more detail in the inductions. Questions?"

"Not right now, thanks. That's great," Barba enthused.

"Oh, and there's a little company car you'll get to share with the other ground girls."

Barba tried not to show the apprehension which came also with pleasure at this unexpected boon.

"Think it works out that you'll get it about once every six days," Karen explained. "Otherwise you're on foot, me dear, unless you get a bike."

"It'll keep me fit anyway," laughed Barba.

Karen gave her the two coral-pink polo shirts with the company logo, two short-sleeved shirts, a navy skirt the same as the one she possessed and two pairs of navy, knee-length shorts. The shirt and skirt were to be worn for airport duty and welcome meetings, with the navy court shoes which had been ordered for her. Navy tennis shoes were to be worn with shorts and polo shirt for daytime visits to hotels.

With a carrier bag full of clothes she would not choose to wear, and a head full of information she had to retain, Barba was glad to stop off at Carol's to talk about it. She was also keen to fulfil her mission for the dog. Carol had received her text and had come to the security gate at their compound of six villas, overlooking gardens bordering a pool with a fountain centrepiece.

The cold white wine and mineral water offered to her were happily accepted.

"It's nearly evening, darling," her hostess had persuaded her, glad of an excuse to indulge.

She listened to Barba's account of the work she would do and read her information sheets with interest.

"Rather you than me," she commented, at the mention of the times of the airport duties.

Barba looked round at the nurtured plants and grounds, hesitating before approaching the subject of the dog. Then the thought of it being exploited for its appeal as a puppy, then heartlessly abandoned and replaced, incensed her again. She conveyed it to Carol, who initially looked unsure as she considered Barba's proposal. After deliberating over the possible problems, her compassion took over her reservations. She agreed that the small concreted yard at the side of her house could be used as a safe place. It could sleep and be fed there, away from the numerous other roaming dogs, if Barba could teach it to come with her. They talked about eventually training it to take a lead, which would make it easier.

"You're an angel," Barba squeezed Carol's hand gratefully.

Feeling that some important stones in the

structure of her new life had been put in place, she collected some dried dog food and plastic bowls on the way home. Atek sent a text message to say they would be another hour at the beach and that he was bringing salad to eat with their dinner. The apartment was empty, so she laid the table, prepared chicken and cut the bread ready for when the men came in just after seven. She would have liked him to kiss her, as before, but his demeanour in his nephew's presence denied such demonstrations, even though Alev was seventeen and about to work in tourism.

Atek peeped in the carrier bags which were on the sofa. She held out the uniform to show him. Grinning, he took the shorts and held them against himself. Discarding them, he pulled out a dog bowl from the other bag with a puzzled frown. She told him the arrangement made with Carol.

"I'm going for shower before to eat," he informed her, as if the dog had not been part of the conversation.

After their meal, during which she told Atek about her day, he described the cleaning, repairing and painting they had been doing. Most of the time, he conversed in Turkish to Alev, who struggled with a few words in English.

"You will have to teach me Turkish, and I'll teach you English," Barba proposed.

Atek showed them a technique by which he had learnt English, writing a Turkish word on a piece of paper, then the English word on the back. She and Alev, with the help of a translation dictionary, began to play a game. Taking turns to write a word, the other would translate then they read them to get the pronunciation right. After ten words, they tested how many they could remember.

It was the first of many evenings she and Alev would spend learning together, keeping each other company. After the first week at the apartment, most nights after dinner, Atek's 'phone would bleep. He would read the message and announce that he was going to talk with a friend for a short time. It invariably turned out to be at least an hour, more often two or three. The first time she protested.

"This is trust?" he snapped at her defensively.

"No, no. It's just that we don't really spend much time together. It bothers me when you just go off with your friends without saying where you are going." She hated the whining edge to her voice as she justified herself.

"You controlling me?" he continued, harshly, "Better in military than this."

"I just think where you put your time shows what is important to you," she reasoned, "and if we want to build a good relationship."

She was stopped by his eyes coldly moving close to hers.

"Listen, baby, I could live with many women in time on beach you know."

"I'm sure you could". Her anger was sparking at this reminder. "And I am talking about me and you."

"Do I always come back to go to bed with you, same time as you?" he asked, as if this was the definitive question.

"Yes you do, and that is lovely," she smiled,

consciously soothing her tone to diffuse their tension.

Although he gave her a sympathetic smile to show he felt she had lost the argument and seen reason, he did not speak to her except when he needed to for three days. This became the behaviour he resorted to whenever she challenged him, as if it was a standard punishment he had contrived. Thus it became less painful for her to accept his freedom in that respect. It was easier to find consolation in the companionship and peaceable fun she shared with Alev. Seemingly content to stay at home, he helped her with chores, learning new words, practising them by playing with the Scrabble she had bought. Often, when she was not using the laptop, he would ask her politely for its use, to talk to his own friends online.

When their work routines became established, her hours were varied, while the men rose at six in the morning and came back twelve or thirteen hours later. Barba was concerned that she and Atek needed to nourish their bond with pleasure and leisure. Sometimes she was free to go to the beach in the afternoon, to lay and swim, but he was becoming more occupied with the increasing number of holidaymakers. She yearned for more privacy. To her, most of their interactions felt on public display, or conducted in the presence of his nephew or friends.

The day before the Easter school holidays began in England, she had called in at her first hotel of the day where a particularly amiable group of clients were staying. Striding contentedly towards her next venue, she felt like a sturdy schoolboy in the polo shirt and shorts, the bag of files pulling on her shoulder, as heavy and cumbersome as a satchel of books. Still, she was glad to be in the sun, out of a stuffy office in a busy high street in Newcastle. Blossoming with fresh compliments and the lovemaking she had enjoyed with her morning shower, the new Barba was elated. She dumped the bag in the sandy dust on the roadside when she felt the vibration in her side pocket. Happy days, she thought, as she read the cryptic text from Lucy, presuming it was written with excitement and haste.

'Hi babe. Great last min deal for hols with ur co. Dreamy hotel. 1 wk. Is it one of urs? X'

Barba read it twice before it was deciphered, understanding that her friend had found a late package deal with Douglas Scott. She replied immediately.

'Fab news babe. Yes, on my way to Dreamy now! Online 2nite for details? X'

Lucy responded as promptly.

'C u 2nite ☺ Booking now ☺ X'

Feeling blessed with good fortune, Barba engaged even more warmly with the guests, including Nille Torid, the depressed Norwegian woman who was staying at the Dreamy. She came to sit with her for the third time that week as she completed her paperwork by the pool. A pallid woman in her mid-thirties, Barba perceived her as looking her own age.

"I am getting a coffee. Do you want one?" she asked, in her wet, dish-rag voice.

"That would be nice. Milk, no sugar", Barba said, feeling magnanimous, hoping that Nille had exhausted her repertoire of ill-fate.

Barba had already heard about her struggles with her mental illness, the lack of support and understanding of her family and the breakdown of her last relationship. It had been one in a series of a few, all similarly doomed. She had travelled alone to Side, she had explained to Barba, for some soul-searching under a therapeutic sun. During the bleak and isolated winter she had contemplated suicide more than once.

"How are you, today, Nille?" She took the coffee from her, thinking she appeared a little more animated than previously.

"Good, Barba, thank you. Are you busy?" she asked, needlessly, in her polite monotone.

"Nearly finished. Just this report."

Nille sat, watching the guests by the pool until Barba put down her pen and picked up her coffee.

"Actually, I wanted to ask you about a hamam, Barba. Do you know a good one?"

"Well, it's something I want to try, and haven't got round to. My company does a package for our clients, but for professional reasons I wouldn't go with them", she said, then at once regretted it. Nille brightened and took her words as a cue.

"Maybe we could go together, as I'm independent," she invited her, producing a leaflet about a hamam another guest had visited and enthused about.

They read the sales copy with hilarity; the English was flowery and creatively misused. The description of the 'enchanting scrubble which leaves you like newborn baby' convinced them of its appeal. Barba was motivated to share her bonhomie of the day. Overriding her intuitive reluctance, she agreed that they could go when she had finished the next morning's round of hotel visits.

"So, I'll meet you here and we will go about eleven?" Nille confirmed.

When Barba returned to her apartment for lunch and a nap before her afternoon duties, Gee-Gee was waiting. Evidently pleased to see her he allowed her to take him to Carol's on the lead. She had been training him, a few metres and minutes at a time. He had also quickly learnt to meet her each day. Lying by the bins near her apartment, at lunchtime, and in the evening, to be taken to the refuge of Carol's yard. Sometimes their paths would cross in the daytime, as she traversed the streets and scrubland between hotels. At Carol's she would groom him and bathe him in a baby bath twice weekly. If she went to the beach in the afternoon she would often take him with her, a stick between his teeth, his tail wagging madly.

After dinner, she asked Atek to walk out with her, suggesting they have a drink at the sea-side bar they liked in. She had changed into a feminine sundress and made up her face before he was due home, optimistic because all the omens had seemed fortuitous that day. There had been an unpleasant exchange at the weekend about the lack of romance between them which she had initiated. The three day distance from him had ensued, which had been dissolved in the bathroom that morning.

"Ok," he agreed readily, "after shower."

He held her hand on the beach as they walked towards the ruins, once stopping to wrap his arms around her and kiss her. She bubbled inside as waves caressed her feet, feeling tides turning.

When they sat down with their cold beers, she told him about Lucy's holiday.

"I know. Berk told me," he said in a disinterested tone. "Good," he added.

"Beach was busy to day," he told her, leaning back with a satisfied grin. "Maybe we could meet for lunch tomorrow."

Barba was exultant. He had been thinking about what she had been saying and planning to take action to remedy it, she thought.

"Oh, baby, I'd really like that."

"About two, I think best, when not so busy."

"Perfect for me. I'll text you to check. Remember that Norwegian woman I told you about? The one who talks about her problems all the time? I said I'd go to the hamam in the morning with her."

He gave her a quizzical look, having already heard about the woman's problems, laughing at Barba's comi-tragic renditions. Containing his displeasure at her visiting the hamam, he said nothing to attempt to prevent her, as it was an indulgence generally enjoyed by her European friends.

Before dressing, after the treatment the next day, she sent Atek a message to let him know she would soon be ready to meet him. Nille had proved to be quite pleasant company when she talked about anything other than herself. She had obviously benefitted from the attentions of the flirtatious young Turkish man wrapped in a cotton sarong. Barba had been thankful for being 'scrubbled' by a masseuse who was respectful. He had sung sweetly as she near-dozed, in a blissful state of relaxation after her first two weeks of walking miles with a substantial load.

Necat had not been amongst the workers soaping

and slapping the lather on bodies on the row of slabs Barba had been lay on. She had forgotten that this was the place where he was employed until she saw him talking to Atek in the reception area.

"Hi," she touched his back lightly, thrilled that he had come to meet her, and so punctually.

"Atek, this is Nille."

"Pleased to meet you." Nille smiled up at him with her narrow eyes that were set close to the bridge of her nose, bird-like.

"We are going to lunch, now," Barba reminded her. She had told her of her plans to have lunch with Atek when they were in the hamam.

"You can come," Atek suggested graciously.

The leaden mass nudged Barba's solar plexus. It hit the floor of her stomach as she heard Nille say she would love to. It crept back up, permeating into her face, turning it to stone. Chewing through a salad she would have relished, in a garden restaurant where she expected to be alone with her lover, it did not soften. Instead, she was glad not to have to listen to any more of Nille's droning questions, her fawning responses to Atek, when he stood up to leave. Making her own excuses as courteously as she could muster when he had left, she walked with Nille to the corner of the street.

Perplexed for the rest of the day because he had given no sign that he was attracted to Nille, certain that her self-absorbed conversation was universally boring, she asked Atek why he had included her when he came home.

"She was alone," he stated flatly, with an amused glint in his eyes.

231

Thinking she would be able to avoid Nille, as she had to do an airport transfer in the evening, she chided herself for being possessive, too easily disturbed by the manipulations of a needy woman. Taking the laptop onto the balcony to talk to Lucy about their imminent meeting, she hoped it would boost her spirits again.

Having most of the following day off, she swam in the apartment complex pool in the morning, deciding to laze on the beach from early afternoon. Her former cheerfulness had resumed. She liked Ray, the male rep she was working with that night, because he was effeminately garrulous and funny. The departing clients had all been ones she had enjoyed a good rapport with.

Almost skipping into the bar area, she looked around for Atek. Her steps came to a standstill as she saw Nille, posed on a high stool at the bar in a purple mesh shift dress over an orange bikini. Sipping from a straw, sallow, simpering at the perfunctory, routine flirtations of the waiters.

"It's part of my job," Atek had silenced her, when she had observed him performing a similar act one day.

He had been attending to two chubby German blondes in black bikinis and white sunglasses, who had dismounted a shared moped and strode, open-legged as cowboys, into the bar. When he came over to her, from them, she had complained to him that she found it insulting. Rather than showing regret, or giving her reassurance, he reacted as if she had complimented him.

She could not see Atek around. Walking around the outside of the bar, she avoided Nille, who had not seemed to notice her. Throwing her towel on an available sunbed, as far away from the bar as she could find, she tweaked with the shade to hide her from view, before slipping off her sundress and flopping down. Some minutes later, Atek appeared at her side. Sulkily, she asked him to bring water.

"And please don't tell that woman I am here," she ordered.

He went off to the bar, chuckling at her chagrin. His amusement fortified her resolve to develop a veneer of dignified self-possession in the face of any further such irritations.

Determination, the warming sea, sunshine on her back, her new novel and certain knowledge that Miss Torid would be back home in two days, comforted her. She consoled herself with the idea that she would never have to give her another thought.

"There are many people like this in Norway," Atek had given her his opinion after the lunch with her. "Egoists," he had labelled them, giving Barba the impression he actively disliked her, and her type.

The beginning of the Easter break meant her workload almost trebled within a few days, leaving her no time to worry about anything except the various demands and concerns which tugged at her the next week. They ranged from the trivial moans of habitual complainers, to sleepless children, fractious in the heat. An elderly man had suffered a stroke, which meant she had to arrange for him to be taken to hospital on one of her evenings off. She prayed for an easier week when Lucy was there.

Her prayers were answered. Lucy arrived with an

easy-going assortment of families, happy to get to a beach in the sunshine after a cold, wet week of entertaining their offspring at home. Fortunately too, she was on early morning airport duty, on the coach which Lucy, Wayne and Phee were travelling back on. She had also mentioned to the manager of the Dreamy that a good friend of hers was arriving, which she hoped would make things more pleasant for them.

After a flurry of emotional embracing with Lucy at the airport, she gathered the rest of group and escorted them all to their bus. Once the journey had begun she snatched conversations with her friend until they stopped outside her hotel.

"I'll catch up with you in an hour or so," she whispered, as Lucy stepped off the coach. "If you can stay awake long enough for a coffee?"

"For you, babe," Lucy replied. "Though I think the kids 'll be in their beds as soon as they find them."

Hearing Phee shriek just as the doors of the bus closed, Barba observed, through glass, the scene of the joyful reunions of the girl with Musti, and Lucy with Berk. Wayne, who was trundling his case up the steps to the Reception, ignored them like a stranger, leaving them behind as if they were nothing to do with him.

The qualms she had felt at the surprise reception from the men dissipated, though not ever quite completely, from the first evening of their holiday. Lucy was radiant in the beam of Berk's attention which was now turned full on her. Lavishing her bounteous affection on him, in every sentence she pronounced him her baby. Phee and Musti resumed their physical bonding, always touching, subtle and sultry, never quite indiscreet. Phee, sixteen and grown more womanly since Barba left England, orbited around Musti in her own lustrous dreamtime. In a way, hers was a selfish condoning too, Barba thought sometimes. The energy of their couplings turned up the low-burner which the flame between her and Atek had dwindled to. It was also her wish that Lucy would want to come back often, as she knew she be driven to for Berk, more than for her.

Alev, with his quiet empathy, took care of Wayne, his fellow outsider for the duration. Lucy hired a car again, more for Berk's pleasure than necessity, Barba guessed. He gained status as their driver, was needed and depended upon. Generous Lucy gave him the keys for the week so he had the advantages of ownership. They all benefitted, as it meant they could squeeze more from their time in between work hours. Lucy and Berk would drive out at nights, which Barba understood was to find compensation for Berk not being allowed in Lucy's hotel, a general ruling for Turkish men in the resorts. Because of this, she had given them the keys to their apartment to use when she, Atek and Alev were all at work. Phee and Musti, she was sure, would find their own opportunities, which she preferred not to think about.

The season was taking off too, at the time that Lucy and her family flew home. The three weeks, between her departure and Barba's mother arriving were tiring and hectic, as the numbers of people and those on the thermometer grew higher by the week. Barba, growing torpid in the heat, yet finding more was required of her, hoped she would acclimatise before the temperatures climbed over the forties.

Her mother came at the right time, when the heat was ideal for basking and bathing. Her flight arrived in the early hours. As the holiday package she and Elsie had opted for included their transfers and a number of tours, they were content, finding it more convenient, to meet later in the morning of her arrival.

Barba found them, shaded under vines and bougainvillea, by the poolside of their boutique hotel, with two men of about the same age. She held her mother like a child starting school.

"Barba, look at you with your tan," her mother exclaimed as she stood back to look at her daughter. "Gosh, you've lost weight too, haven't you? Not too much now, though, be careful."

Laughing at her mother reverting to role so quickly, Barba thanked her for the compliment. She kissed Elsie and asked about their journey.

"Marvellous, wasn't it, Tony? Barba, this is Tony, this is Ken," Elsie touched the shoulders of their companions as she named them. "We're on the same tour together," she said with a shiver of anticipation.

"Nice to meet you." They shook hands. "Mum, you look really well yourself. So do you, Elsie."

The two ladies were an illuminated version of the Newcastle selves Barba recalled. Observing the already familiar ease between the four travellers as they told her their itinerary, she attributed the change to the presence of Tony and Ken.

Their holiday was filled with activities they hated to miss. Apart from drinks in the evening with all four of them, once with a charming but reluctant Atek, there was little time to meet. When they did, Barba felt superfluous, hearing the banter flow between them, listening to their recounts of historical relics, jeep safari, island boat ride, hamam, dance show in the amphitheatre, shopping and dining.

Before she went home again, Barba asked Dot if they could spend at least an hour alone. They arranged for her to come to the apartment on her last evening. Atek said he and Alev would be late back from the beach when she told him her mother was coming about seven.

"We're all going out for a meal, you see, as we won't be seeing Tony and Ken for a while," Dot apologised.

"Don't worry. Enjoying yourself is what it's about, Mum. Anyway, what do you mean, a while?"

Dot pressed her lips to hold back a smile, shaking her head evasively.

"They live in Manchester, but we've all had such a good time we might do it again."

Pushing aside her inquisitiveness, Barba left it at that, saying a private prayer that this joy would continue for her mother, who seemed to shrivel after her father died, three years before. Her thoughts went to him, and the house she had grown up in, which he had left to her in his will, having inherited his own childhood home.

"Have you seen much of Sean, Mum? The house sale isn't as quick as I'd expected," she enquired.

"He seems fine, love. Always at the Golf Club but manages Sunday dinner at Beth's usually."

Wondering if she was normal to feel so dispassionate about him, she considered speaking to him about letting the agency do the viewings if he was out so much. Once her job there had begun, it was for the duration, which meant the matter of the house sale would have to wait until the end of the season, if necessary; another five months.

"That's good. How's Beth and the children?" She felt the need to ask, even though she called them weekly, speaking to them all in turn for a few minutes, even baby Lou, who was saying more each time.

The hour was soon absorbed, the buzzer stopping their dialogue like a school bell at the end of a lesson, letting them know her companions were waiting downstairs. She made Dot promise to call her from the airport and found it hard to unwrap her arms from her, to let her go.

June, she imagined, would always be her favourite month over there. The April rains had prompted a succulent greening, the sun encouraging an awesome spurt of growth in May. Vines, jasmine, honeysuckle, bougainvillea and roses. Rich varieties, temperate and tropical, stretching and blossoming in harmony. Reaching to full glory before the withering heat of the high season.

Her customers were generally couples and friends who had a fondness for the place, revisiting each year. It made Barba's job easier, as they were used to being there, knowing what they wanted, liked and expected. She was told, by the other experienced reps, that the clientele in September and October were usually similar.

The month, which began so pleasantly, was more eventful than she would have predicted.

Lucy had spoken about coming out on her own

for five days at the end of June. She was awaiting definite plans, knowing that Lucy was anxious to see Berk again, speaking to him every evening.

Alev's parents stopped for two days at a friend's house near Manavgat, so they arranged to have dinner at a riverside restaurant on their second night. Alev's mother, Asya, was handsome, very much like her son, with the gentle charm which Barba admired in him. From his father she thought he had gained the air of strength and a kind of modest nobility. Asya, Barba knew, was fourteen years older than her brother, yet looked no more than maybe five, having kept out of the sun, dressing as she was then, in a headscarf and covered from head to toe. She spoke little English so they communicated mostly without words, which Barba thought was probably the most authentic way. Certainly, she felt the joy then compassion when she indicated Asya's pregnancy and asked in Turkish when it was due. She told her it was August and that she had lost a son after Alev.

"Ben de," Barba replied, with her hand on her chest. Me too.

Asya reached out for her hand and looked over at Atek. The troubled pallor that crept over her face was briefly mirrored in all of theirs, except his. His expression was of distant boredom, which Barba had noticed was growing more frequent. An ennui that punctuated periods of frenetic activity, rushing and busying, or manically high spirits, when he saw the funny side of everything. When he was quiet she assumed he was lost in thought.

"My brain just stopped," he would tell her, if he

did not hear her or understand at first when she was speaking to him.

She was not sure what he meant.

For three nights after the dinner with his sister, he was in that withdrawn state, lying on the sofa in front of the television after eating, then dragging himself to bed. She followed him into the bedroom.

"How much hashish do you smoke, Atek?"

Lunging at her with the eyes and unnerving speed of a crocodile, he pushed her into the door. She cried out as the handle jabbed painfully into her back.

"Why do you look only from one side?" Pushing her again as she moved away from him.

"What do you mean?" she shouted back." I just think you are acting strange, these days. And you don't need to push me around."

His pin-prick eyes were fixed, cold as a reptile's but his voice became soft.

"You just don't think I have problems", he uttered, as if it was a superhuman effort to keep his patience. "It's not the same here in Turkey. Always problems."

"What problems?"

"Maybe better for us if you sold your house."

"Why? It takes time anyway. If you're talking about money, you don't pay for anything here," she reprimanded.

He began undressing, yanking his clothes and flinging them to the floor.

"I give you everything," he said slowly, emphasising each word.

She went into the bathroom, not wanting to

consider what he truly gave, in her mind. He brought food home from the beach restaurant. Whenever that contribution was discussed it escalated into a conflict. When she emerged, the fury in her head was diminuendo. As before, their anger simulated passion before it dissipated. It was not the healing fusion of true connecting, but for her it was better than an abyss.

After the next morning at work, she found Gee-Gee to take him to the beach with her. Hoping that she and Atek could sit together for a while; an act of reconciliation. First she played with the dog in the waves, throwing a stick while he grunted and galloped in the spray. A little boy with dark curls clapped and giggled. He began to call "Gee-Gee, Gee-Gee," copying her. His mother who was watching him from a sunbed close by, came over.

"Hi," she said to Barba as she held her son steady in the waves. Sounding German, she did not look typically so, with short brown hair and eyes, a little taller than Barba.

"Hi. He likes my dog," she replied. "How old is he?"

"He was three in January."

"Are you on holiday?"

"Yes, a kind of holiday. We are visiting his father. He is Turkish, so we come a few times a year usually. Also he comes to Germany, when we can make the plans."

"How long are you staying?"

"Another three days. Already we are here for a week." Barba noticed the dulling tinge of sadness in her face. "How about you? You live here?"

241

"Yes, with my Turkish partner. " Barba felt herself opening up. "I work as a rep for Douglas Scott."

"I too used to work as a rep for German tour," she remarked, "That's how I met his father. My brother jokes that it was a work-accident," she laughed.

Barba laughed too, and waved at Atek, who was carrying a tray by the front row of sunbeds. "That's my partner," she pointed him out to the woman.

"You are with Atek?" the woman exclaimed. "Then you know Berk, my son's father."

"Yes." Barba put on a smile which she had practised at work.

"You must come to my little sister's party at the Temple tonight," she insisted. "Did you hear? There's going to be a little surprise," she added mysteriously. "So get there about eight."

"I'll see what I can do. I have to go now. See you later." Calling Gee-Gee, she waved as affably as she could to them, before jogging off the beach with the dog, for a hasty exit rather than exercise.

Atek contended that he was going to invite her to the party at the Temple when he got home. Insisting he had not been sure that it was definitely happening, as Mari, the eighteen year old little sister, did not know about it. Stunned, she had decided to postpone any discussion about Berk's German connections because she felt the outcome would be predictable. Gagged, guilty of a complicit betrayal of her friend, yet fearful of the conspiracy of their brotherhood, which approved loyalty above morality. At times, she read the same discomfort as hers in Alev's face; the impotence of good men who did not know what to do in the face of evil.

There was also the cruelty of driving the sharp pin of truth into the heart of a friend swelling with love and happiness. Neither was she ready to brace herself for the battle which would inevitably ensue with Atek, if she denounced his friend.

The three of them showered, dressed and walked to Side in silence. Round the pillars of the temple, some German friends and those from the beach were gathering. Clutching cold beers from the nearby shop, they stood chattering and laughing. There was a low cheer when Mari arrived hand in hand with Musti. Barba stared at him in disbelief.

Music started up intrusively, from the system behind the wall where the disco functioned each night. The theme from 'The Bodyguard' echoed around the Roman stones and Mari's party. She looked around nervously, as Musti manoeuvred her into the centre of the temple. The song stopped abruptly, he dropped to one knee and with great force, shouted out his proposal to her. Mari, as open-mouthed as Barba, looked around as if uncomprehending. Blinking and blushing, she scanned the attendant faces, put her hands to her mouth and said yes. The consent was audible through the utter silence as they strained to hear. Instantly, the temple was filled with dancing, hugging people, and more fitting music.

Atek left Barba with Alev, walking away with Berk and three other men without explanation. Dancing back to her, about thirty minutes later, his eyes were bright and dilated. Carrying beer, in a jovial mood, he handed them a bottle, urging them to drink and dance. She thought she might as well.

Berk had been the most frequent visitor to their apartment. There had been periods of a few weeks when they did not see him, about which Barba now had a theory. Atek had been the one to go out visiting in the evenings but in June, Berk, Musti and Mehmet gathered almost every night with Atek. Glasses of Turkish tea, the laptop and equipment for rolling cigarettes were taken out on to the roof balcony leading from the living room, which was sunken and very private. Sometimes she and Alev would join them with a drink, but always declined the hashish when it was offered.

Barba realised that Atek did not know how well she was beginning to understand Turkish, as she still felt less confident about speaking, especially to him. He and his friends were careless about what they said in her presence. One night they were commenting and guffawing, hunched around the laptop on the table. She knew they were on Talkbook, that there was a picture of a woman, possibly pornographic, from their comments.

Atek called her to them.

"Barba, what is slapper? A woman called a slapper?"

"It's hard to explain. Why do you want to know?"

"Mehmet has Talkbook friend, Sexy Slapper." They all slapped each other and nudged the table with their laughter.

"Usually it means someone cheap, you know. A woman who sleeps with a lot of men." She could smell her thought. A goggle-eyed fish being banged around on a slimed slab in a crowded, noisy market hall.

"I understand," Atek waved her away. They set off laughing again.

When Atek had let his friends out, he walked straight into the bedroom and put himself to bed, leaving the mess and the computer on the balcony table. Barba cleared up the debris and brought the glasses in. As she went to collect the computer it glowed to life as she touched it, revealing that the windows of Atek's Messenger and Talkbook were left open. Clicking to view all his friends on Talkbook, scrolling through, she was suspicious and confused when she saw Nille Torid there. Sexy Slapper Teena was easy to pick out. Possibly forty, probably fake-tanned, she was holding up strawberry blonde hair by its dark roots. It looked as if she could smell something bad but Barba discerned that a pout was intended. Wearing a vest with spaghetti straps over her androgynous rolls of flesh, low at the front so the black bra underneath could be seen. The word 'Sexy' was visible on her right breast. Barba presumed it was a tattoo, though the style and quality of the calligraphy was suggestive of scrawl with a permanent marker. She was holding one hip, her comparatively thin legs sticking out from denim shorts rolled up to her groin.

Remember me, the box offered. Barba accepted electronically, once for Messenger, once for Talkbook, before closing down.

CHAPTER 10

"I think there will be party on the beach tonight," Atek told her as he kissed her goodbye in the morning.

"I'm on airport duty tonight, remember", she responded as if it were an invitation, which she felt it was not. "What time will it finish?"

"By midnight for sure. If the Gendarme get to know we will have problems."

Trying not to think of ways to anonymously alert the Gendarme, she reminded herself that the beach parties were part of his work. He had explained that they were lucrative when there were more tourists seeking entertainment at night. By June it was warm enough and busy enough to plan them.

"Hope it goes well. See you when I get home."

Barba engaged as much as she could with the outgoing clients that night. Their skins told the story of their spell in the sun, from prickly-heat pink, patched, blotched, smoothly golden or caramelised. Listening to their anecdotes revealing the successes and the failures, asking questions, laughing at their jokes, she crowded out her mind with their chatter. Until there was no room for visions of loosened females letting themselves go on the beach at night. When they had re-loaded with the incoming people, she looked at her watch and relaxed. The party should have been over.

Breathing out a silent thanks, she placed her court

shoes beside his sandals outside the front door. The lights were out, so she crept into the bedroom by the light coming from their bathroom. He made no movement as she undressed, listening to his breath behind the sheet pulled over his face.

In the final week of June, another beach party was organised, which coincided happily with Lucy's five day stay in their apartment with Berk. Alev had arranged to visit his uncle in Fethiye, and she had some rare time off.

Whenever English people were around, Atek became more attentive to her, particularly in the presence of friends and work colleagues. With Lucy and Berk she really felt part of a couple with him, which was bitter-sweet, as it made her aware that too often she did not. It also made it harder to warn her friend of Berk's duplicity, or even triplicity, when the atmosphere was so romantically upbeat and amicable. There were also few opportunities to speak to Lucy alone, as Berk expected her to be at the beach while he worked, and Barba had her own responsibilities.

"Haven't had much chance to really talk to you, honey," Barba said as they put their flamboyant cocktails on the nearest table to the sea that was available. Even though they had joined the beach party early, the seats were filling quickly.

They had got ready in Barba's bedroom like two teenagers, when the men had left to prepare. After they had finished painting each other's nails, coiffing and giving advice, they agreed that they were gorgeous. The lift of the men's eyebrows, when they arrived at the beach, had confirmed it for them.

"It's not much time really," Lucy sighed, "but I don't feel I can take any more time away from the kids at the moment."

"How is Phee?" Barba asked, hoping to find out what she knew of Musti. She had been biding her time, to determine whether she needed to reveal the news of his engagement.

"She has a boyfriend at home, now."

Barba felt her shoulders lift. "Does she have contact with Musti anymore?"

"Don't think so. She doesn't tell me much." Lucy sipped her cocktail thoughtfully.

"Just as well, eh?" Barba indicated their subject with a cock of her head. At the adjacent table, Musti's back was being stroked by an inebriated girl in a sarong. Casually, he took bottles of Efes from his tray and placed them in front of her companions. The body language and manner of interaction between the two young men and another woman in the group suggested they were friends, or related, rather than romantically attached. The other attendees, it reassured Barba to note, were couples.

"What's the deal with you and Berk?"

"Good fun. Take it as it comes. Enjoy it for what it is," Lucy shrugged. Somehow Barba felt let off the hook.

The grilled meats were succulent and perfectly spiced, the salads fresh and well-mixed. Mingling more fluidly after the meal and more drink, the party-goers were lively and friendly, without excess, once the girl in the sarong had vomited by the bamboo and staggered away, supported by her companions. Dancing on the sand, they created, aligned with the choice of music, a heady 'Turkish meets Caribbean' experience.

"Let us know when the next one is," Stuart requested when she had given her account of the fun they had. "We'll see if we can get a group together."

The events were planned to occur in the first week of the months of the high season, with flexibility, as the weather and potential guests were variables. In July, Barba was able to give her colleagues three days' notice, feeling fortunate that her schedule again allowed her to go, and to have people to go with.

Stuart, Karen, Courtney, Helen and Ray met her there with their own partners. Helen and Courtney had Turkish boyfriends, who worked for the company as escorts on the coaches, Stuart's girlfriend was English and worked as a hotel receptionist, Ray's boyfriend was a more reticent Dutch holiday rep. Ray, uninhibited and unconcerned, always attracted the attention of the wary Turkish waiters with his theatrical shrillness and uncontrolled hilarity.

Rushing over to her when she arrived, Atek surprised her with his effusiveness. Leading her by the hand, he took her to the reps table, as if presenting them with a gift. Charming her was a medium for winning their respect and hopefully, the advantages of their connections, she suspected, despite her pleasure. Unaware of how much he resentment he had shown on the few occasions she had gone out with them socially, they embraced like actors, exchanging brief updates and witticisms. Atek took their order, happy to have them drinking copiously, leading their clients behind them. Expert party beasts, they were welcome on his terms.

There were more singles than couples there that night. Some of the girls took off their dresses, intending to swim in their underwear when the barbecue had finished, having been drinking and dancing around the bar for about two hours. The waiters watched them undress first, before Mehmet intercepted their giddy stumbling to the sea.

"Go back," he commanded, "tonight is too dangerous."

In mid-August the water was consistently warm. Barba preferred to wait to swim until the last beach bus left at five in the afternoon, when only a few bathers remained. One sultry evening, when Lucy had returned for a fortnight break, they planned to have dinner at the beach. Atek followed her when she waded in and was stood on her tiptoes with her chin above the water.

"Something is nibbling me," she giggled.

Lifting her up by the waist, he caught her legs and placed them round his hips.

"No one can see," he breathed in her ear as she gasped.

There was something in Berk's expression when they returned to the sunbeds, where he was resting with Lucy, which made her suspect that he knew. Of course he would know, she realised with brutal disappointment; the second-handness of the thrill shooting out the excitement of novelty.

The original plan had been for Lucy to come out with both her children in the school summer holidays. Phee was invited to Spain for two weeks with the family of her best friend, so Lucy had rented a two bedroomed apartment. Conveniently, it was in the next block to Barba's, belonging to a friend of Carol's.

"Alev, would you mind sharing your room with Wayne while Lucy is here?" She had considered it reasonable to be able to use her spare room to some advantage. Wayne would appreciate Alev's company.

"No problem. I am happy to share with him".

"Thank you. You are an angel."

"I know," he fluttered his eyelashes.

The absence of Phee had another advantage, apart from the reduction of angst. Barba and Atek were able to spend most nights in the apartment with Lucy and Berk, recreating the early ambience of playful and sensuous intimacy. Increasingly, Barba perceived a growing intensity in Lucy's feelings towards Berk, which made her feel protective. Although she had not seen the Swedish or the German woman with his children, for the first two weeks in August she had not seen Berk at all. In her mind she scolded herself for making assumptions about his behaviour, as she rarely went to the beach before evening, finding it too crowded and tortuous in the fifty degree heat. Everything seemed so much easier when Lucy was there. The dragons of deceit and mistrust were slain and she could believe in happy endings.

Her friend left just before the beach party at the beginning of September, when all the families were starting to return by the end of the week, in time for the new school year. Barba was on airport duty again that night, Atek had gone to the beach a few hours earlier, and she was ready in her uniform when she received the histrionic call from Ray. It was about an hour before she was due to join the coach.

"Barba something's come up, love, and I really need to swap my airport duty tomorrow night."

Barba had learnt that it was better not to delve with Ray, no matter how serious his problem sounded. It usually had something to do with his lovers.

"Are you ready to go?"

"Yes, I'll be in uniform in two minutes, sweetie. I can be round for the list in fifteen."

"That's fine, then," she agreed, "just clear it with Stu first."

Pouring a glass of wine while she waited for him, she decided she would ask him to drop her off at the beach on his way to work. The food would be finished by the time she arrived, which did not matter as she had eaten earlier. A long, silk sundress and her sandals replaced the uniform.

As they approached, the music could be heard competing with, somewhat camouflaged by, the din from the superior German hotel further down the beach. It made it harder for the Gendarme, who were well-occupied in the town centre in the peak holiday season, to detect that anything unusual was happening.

Shouts and loud laughter rose above the dance music, as she opened the car door.

"Thanks hun. Have a good evening."

"You too, Barbs. You saved my life."

Twenty or more people, she guessed, of different ages and nationalities, were bobbing and bouncing around the impromptu dance floor of the bar area. Berk was busy serving drinks behind the bar with Mehmet, while Musti was bantering, clearing and taking orders at the tables. Atek was nowhere to be seen in the covered area. She surveyed the rows of sunbeds where a few customers were drinking and sitting, some couples watching the sea or the sky, sharing a bed.

Walking towards them, she saw that there were a few figures already in the water, quite close, as the tide was coming in. A woman was writhing, posing in the waves at the edge, for a photographer, as a pale man looked on. Another, heftier, female was waving her arms, further in.

"Atek," the woman yelled gleefully.

Barba surged forward as if she had been shot at, identifying the target as the figure moving towards the woman in the water.

She knew she was still running, watching in slow motion as he was shoulder deep, his back to her, level with the woman. Rising, her head thrown back, shouting, laughing. As she was lifted, the camera flashed three times. On her right breast, Barba glimpsed, before she was lowered, her arms around Atek's neck, the word 'Sexy' tattooed on her breast. The shutters of the lens closed, it seemed darker. He was moving away from her, with her.

"Atek." The scream sounded to her as if it had resounded out of the sky rather than her own mouth, an accusation more than a name.

The woman toppled back as she was dropped, when he jerked away from her, round to face Barba. She heard her scrabbling at the water to stabilise, as if it was something solid, spluttering as she breathed in the brine.

"Tina." Another figure was swimming towards her.

Barba hoped Sexy Slapper Teena was drowning

as Atek, his fists and jaw clenched, cut through the water. He grabbed her arm and carried on walking, not stopping, shouting in Turkish to Berk, who looked at her then to the shore, where the woman was retching on all fours.

His fingernails still digging into the flesh he was clenching, he dragged her on to the dirt path.

"Let go of me." She yanked her arm from him.

He punched her in the shoulder with the released hand.

"What you doing? You a spy now?" he jabbed at her throat.

"Ray asked me to change my airport run with him. I just thought it would be nice to come to the party."

"You don't trust me?" His words were tight, like the notes of an over-strung instrument,

"What were you doing with her?" she shouted, her voice raucous and raw.

"She was playing. You don't believe me?" He pushed her hard on the forehead.

Staggering backwards, hitting a rock with her heels, she fell, hearing the crunch as her head collided with another stone.

"You stupid woman." He bent over her, snarling. "If you sold your house we have real estate business and I would not work at beach."

This reasoning stunned her almost as much as her injury. She pushed the ground to raise herself. With a petulant kick to each of her shins, he started to walk away. Precariously following him, she was surprised and fearful when he abruptly turned and came back to her.

Reaching her, he raised his arm. She flinched, but he was putting it around her and leading her to the road, where she saw the cause of his concern.

"Barba. What happened? Are you alright?"

Carol and her husband were walking their dog. She guessed that they had been on the other side, ready to cross the road to the beach path, when Atek saw them.

"I think so. I tripped over a rock and hit my head." Putting her hand to the back of her skull, touching the blood soaking her hair, trickling warmly down the back of her neck.

Atek was silent, his distress obvious to them all.

"Oh my God," Carol exclaimed when she saw Barba's bloodied, dirty fingers. "We'd better get you cleaned up."

Nobody protested as she handed the lead to her husband and supported Barba back to the apartment, with Atek following wordlessly. Inside he stood aside, while Carol fetched hot water and antiseptic, dabbing the grit and gore from Barba's skin and hair. Engrossed in her task, there were no more questions. The skin and veins on Atek's face shifted as he watched, as if struggling with foreign organisms under the surface, reining in his rage and frustration.

"Here, take these," Carol ordered, handing her a glass of amber liquid and a white pill.

"Together?" Barba sniffed the drink." Brandy and paracetamol?"

Carol nodded like a stern nurse, Barba did her bidding.

"You've been really kind, Carol. I'll get a bath now and get to sleep. Thank you so much."

"Glad I was there to help. Look after yourself now. Let me know if you feel strange or need anything, won't you?"

"I will. Goodnight and thanks again."

"Goodnight, love."

Atek let her out. She heard Carol instruct him to take care of her. He closed the door and went into Alev's bedroom.

Sleeping there for five nights, he stayed out until she had gone to bed, except when she went to the airport. Assuming he had told Alev to inform him with details of her moves, she felt unable to ask his nephew if it was so, knowing that their code of male loyalty would be given priority over truth, as always.

This sealing of lips, even in the face of dishonesty and brutality, could seem like the incarceration of hope and honour to a victim.

Her head was sore in the morning as she brushed her hair gingerly around the drying wound. She put on navy trousers with her long sleeved uniform shirt to hide the marks of violence on her body, rehearsing the excuse about neglecting her laundry, the self-deprecating joke that would divert her colleagues. The men had left before her as usual. Drinking coffee, she ate a banana alone, not really thinking, not tasting bitter or sweet.

Adrift in broken fantasies, she carried herself through her hotel rounds, drinking iced water at each stop to quell the itching and the sweating beneath the polyester. The moment she entered her apartment in the afternoon, she stripped, lying under her white cotton sheets with the air-conditioning blasting cold air around the bedroom. Sleep was given to her in short, palliative doses, like medicine.

Alev came in as she was coming out of the shower. While she dressed for the airport duty, she listened to him moving about in the kitchen, preparing a meal; their usual routine. Wondering whether she had an appetite for anything, she found some tights which would mask her legs, shuddering at the thought of nylon sticking to clammy skin.

"I made you," Alev offered the grilled lamb and salad he had prepared.

"Bless you, Alev," she smiled, sitting with him, to eat for him.

She did not ask why Atek had not come home.

After the walking and talking she had to do most mornings as a rep, she liked to eat a small lunch, then base herself by the poolside or at the beach, to lounge, doze, read and swim.

In the furnace of August, she frequently found it more relaxing to cool in her shady bedroom with the cold fan and the blinds half-closed. The first week of September was as hot as the previous month, the heat sucking out her energy, as well as the fluid through her pores, leaving her more sluggish in her depressed state. It would have uplifted her to immerse herself and swim. Longing for cool water, but not wanting anyone to see her bruises; the violet and pus-yellow shapes, like distorted hearts, stamped on her arms and legs.

On the afternoon of the sixth day after the party he came back. Into the bedroom she heard him stepping quietly. At the end of a tunnel she heard her name whispered. His hands were stroking her through the thin sheet, from her feet, up her legs and round her body. His belt fell heavily to the floor, she heard the impact of leather on metal buckle. Naked as she, he lay beside her, kissing her, his mouth like falling petals on her lips and face. He rose, peeling the sheet down her body, exposing her, moving behind her. She wanted him. Because she thought that was how he wanted her, she raised herself, on her hands and knees, but he was probing higher. She froze, suddenly lucid.

"No, not that way. I've told you."

"Please Barba, I'll be gentle with you."

The shock of violation could not be distinguished from the physical pain as he thrust himself into and down on her, flattening her with the weight of his body. The force with which he rammed, pushing her face between the pillows with his head, smothering and struggling. Where she drew her breath or her strength from, she could not say afterwards, just aware that might was hers as she pushed herself up and him off her back.

"So you are crying now?" he commented tightly as she sobbed.

He put his shorts on, bunching up the sheets stained with blood and mascara, carrying them out in the manner of a humble but conscientious maid.

A strange normality was affected, which lasted for no more than forty-eight hours, as if acting so would become real. Barba could move and converse as if she were untouched by his benign savagery. Each time a door opened or closed, or a key turned in the door, her unconscious emotions betrayed her, making her jerk like the pulling of a tendon of a dead chicken's foot. When she was alone, sometimes she found herself shaking, though she tried to tell herself a more palatable story. In bed that night and the next, he joined her, not touching her as she lay close to him, telling her he was exhausted before lying down.

Undisturbed during the afternoon in between, she had eventually slept. The following one was restful too, until she heard him come in. The replay of the shameful scene; breaking open the lovely, soft flesh of a fruit and finding it rotten inside. Somewhere in her mind she had chosen to believe that the first time had been a thoughtless misjudgement, that his remorse would demand respect for her, that a second temptation could correct a first mistake.

"Please don't," she screamed out this time. Volume, pain, horror; the power in her voice shocked him motionless.

Lifting off her, he sat back on his haunches. She did the same, mirroring him, facing him, searching his eyes.

"It hurts," she said.

"I know," he replied.

Their eyes communicated the truth. Without the spoken word, her soul saw and understood everything.

There was a tapping on the bedroom door.

"Alev is calling me. I have to go."

She sat on the bed, hearing, though not trying to listen. Atek jabbering, Alev speaking, calm and even. The 'phone ringing, Atek explaining, his tone defensive and impatient, then angry and rising. She thought the 'phone was thrown across the floor. A voice inside her urged her to keep moving. Washing, dressing, trusting the voice of survival, because she knew it was telling her that if she lay down she might not be able to rise again.

They were smoking in silence on the balcony when she came through. Atek met her gaze directly, something defiant, even taunting, in his stare and the set of his mouth. Alev's eyes were lowered.

"Who called?"

"My big brother," Atek answered with contempt. He turned his head down vehemently, as if he was about to spit on the floor. "So correct," he added, gnashing out the words.

Like an unseen ghost touring the landscape of the living, she wandered on the rocks, by the shore, through the pillars of the temple and the scattered ruins. Timeless and still within, her ego battered into submission. Finding that the giving way allowed peace in, like rays of light. That there was something very pure, still and tranquil in her being, that nothing in the material world could actually ever touch, break, or alter its wholeness.

When she went home, just before dark, they were gone. The wardrobes in both rooms had been emptied of their belongings. She had checked when she read Alev's note on the kettle.

Barba,

I am sorry. My uncle Alaatin wants to see Atek and I must go too.

Goodbye, take care.

Alev

CHAPTER 11

"I know some people enjoy it that way," she began, unsure of how to explain.

Fern listened patiently as she found the words to contain the feelings. They were sat in wicker chairs by her hosts' courtyard pool. The smell of jasmine stirred her; powerful scent from tiny, delicate, white stars.

"But I made it clear from the start, I didn't want to." Barba winced. "It's not even as if he, or I, had been drinking." She shook her head, as if burrowing for comprehension. "And he forced it on me." The last four words sounded like a feeble testimony to the terrorism of the act. "So ugly."

Fern seemed to understand.

"So he raped you?"

Barba turned over the word in her mind, an acid-leaking capsule.

"That's what it felt like," she murmured, with uncertainty, as though it could only be made up, never something that could be done. By anyone. By him.

"Have you spoken to him since?"

"I sent him one text. I asked him to help me understand. I said that I kept thinking that there was something wrong with me. I said that is how a child feels isn't it?"

"What did he say?"

"Nothing. He cut his 'phone off."

Fern had called on her the day after Atek moved out with Alev. She took one look at Barba.

"What has he done?" she asked, searching Barba's eyes and face.

Barba could not speak at first. She did not think anything showed on the outside yet Fern had seen something.

"I don't know," she answered, finally.

Fern ensured that she called the office, told them she was sick and would not be in work for three days. Carol promised to take care of Gee-Gee.

"Pack a bag, Barba. You can stay with us for a few days while your nerves calm down."

Cem was very gracious and hospitable. She did not know what Fern had told him, only that he was very kind to her and their children made her laugh, which made her feel normal.

"Did he ever ask you for money, Barba?" Fern asked her on the second day.

She thought about it.

"Not directly, really, though he did go off with the motorbike I bought. It's in his name so I can't do anything about that. There was always some problem with a friend or in the family so he regularly got handouts that way, I suppose."

"How much?"

"Varied. Couple of hundred when his friend's father died. Fifty quid here and there for medicines for the family. Hospital treatments for relatives. Gifts. Subs all the time which never got paid back."

"Adds up, eh?"

"Yes and I'm beginning to see just how it does,"

Barba sighed. "I've not even mentioned that he didn't pay for a single thing in the apartment. Just bought leftover food from the restaurant, and wouldn't let Alev give anything either. At least Alev helped clean and everything."

"Alev's pretty special, I think," Fern commented.

"Yes, he is. Another thing, we talked about setting up a business together when I sold the house. Thank God he didn't know I had no mortgage. He used to get really angry that it hadn't sold whenever we had an argument."

"What business?" Fern was interested.

"Real Estate." Barba laughed then. "Not to compete with you here. I always fancied Fethiye."

"Why not?" Fern smiled encouragingly.

Barba declared herself ready to leave on the third night. She was keen to get back to work, feeling she had no good reason to extend her sick leave. Protesting, Fern made her promise to say if she felt at all unhappy in any way.

"Bless you darling. You've all been wonderful."

Fern drove her home. She accompanied her to the security booth and listened while Barba explained that Atek no longer lived there and had no right to access the building anymore. Fern's face was steely, which prevented Barba from succumbing to tears. Fern repeated her instructions in her perfect Turkish to the security man, to ensure he understood. She extracted a guarantee that his colleagues would be informed. Knowing that Alev would not be able to live there without his uncle, Barba asked Fern to make it understood that he was a welcome visitor.

Inside the apartment, her world once again felt emptied of meaning and goodness. Feeling she could not sleep for at least another few hours, she put the television on, to see people moving and hear them talking, poured out vodka and set the laptop on the coffee table. She sent Lucy a text to ask her to come online. She was there in ten minutes.

Lucy says: Hi honey. How are you?

Barba says: Ok. How are you?

Lucy says: Excited! Berk wants to set up a business. Turkish confectionery. ☺

Lucy says: Wants us to be partners- live together in 3 years when Wayne's 16 ☺

Barba says: Wants you to invest?

Lucy says: Yes

Barba says: Don't

She invited her to share the cameras. Lucy was frowning.

Lucy says: What's up Barba?

Barba says: Atek and I are finished. He's done some bad things. I have something to tell you about Berk.

Typing frantically, she did not pause to read Lucy's expression until she had finished. She told her she would explain more about Atek when they were face to face, something too personal and difficult to write there. Sexy Slapper Teena, Berk's relationships with his children and their mothers were described in an honest summary, devoid of blame or bitterness. Lucy read without comment, her face visibly palling, even in the gritty image of the webcam.

Barba says: I'm sorry Lucy. Maybe I should have

264

told you before.

Barba says: You must know now because I don't want him using your money and you!

Barba says: Not even like it's just a double life. With you it would be a treble life.

Barba says: Lucy, are you still there?

Every day for three weeks she called her, to find the landline ringing until the messaging service switched on. The mobile was switched off so she ceased sending texts too. Every night she turned on the computer to find she was not there.

Ray came round for a drink one night when he was passing on his way home. The reps seemed to be getting closer, as the time came nearer to the end of their season. In one more month a few chosen ones would be jetting to winter resorts, whilst most of the rest shivered at home on Jobseeker's Allowance. Barba was waiting to hear if they had any winter work for there, knowing it was competitive, her chances small.

"God, are you on Stalkbook again?" he teased, when he saw the page open on her screen.

When she had poured them both a drink of wine, she showed him Sexy Slapper's profile, pointing out the teenage children flanking her in the photographs. There was a gawky, hostile-faced son, a tubby daughter in a dress that could have been a long, tight vest, with Ugg boots.

"Bit fow, isn't she?" Ray always used the Lancashire dialect with flair.

"Right response, baby." Barba blew him a kiss. "How old d'you reckon?"

"Forty-ish. Doesn't look younger than you,

anyway. And you're much more attractive."

"Thanks babe. I love you."

"Love you too. Pity you're a woman."

Barba scrolled down the posts on the woman's wall, until she reached the first.

9th September: Bugger me, baby! Miss you...LOL!

"Ooer," Ray commented.

Barba still wanted to cry whenever she read that, which by then must have been fifty times.

16th September: Miss my baby so much! Now I've got some beaut pics to look at ☺

She let Ray look at the photographs of Tina entwined around Atek. The background was the beach bar.

"Not nice is it?" Ray concluded, hugging her.

"Looks like she's coming back soon, too." Barba scrolled up.

24th September: Can't wait! Just 4 weeks until I see my baby again ☺

Exactly a fortnight later, Ray rang the doorbell of Barba's apartment. This time she was already affected by alcohol. She offered him some chardonnay from the open bottle on the coffee table next to the laptop. Within seconds, he was viewing the latest status posting on the Talkbook wall of Sexy Slapper Teena.

1st October: YAY! I'm having my baby's baby!

8th October: My baby's asked me to marry him! And I've said Yes!

Barba cried and drank uncontrollably, until Ray put her to bed bossily and went to sleep in the spare room.

Her timekeeping was punctual, she still had a good rapport with the guests, whose dwindling numbers made her job easy, but her targets were down. Barba was not making enough sales on tours. She suspected that her deteriorating performance was the reason she was not offered winter work.

Drink anaesthetised the times alone which were not filled by having to work, attend to Gee-Gee or maintain some kind of composure for her loyal friends. These included Alev, who regularly brought her bowls of food he had prepared. Handing them to her with smiles and a few words, before placing his fist on his heart to say goodbye.

The Douglas Scott reps in Side arranged to go to a disco just outside Manavgat town centre on the twenty-fourth of October for their farewell party. All their flights had now been arranged between the twenty-sixth and last day of the month. Barba decided to stop feeling sorry for herself, vowing to make a huge effort to look her best and enjoy herself for her friends' sake.

She booked to have her eyebrows trimmed, her face smoothed by threading and a cut and blow dry at the hairdressers. Fern took her to Manavgat where she chose a silvery, silk, knee-length dress. It had an asymmetrical hem and neckline, sewn with inserts of fabric to create a waterfall effect. Aware that she had lost weight, she was still amazed at the size six to eight label on the one that fitted her. The shoes she bought were higher than she usually chose; silver, with crystal drops hanging from chains around the straps.

The 'phone alerted her when she was waiting for

Karen to pick her up in the car. She was intrigued to see that Sean was the sender.

'Hi. Hope u r ok. Moving out 2moro. Met someone. B in touch. Sean'

She re-read the text numbly. If someone had asked her at that moment if she felt happy, relieved, grateful, dejected, rejected, jealous or nothing, she would have said yes to all of them.

"You look stunning my darling." Ray spun her round the entrance to the disco.

They were waiting for everyone to arrive before they found the booth they had reserved. She had gone to Karen's to get ready, making sure the false eyelashes her friend had promised to put on her were applied, before the wine was opened.

It was impossible not to feel festive with the extravert reps who always threw themselves into frivolity as if it was crucial to their careers. After a few vodka mojitos, and consecutive soul tracks from the sixties, Barba was believing that she could enjoy life again.

"Hiya Barba."

She picked up her drink from the bar and turned to the voice, not a stranger's. It was Maggie from Sheffield, still recognisable, although she had gained weight, bleached her hair and was now wearing make-up and a short dress. The Turkish man she was gripping by the arm had spiked hair and a tear tattooed at the corner of his left eye. He was introduced as Oz.

"How are you, Maggie?"

"Good, thanks. How about you?"

She knows, thought Barba.

"Did you hear that Atek is getting married?" she asked Maggie brightly, finishing her drink and ordering another.

Maggie feigned ignorance.

"Everything's changed this year," she said nostalgically. " Musti and Mehmet have married German girls. They'll be living in the next town to each other, when Mehmet gets his visa."

"I met Mari, Musti's wife. I didn't know about Mehmet," Barba said. "Who did he marry?"

"She's called Gudrun. Apparently he met her last October."

The surprise of the name turned on a faint memory, of the girl Musti had kept waiting, the one on the balcony. Suddenly, it made sense, like a dimmer switch turning up the light. Recalling the scene in the pension, on her last night, the first time she had visited Atek. Gudrun, on the balcony with Musti. Barba, walking through to the downstairs bathroom from the bar. Glancing up, seeing Musti begin to lift Gudrun's top, up from her waist, over her ribs. She, objecting, pulling it down, walking back into the bedroom. Musti, an angry scowl of frustration on his face, looking down before he joined Gudrun. Beyond Barba, who had turned to see Mehmet, watching the show from the small glass booth, the makeshift office.

"Almost as if there was a plan," Barba muttered, not expecting Maggie to understand what she was implying.

"Best to be friends, I always say," advised Maggie with an air of wordly wisdom, when Oz had gone to the bar for their drinks. "They've always got problems, always need money. That lot used to be running in and out of each other's rooms, taking drugs, when they lived together in Side."

Oz came back with their beers. Maggie excused herself to go to the bathroom.

Barba asked Oz if he worked in Side too.

"No, I have been working in Bodrum," he told her. "We are here for friend's engagement. He is marrying an Englishwoman. They are having baby."

"What's your friend's name?" She had to be sure.

"Atek."

Excusing herself, telling him she was pleased to meet him, she went to the bar. The scene seemed like a goldfish bowl she was on the outside of, looking in, watching the bright fish dart round. Sitting at an empty table, she swallowed the vodka cocktail she had just bought, without tasting. Fumbling around her feet for her handbag, she realised she must have left it on the shelf beneath the counter at the bar. Thankful to find it still there, she grabbed it, walking out unsteadily in her heels into the cold night air. She lifted her arm to alert the driver in a taxi out side. As he pulled up beside her, she opened her bag to find her 'phone, intending to send a text message to her friends to explain that she had left the disco. Fishing it out, she discovered it was the only object left in there. Her purse, with her cash and credit cards was gone, even her cigarettes and lighter. She tried to call Ray, then each of her friends in turn. When none answered, she came to the conclusion that the music and the din was drowning out their 'phones. Not wanting to go back in there, uncertain she would have been permitted to, with no money.

Panicking, she tottered over the road to the building where the sign of the Gendarmerie seemed to promise some protection. An officer was writing notes at the reception desk. He eyed her wearily as she reported the theft, enunciating slowly in the hope that it would counter the effect of her drunkenness. She was led into a side room where four more officers were drinking glasses of tea. The officer on desk duty spoke briefly in Turkish and went back to his desk. One of them stood up, a tall, bear-chested man with grey hair and eyes which seemed almost closed.

"How can I help you? he asked in cracked English.

Repeating her story, she halted when she heard her rushed, less than coherent speech. She began again, emphasising each word. One of the men sitting at a desk mumbled something to his colleague, who sniggered behind his papers like a schoolboy.

The one standing told her to sit, so she placed herself on a chair by the wall. He stood in front of her with his hands on his hips, now level with her face.

"You have problem. I am thinking how can I help you?" He leered at her and turned his lower body towards the other officers. Looking down, then rolling his eyes as if he had committed an unfortunate but amusing faux-pas.

Every hair raised as she stiffened. Frozen needles piercing every inch of her skin, when she saw the unmistakeable bulge pushing the zip of his uniform trousers away from his groin. He was smirking proudly, while the two men mocked her, with their hands over their mouths and their shaking shoulders. The gendarme at the other desk kept his eyes down, continuing writing, his face stern and unsmiling.

Frightened sobs burst out of Barba's body, clattering the unstable legs of her chair on the tiled floor. The erect officer looked disconcerted at her commotion. She was oblivious to any attempt to speak to her. Only one sound got through, the ringtone of her 'phone in the bag on her lap. She fumbled for it, as desperately as a sinking swimmer grabbing a float thrown out to her.

"Ray," she called, when she saw the name on the screen and pressed to answer.

"Barba. I missed your call. Where are you?"

"In the gendarmerie across the road from the disco," she wailed, in between involuntary gasps.

"Wait there," he instructed her reassuringly, with an authority she had never heard in him before.

The officers were exchanging glances. She wiped her eyes with a tissue. The serious man filled a plastic cup of water from the cooler in the room and brought it to her.

"Thank you. My friend is coming," she whispered to him as if he was her ally.

He seemed to have understood.

Ray flounced into the room purposefully.

"Everything is fine, now, gentlemen," he declared, as if he was taking official command.

He held out his hand like a courtier, for Barba to rise. There was a look of repulsion on three faces as they watched Barba being lead out by Ray. He threw an insolent glare back at them as they left the office.

Once again she was laid on her bed by her fussing friend. He unstrapped her silver shoes and covered her with the sheet before turning off the lights.

Ray was making coffee when she shuffled into the kitchen space at noon the following day. Still in her silver dress, peeling off the eyelashes which were curling away uncomfortably into her lids.

"Thanks for saving me last night". She hugged him.

"No problem. All in the course of a hero's day."

He made sure she contacted the banks to report the stolen cards before he left to begin the packing for his flight in three days.

"You know, I need to start too," She looked around the apartment she would have to leave in a week's time. "Wish I didn't feel so rough."

"Look after yourself, sweetie. I'll call you later."

"'Bye Ray. And thanks again for protecting me from the agents of the law."

He tipped an imaginary hat to her, saluting as he departed.

The shower was running, she was forcing herself to drink another pint of water when the doorbell rang. Thinking Ray must have forgotten something, she peeped through the spyhole. It was a dark-haired female, which made her assume it was one of her kindly Turkish neighbours, or Courtney from work.

She opened the door and screamed.

"Lucy! Lucy!"

"Hello babe. You going to stand here yelling or let me in?" She gently removed the arms around her neck and picked up her case.

"How?" Barba stood aside, stammering with disbelief.

"I am so sorry, babe. I've been really out of it for the past six weeks."

"Me too. Why didn't you tell me you were coming?"

"I checked with Fern. She told me you were having a hard time of it, and I just went off your radar, which couldn't have helped. I thought it best to just come out, give you a bit of support and travel back with you next week. Fern gave me the details so I could get a ticket on the same flight."

"Oh, Lucy." Barba embraced her friend again. "Come and sit down. Tea? Coffee?"

"Coffee, please," Lucy said then looked Barba up and down. "Girlfriend", she asked in an exaggerated Southern States accent, "are you going somewhere?"

Barba laughed, in spite of her crumpled party dress and the black smudges stinging her eyes, making them run even more. Lucy joined in.

"Oh, honey," Barba said, pulling a tissue out of the box, "you're a great all-round doom and gloom and hangover cure."

They agreed they needed a shower and fresh clothes, before they talked about what had been happening in their lives and how they had become separated. Barba fetched Lucy a robe and towel so she could use the main bathroom while she was in the en-suite.

Cleansed and refreshed, they made more coffee and sandwiches to take on the balcony. Barba filled the gaps in her story first, which did not take her long. She brought the laptop out to show Lucy the posts on Talkbook, as she had shown Ray.

"Poor babe," Lucy kept iterating.

"Now you." Barba leant back to listen when she had horrified Lucy speechless, with the details of Atek's atrocity and the sordid scene in the Gendarmerie.

"Basically I had a kind of breakdown," Lucy began, "what I didn't tell you the last time we spoke was that I had just found out I was three months pregnant."

"Pregnant?" Barba stared, trying to absorb the ramifications.

"Berk. When I came in June I messed up my pills one night and forgot all about it. I was losing weight so it never occurred to me it was that. Thought it was stress."

"Why didn't you tell me?"

"I was going to. But then you said about Atek and told me about Berk. I was out of my mind. I miscarried that night."

Dark rivulets were trickling down Barba's cheeks as she stared dumbly at her friend.

"I shouldn't have told you," she whispered guiltily.

"It's for the best, really. You did the right thing. It's better to be hurt by the truth than a lie, I think. 'Cause it cuts through the crap and frees you for something better."

Barba held her face in her hands.

"Lucy," she wept, "you have been through hell and I have been so selfish, feeling sorry for myself."

"You couldn't have done anything. I stayed with my aunt until I felt better. Alan moved back in to look after the kids." Lucy read the question in Barba's face. "We'll see. I've finally learnt it's up to me to set standards. Value myself if I want someone to value me."

The importance of Lucy's words resounded with Barba a few days later. They were sorting out which clothes she should keep or throw away as they cleared the apartment.

Barba was holding up some fashionable but unworn sandals she had bought in Side when she had first moved there.

"They look good but they hurt me," she told Lucy.

"The quality looks a bit poor," Lucy assessed them.

"They were cheap," Barba confirmed. "For some reason, I had to have them at the time. I don't even think they suit me now. Haven't got much wear out of them, though."

"Do you want to know what I say to myself?" Lucy asked.

"Go on."

"I see myself in something better."

Barba repeated the sentence then again, loudly and triumphantly.

"That's it, Lucy! It applies to everything that's not worthy, doesn't it?

"I suppose so."

"Absolutely so. Anything that doesn't make you feel really good. Shoes, food, situations with people. Men."

She walked up to the rails of the balcony as if she was a princess addressing her subjects below. "I see myself in something better," she pronounced regally, raising an arm to heaven.

CHAPTER 12

It was as if, having declared her intentions, the universe shifted to grant her wishes. Chains which had held her back were being cut with the blade of truth, as she took responsibility for her life.

Lucy, having helped her vacate her apartment and flown back with her to England, spent the next consecutive seven days doing more of the same. When the clutter was removed from Barba's house, they began painting all the walls magnolia.

Their labour was rewarded at the end of the second week. Barba had instructed a new estate agents. Their niche was to achieve quick sales, with a fixed five per cent discount off the valuation price, working only with potential buyers who had their finances organised. Barba made notes about the way they worked in the project book she had bought, to record any ideas and useful information for the real estate business she was planning.

"Honey, can you come round tonight?" Barba asked Lucy on the 'phone.

"No problem. About eight-thirty okay?"

Barba said she would pick her up and pay for her taxi back home.

"Good news. I've got a cash buyer," she greeted Lucy at the door with a glass of champagne.

"Wow! That's great." Lucy handed back the glass

while she took off her coat and gloves.

"Want to get settled before Christmas. Moving here with the guy's work from London. One teenage son."

"Sounds good."

"So planning to exchange contracts in three weeks, and be completed by the middle of December, maybe earlier."

"Fantastic. Where will you live until you go back to Turkey?"

"With my mother." Barba chewed her lips in mock consternation. "Be quite nice to have Christmas with her. Might be the last one."

Lucy looked upset. "What do you mean, last one?"

"She might be wed to that Ken bloke she met on holiday in Side," Barba laughed. "They're going on a Turkey and Tinsel type thing for New Year, in Cyprus."

"Good for her. Pass the champers and we'll drink to that, too."

It seemed appropriate that they were celebrating thus, when Barba told Lucy she had the impulse to look up the Sexy Slapper on Talkbook. The engagement photographs had been added; her latest post announced the date for her wedding to Atek.

"Christmas Eve," read Lucy." Not much of a present, is he? Is this a joke? Sexy Slapper Brit marries Turkish Love Rat."

Barba had to laugh at her friend's sarcasm and moved on to the album.

"This could be Musti's engagement with their faces pasted on," Barba scoffed. "It's even got a caption on this one." She poked at the picture of Atek on one knee." It says the theme from The Bodyguard was playing. Just the same."

"How do you feel about it, really, Barba?"

Barba screwed her face in pain. "It still hurts, Luce. I can't pretend it doesn't. Especially when he's posting things like 'my beautiful fiancee' and 'my unborn child' and how he can't wait to marry her. Then I think he must have changed or it was me, because he loves her so much."

Lucy blew her wretched words away with a blast of scorn.

"If he loves her so much why does he have to say it on Talkbook? He's still trying to manipulate you, Barba, by shoving it in your face. And keeping her sweet. I'll give him two years doing the same, until he gets the right to stay here. Then I see him dumping her like an unpinned grenade and going to work in a kebab shop near his mates. The sad arse'll be screwing every doner-munching female who wanders in after a night out without pulling."

"Whooo, Lucy. Calm down. Don't worry. I said it hurt. That doesn't mean I want that again. See myself in something better, remember?"

They chinked their flutes to that.

The house sale proceeded without complications. A few days before the completion date Barba began to experience an ache of nostalgia. A gift from her father, his childhood home which her grandparents had passed on to him when they died. Wandering around the rooms she was telling him how she felt when she was suddenly enfolded by calmness. It passed through her, leaving her

279

with a sense of certainty that she was on the right path. He was looking after her, she thought, telling her that the house had been given to aid her on her true path, not to hold on to, not to be held back by.

Bethany too, approached her with a new faith in what she was setting out to do. She asked her many questions when they were discussing her plans on Christmas Eve. Her daughter seemed as eager as her grandchildren, to paint a picture in their mind of how her life might be there. It reminded her of her vision, refuelling her excitement. The misery of recollecting that it was the day that Atek was marrying that woman, was easily dispelled.

"I'll definitely have my own house this time," Barba promised her daughter on Christmas Day. "So there's no excuse not to come out. I'm determined to find something big enough. As long as you don't have any more babies," she teased," three bedrooms and a bed settee might do it."

"We've already started saving, Mum."

"Really?"

"Really."

With her mother away with her lover at New Year, Barba decided that if she was to see it in alone, she would prefer to be somewhere meaningful. To her that was Fethiye, where she wanted to start her new life.

Picking out the constellations, recalling some of the heroic scripts, she toasted the gods at midnight. Inside Olive Cottage, the old fireplace was alive with burning logs, the candles scenting the air were cinnamon and apple for the season. With more champagne she blessed her family and friends, even Atek, for his part in freeing her.

On New Year's Day Barba sent Alev a text asking him to come online. She had to wait until the evening to talk to him.

Barba says: Happy New Year Alev

Alev says: Happy New Year. Good for you, I hope

Barba says: Sen de ☺

Barba says: That is what I want to talk to you about

He did not have a camera set up on the computer he was using. She had to rely on his language to gauge his response to her proposal.

Alev says: ?

Barba says: I am going to start a real estate business here in Fethiye

Alev says: Good

Barba says: Are you interested?

Alev says: Of course

Barba says: I mean would you like to work here?

Alev says: For you?

Barba says: Yes. At first, I would pay you to help me get the office ready and any other help

Barba says: Then you could learn more about the business – selling

There was a long pause. Barba waited, assuming he was absorbing the information and considering his decision.

Barba says: You don't have to decide now

Alev says: I am very happy to do this Barba. I can live with my uncle Alaatin, I am sure.

He is accountant

Barba says: I will need an accountant too

Alev says: Thank you :D

Barba says: Well, remember I will just be starting

Alev says: I know

They agreed that he would come when she had found an office. His contract with her would be for nine months initially, at a basic wage which a waiter in a holiday resort might expect. Her plan was to give him bonuses when they made sales.

She travelled back to Side by coach the next day, frothing exuberantly, her head full of plans. Looking forward to spending two weeks with her friends, learning the business with Fern and bringing Gee-Gee back with her. She had bought him a kennel for the winter, which Carol had been kind enough to allow her to keep in her back yard, so the dog could be more comfortable whilst Barba was in England.

Fern had recommended some books to help her learn about selling property and marketing. Proving to be a firm, if not hard, taskmaster for Barba, she gave her a list, instructing her to have done the reading before she started teaching her. Fern assured her that she was happy to spend time doing it during the quiet winter spell in the market. Barba was anxious to reward her by being a good student, maximising the time so she was well prepared when the season began.

Cem had been looking around for a car for her and was ready with a few options when she arrived. In one day she was driving her own vehicle, a white Fiat Punto. Singing to herself about having her own wheels again, she felt ecstatic. It helped to quell her nerves at coping with erratic, Turkish driving styles.

Every morning Fern took her into her office at home or they drove to Side, depending on what the agenda was. Fern introduced her to her own webmaster so they could plan her website, which he would maintain and find ways to get traffic to, once she was operating. They wanted to include mutual links between Fern's site and Barba's, anticipating finding more ways to cooperate and support each other's business in time. Cem helped her with her business plan, taking her through each step thoughtfully and patiently. He used his contacts to locate some available office spaces in central positions in Fethiye, giving her four telephone numbers to call when she returned. She admired his ability to think of every detail; he and perfectionist Fern seemed like the ideal team in work, as well as love.

When the intense fortnight came to an end, she was dizzy with new knowledge and nervous excitement.

"I feel as if I can't find the right words to show you how grateful I am," she told the couple at her emotional farewell.

"Don't be silly. Just make it work," Fern replied in her bossy professor voice, then laughed and hugged her tearfully.

Cem kissed her on each cheek and wished her well, sincerity radiating from his face and warming his words. She cuddled the children who had kept her spirits high when she most needed it, and promised to visit as soon as she could.

Gee-Gee welcomed her deliriously and, keen to do whatever she wanted him to, bounded cheerfully into the car. He was unused to travelling that way, however, and quickly became subdued, lying on the back seat, occasionally whimpering. Barba felt sorry for him and talked to him reassuringly all the way, able to drive better with him in that state than his earlier giddiness.

"Alev, how are you? I've got good news," she told him, resisting the urge to whoop loudly. That was partly because she was stood in the street, outside the building where she had just agreed a rental contract for her first office. She wanted to hear Alev's voice when she told him, rather then via text.

He was as thrilled as she.

"I will call my uncle to talk about when I will come," he told her, sounding as if he was skipping about, the way she wanted to, at that moment.

"When do you think that will be? Alev, I am so excited."

"As soon as he says I can do. Me too."

"Text me when you have spoken to him and I will call you back. And let me know how much the bus ticket costs."

Alaatin was apparently delighted to have his nephew join him. Barba sensed this for herself when he brought Alev to Olive Cottage. They arrived for breakfast, as arranged, when he had collected him from the bus station, three days after she had found the office. Her first impression, as she walked to the gate to welcome them, was how like father and son they were. The second thing that struck her was his eyes, the only feature he really shared with his younger brother. When she had first seen Atek's eyes in sunlight, she had recalled an image of the Aegean Sea. Greens and golds marbled with brown. Alaatin had those eyes, only softer and more luminous. His hair was grey, with flecks of the black of his youth. He shared the same leonine features as Alev. Though more deeply lined and marked with age, they were handsome in an unconventional sense. His uncle was taller than Atek too, being of similar height and build to Alev, with a muscular, well-proportioned frame.

Another characteristic of Alev, which she immediately perceived in Alaatin, was how he made Barba feel natural and relaxed in his company. Experiencing none of the embarrassment she had feared on being introduced, just a sense of having known Alaatin much longer than a few minutes. Sitting with them, eating the Turkish breakfast she had prepared, they conversed easily, discussing Alev's journey, the new office, and the preparations needed before the business could begin.

"Because it was an estate agent's before, the rooms are ideal. It has the main office and reception, with a small office I can use for private meetings with clients. And there's a small kitchen. The toilets are shared with the other businesses there. They're on the first floor," Barba informed them.

"What do you think we will need to do to get it ready?" Alev asked, eagerly.

"Cleaning first, then decorating. The marble floor is nice but everything else needs to be changed. Then we'll have to get new furniture, the computer and printer and all the other things." She and Alev exchanged excited looks.

"I will help when I have time," Alaatin offered.

"Certainly at weekend I can help you."

"If you can that would be great," Barba responded, hoping he would.

"Can we go and see it now?" asked Alev.

"But aren't you tired?" she replied.

"Some," he smiled, "but I really would like to see it."

Alaatin assured them he was happy to drive them the few kilometres into Fethiye centre. Olive Cottage was equidistant to Fethiye and Olu Deniz, where Alaatin had an apartment and his office for his accountancy business.

"I have many people I would like to introduce to you, Barba," Alaatin told her as he was driving. "It will be good for your business."

"Sounds fantastic," she commented gratefully.

"We have business network dinners every two or three months also. If you like I will take you to the next one, so you can meet people."

"Yes, please. Are they Turkish? English?"

"Mixed, and a few other Europeans, German, Scandinavian. Most are English and Turkish from the local business community."

"When is the next one?" Barba could feel a thrill spurting up inside her. She knew it could not be attributed solely to the prospect of a work-related meeting.

"I think end of February. I will let you know exact."

"Thank you. That will be good timing as the office should be ready by then."

She showed them round the dusty, unkempt

offices proudly. Illustrating with some swatches and wood samples, she described the lavender-grey colour scheme, with pale wooden blinds and furniture. The men looked around and listened to her with approving smiles and nods.

"What time should I come tomorrow?" enquired Alev keenly.

"Call me when you are ready," Barba said." You need a rest first."

At nine o'clock the next morning they were entering the offices carrying brooms, buckets, dusters and bottles of cleaning fluids.

"Good luck," called Alaatin, as he drove off.

When he came to collect Alev at four in the afternoon, they declared that they were ready to begin painting the next day.

"Good job," he praised them. "If you need anything, tell me," Alaatin instructed her. "Usually I know someone who I do accounts for, to help you find what you need."

Barba felt as if she was constantly thanking him.

In ten days, by the first week in February, with Alaatin's help during the weekend, the decorating, inside and out was complete. She and Alev moved on to the next task; choosing and ordering the furniture.

A parcel arrived while Barba was listening to Alev discussing the delivery time for their desks and office chairs. It had Turkish stamps.

"Oh, it's from Fern and Cem," she exclaimed, reading the handwriting on the back. "That's so thoughtful of them."

Alev put the 'phone down and watched her open

it with interest.

Inside was a card with a beautiful watercolour painting of a beach, with a box, gift-wrapped in purple foil and silver ribbons.

"Barba. It's your birthday! Why did you not tell us?" Alev reproved her lightly, as he read the words inside the card she had handed him.

Smiling, shaking her head dismissively, she held up an exquisite fountain pen with delicate silver filigree on each end. There was a matching tray, containing a notepad and a holder for pens.

"For my new desk."

Alev admired them all. "Would you like to do something this evening?" he asked her, solicitously.

It touched her that he wanted to make it special for her. There had been no thought of celebrating until now, her life was so different, preoccupied with getting the business ready. She was thinking about it as he walked into the kitchen to make a call, speaking quietly into his mobile.

"Would you like to come to dinner with my uncle and me, Barba?"

"Well, yes. But I just had the idea that I would like to make you dinner at my house. Then I can say thank you to you both, too."

Alev looked uncertain. "If you are sure it is what you want?"

"I am sure."

"I will call Alaatin Abi. What time?"

They arrived just as Barba, not knowing what to make in such a short time, was putting the Shepherd's Pie in the oven. She explained that it was a traditional

English meal. Alev pronounced it 'Shepherd's Pee'. When she pointed out the error, it kept them all laughing and set the mood for the evening. The nods which showed their approval when it was served, and their clean plates, convinced her of their enjoyment. She had found a small cake in the patisserie, where they included a small candle when she told them it was for a birthday. The men sang 'Happy Birthday' heartily to her, cheering when she blew out the candle.

"Shall we sit by the fire?" Barba suggested.

They took their glasses into the living room, where Barba had several candles glowing around the hearth. Alaatin said they had to fetch something from the car. She put the mellow Turkish guitar music on the player while they were gone. Alev walked in first, his face concealed behind a bunch of vivid blooms. She grasped them like a bridesmaid catching the bride's bouquet at a wedding. Alaatin followed, holding out a tissue-wrapped parcel. Peeling off the layers, like a child playing 'Pass The Parcel', she uncovered a carved walnut box. It had a lion's head on the lid, and four legs with the feet of the beast. Alaatin showed her the secret method of opening it, by pushing in concealed levers at each side.

"It's beautiful. So unusual." She traced the intricate carvings with her fingers. "Was it yours, Alaatin? You shouldn't have."

"I wanted you to have it. It was made in my village, you know? And I can get other one."

Hugging them both tenderly, no longer self-conscious about expressing her affection, she thanked them for making her birthday so wonderful.

Making themselves cosy by the fire, they joined Gee-Gee, who was a contented curl in the centre. Alaatin said he was so comfortable, and having such a good time, he might ask a friend to drive them home, so they did not have to worry about drinking.

"There are two beds in the spare room if you want to stay here," Barba invited them on impulse.

They looked inquiringly at each other. Alaatin made the decision.

"Thank you," he accepted, "if it is no trouble. Why not?"

Barba commented on the likenesses between them, which initiated the telling of their histories. Alaatin told stories of Alev growing up with his two daughters, who were both, by then, university students in Istanbul.

"When did your mother die?" Barba asked, when Alaatin mentioned her.

"Nearly five years ago."

"Same as my father. What did she die of?"

Alaatin shrugged sadly. "I don't know. She just died. Three months after Atek went into the military."

It was the first time Atek's name had been spoken. Barba could not stop herself asking the question.

"You think Atek going into the military had something to do with your mother's death?"

"Not exactly."

Barba did not ask what he meant. The struggle of sadness, and something else in his features, prevented her. Alev said he was going outside to smoke.

"I'll come too." Alaatin got up to follow him.

They had dinner together four nights each week for the next fortnight. Barba cooked for them at the cottage on two nights. Apart from the pleasure of cooking and their company, it was the only way she could repay Alaatin. He insisted on taking them out for a meal on Friday and Saturday night and would not hear of her contributing anything.

With the office ready, with furniture, equipment and supplies arriving daily, Barba and Alev would spend the afternoons sharing ideas. Planning each step towards the success they both felt in their being they would achieve. To Barba, it was as if an inner chain had been forming, each link connecting and strengthening. Externally, it manifested through the flow, the coming together of events and the forging of relationships. The complementary partnership of the conscientious and creative Alev blended with the forethought, action and connections of Alaatin. It seemed like a fabulous structure was being put into place by master craftsmen, just waiting for the finishing touches to be added.

Alaatin gave her the date for the Business Network Dinner at the end of February.

"If you get your business cards, the flyers and invitations to the launch ready, you can give them to people. And remember your diary."

Barba got to work immediately with Alev, designing and choosing. They set the launch date for the first week in April, as it would give time to plan, benefit from the contacts made and operating in time for the Easter holidays. They needed a name.

"Express Wish," Barba announced, circling the words on a page of scribbled possibilities.

Alaatin had arranged to go to Istanbul, combining a business trip with spending time with his daughters and old friends. He was leaving mid-February and expected to be gone for approximately ten days. It was an opportune time for Alev to go home to visit his family, particularly his new baby sister. They had received the delightful news of her birth a few days after Barba's birthday. It was decided then that Alev would go, as soon as the office was ready.

It was only when they were gone that Barba became aware of how much joy and comfort she found in their presence. They came into her thoughts often, when she was walking Gee-Gee or immersed in her books about business and marketing. Any time there was a space in her thoughts that could be filled, they flowed in. What unsettled her was how these streams in her mind began to teem with images of Alaatin, to babble with the rising and falling of his voice.

He came back first, a few days before the Network Dinner. Without calling he arrived at the cottage as she was preparing dinner. Shy, for the first time in his presence, she invited him to stay.

"I've missed you," Barba heard herself saying, then qualifying, which increased rather than decreased her embarrassment, "it's not the same without you two."

"I brought you something," he replied, as if that was enough to reciprocate.

It was. He placed a cardboard box on the table, which she opened, trying to control the foolish smile she felt was making her a clown. She pulled out a chain attached to a short post with a hook. A lamp emerged, fished out by the chain. A brass oil lamp, decorated with swirls of flora, with a spout and a lid that had a small eagle's head on it. Barba held it to her, her eyes shining.

"It's perfect. I don't know what to say." She put the lamp down, her arms around him. Resting her head for a moment on his chest, she breathed with him.

"Just make a wish," whispered Alaatin.

He released her slowly, moving away.

"Sit down please, Barba. I want to talk to you. I want you to know all about me, whatever happens with us."

Barba sat opposite him at the table, the lamp between them, his last few words echoing in her mind.

He took a deep breath and closed his eyes. She watched the same conflicting emotions wrestling in his face, as they had when he had spoken of his mother's death.

"I know everything that happened between you and Atek."

It was Barba's turn to inhale for composure.

"It is not easy for either of us to talk about him. I know he is my brother in blood, and I wish it felt like more." He hesitated. "But I will not be silent again, when it is wrong to say nothing. Too many times I did this before."

He reached for her hand before speaking again.

"It was I who made him leave you then. I wanted to stop him hurting you more. I said I thought you would call the Gendarme to him. You see, Barba, he is his father's son. And when my mother saw this for herself I think she chose to die. She did not want to see."

"How ?" she asked in a low voice, as if others were listening.

"When he was nearly twenty, he had a girlfriend he met at the beach. She was seventeen, half-Turkish, on holiday with her English mother and grandmother. She believed in her pink dreams of him. How could she know he was sleeping with many other women, most of them older than her? Women with more money, who came on holiday two or three times a year. Two months after she went back to England he was sent to the military. A few weeks later, some men from our hometown knocked on my mother's door. They said they were uncles of the girl and they were looking for Atek. They were angry, saying they were going to kill him because of what he had done to their niece."

"What?" she asked hoarsely.

"They said he had asked her to be his wife, that he had forced her to do things in bed that she did not want to. She was having his baby. She had an abortion and was going crazy because he would not speak to her."

"What happened?" She could barely hear her own voice, for the clamour of the ones in her head.

"My mother told them Atek was a soldier by then. They said they would be back. Luckily for Atek, again", he said bitterly, "the next time they came was the day of my mother's funeral. We never heard from them again. Even they had some respect."

"Why are you telling me this?" She put her hands to her ears, as if she could stop all the voices, including his.

"Because I want to have a clean heart with you. It was not always so. I worked in tourism too. I took many things from people. I slept with hundreds of women whose faces I can't remember. Made them pay, while I had a wife and two daughters back in my village. It was arranged that I married my cousin when I came out of the military."

"Why did you get divorced?" She was hearing him exclusively now.

"To set her free. I could see I was losing something important by continuing this life. One day I knew that you can tell yourself anything. What you are doing. Why you are doing it. The truth is, you are selling yourself. Do you understand me?

"I think so. However you dress it up, it smacks of prostitution. The women who go there with their freedom and their money. They're looking for fun, sex, romance, love, but they end up paying for it."

She could see he had not understood her speech.

"We are not toys," his voice raised angrily.

"Who are the toys?" she asked emphatically.

"At first it is like game. You feel like you have some power, playing the game. Winning."

"But no-one wins that way."

"You are right. When I looked at my daughters growing up, I wanted something different for them. For myself too. To earn my own money by working hard. Believe I could do it. Respect myself again. Respect other people. So I saved until I could train as an accountant."

"What made you change?"

"An English woman," he smiled. "She finished with me after three years."

"Why?"

"Many things not good really. I was always trying to control her, pressing her for money, expecting her to pay. It was too late when I saw how she had done her best. She wanted to help me to see that I could do better than that. That I was responsible for my life. When she was gone it was too late to show her that I had loved her too."

"So she did help you in the end? Like me. I mean, in a different way, because of Atek I learnt to value myself too."

He nodded sadly, squeezing her hand harder.

"When did you last have a relationship?" His honesty had given her the courage to ask.

"Just over a year ago it finished. German, a foot doctor. Her mother works in tourism here."

"Why did it end?"

"She got engaged to someone in Germany. She told me that it was too far, too difficult to have a long-distance relationship. Said thank you, it was fun. Now she lives here with him."

There was irony in his tone, but no regret she could hear.

"I'm sorry."

"Now I am not."

He picked up her hand and kissed it before walking out of the door.

Barba thought of a baroque dance; the coming together with grace, the steps away, the circling, the crossing, turning, joining.

The true 'belle danse' did not begin until the night after the success of the Network Dinner. Barba had been driven home by Alaatin, with a hotel-owner who had asked for a lift. Barba got out first. Saying goodbye formally, her eyes engaged warmly with Alaatin's. Her head and her diary were full of encouraging exchanges, appointments, telephone numbers, useful information and links.

One of the meetings they had arranged was for the next morning. Alaatin had introduced her to a Mr Aknar, a local property developer. His current project was the refurbishing of several village houses a few miles away, in the surrounding hillside. Barba was interested, personally as well as professionally.

"I love the old style of Olive Cottage with the fire place and all, but modern enough, with the pool as well. I need to find something by the end of June," she told Alaatin as they drove to Aknar's site.

"I too am looking for something bigger," he said. "With Alev now, I need more room, for when my daughters visit."

Mr Aknar showed them three houses, one complete and two in progress. They praised the workmanship and the care with which he had retained the traditional features, whilst bringing them up to date.

When they had discussed how they would market the properties, they agreed on a commission rate of eight per cent for the first three sales, rising to ten per cent thereafter. Agreeing to meet soon to sign the contract, they shook hands like old friends.

"I want to show you another house a little further up the hillside," Alaatin told her, mysteriously, as they got back in the car.

"Well, I loved the little village houses but this is something else, isn't it?" Barba exclaimed.

He explained that he had the keys to a house which a friend of his had told him about. It was in need of renovation, but he had clearly been captivated by it. Barba could see why. It was faced all round in ornately carved wood, with a traditional verandah over the entrance. There were two rooms downstairs, apart from the kitchen, with three bedrooms and a bathroom upstairs. Alaatin led her through, sharing his ideas of how it could be transformed with her.

Outside, he pointed out the spaces where he imagined the pool and the gardens for fruit trees, vegetables and flowers, and a small, two storey, stone out-building.

"That could be stables, or a lodge for guests," he suggested.

"Nice idea to have a guest lodge. Stables? Do you ride?"

"It's one of my dreams to have horses and ride again. What about you?"

Barba was enchanted, not sure whether she was walking in his dream, or he in hers.

"Me too. I loved to ride as a girl."

"I have a friend with a horse farm in Antalya. In a few months we could go there, and you could visit your friends in Side."

Putting his arm around her, he pulled her closer. For many minutes they stayed like that, sharing a vision.

They slept, joined together, that night. That consummation was the fanfare of the dance that was to be the expression of their eternal flame. However the mood, tempo or pace changed, they would move with it. Connected, in the choreography of their enduring passion and ever-deepening romance.

CHAPTER 13

In the autumn of 2009 the best-selling magazine, 'Take a Break', launched a 'Holiday Justice Campaign'. On the feature page was a passage condemning the exploitation of women on holiday. It referred to its growing dossier of scandalous stories, particularly those taking place in Turkey, where increasing numbers of women were subjected to trauma, abuse and fraud. The absence of equal rights, afforded by the Turkish authorities to women in such circumstances, was denounced. The report pointed out that millions of Britons supported the Turkish Tourism Industry annually, by visiting resorts in Turkey. A challenge was made, urging the Turkish Prime Minister to address these issues, and to sign the magazine's petition for Holiday Justice.

Berk was bored. He expected more action on the beach in June. The owner of the bar was discussing the merits and disadvantages of joining the E.E.C., from the viewpoint of someone who had largely benefitted from crime. The other waiters were predicting the outcome for Turkey in the forthcoming World Cup Games. Half-listening to their conversations, he carried out a mental inventory of the customers on the beach. Specifically, he was trying to analyse what had happened to the quotient of available females.

Two teenage girls in different families. Both with fathers who glared belligerently if their daughters were addressed less than formally by the waiters. Two pairs of lesbians. The other women were either single women on holiday with their partners, or married women with husbands, many with children. No single mothers, no shy or self-conscious spinsters in their thirties, no confident divorcees over forty, not even a sixty-plus widow could be seen there.

The hotels were becoming stricter too, he reflected. Unwilling to do business with any of the beach restaurants who had employees reputed to exploit the guests in any way. Some were even threatening, if there was so much as a hint of inappropriate approaches to the customers.

As he scanned the scene, a pair of horses rode out of the woods, into his peripheral vision. From experience, even from a hundred metres, he could guess that the male rider was Turkish, the female English. Thinking that there was something familiar about them, he watched as they dismounted and kissed. The horses' reins were tied to branches of pines, they took off their boots and walked hand in hand to the sea. The man picked up a stick, scrawling something in the sand which made the woman put her hands to her face and kiss his head. He remained kneeling on the sand, adjusting his position until he was resting on one knee. Taking one of her hands in his, he looked up at her and spoke. Berk heard the elation as she shouted 'Yes,' at the top of her voice.

People were sitting up on the sunbeds, looking over at the couple. Berk considered that, if things were going to continue this way on the beach, it might be time to get married himself. Contemplating Lucy, he regretted his indifference to the end of the relationship. For him, England was a more favourable prospect for a visa than Germany or Sweden. He had been told it was a good place to be if you worked hard, and he liked the people better. Atek, as well as other friends, was there, he thought, wistfully.

An Englishwoman's laughter drew his attention. Two well-maintained women, he guessed to be in their early sixties, were setting their bags down by the sunbeds in front of him. He observed them for a while, noting the abundance of weighty gold jewellery around their necks and ears, absent from their hands. The beachwear was expensive.

Deciding he favoured the high-spirited lady he had noticed first, he removed his t-shirt, moving over to them, employing his smoothest tones, his suavest smile.

"Welcome ladies." He stood before them, pushing his sunglasses up. "Where are your husbands?"

"We're here," answered a deep, jovial voice behind him.

They all laughed.

Printed in Great Britain
by Amazon